HEAVEN

HEAVEN

ANN BUTLER ROWLANDS

Published by Alogo Publications

A CIP catalogue record for this book is available from the British Library.

ISBN 978-0-9955769-0-2

Book layout and design by Clare Brayshaw

Prepared and printed by:

York Publishing Services Ltd
64 Hallfield Road
Layerthorpe
York YO31 7ZQ

Tel: 01904 431213

Website: www.yps-publishing.co.uk

For my brave beautiful children and grandchildren

Photograph: Elena Cherubini

Ann Butler Rowlands found the real Kapotheni many years ago and has returned frequently to draw energy and comfort from the wisdom and playfulness of the people, whose home is one of the most beautiful places in the world.

Contact: abutlerrowlands@gmail.com
            www.annbutlerrowlands.co.uk

Thanks and Acknowledgements

Ευχαριστίες και την αγάπη μου σε όλους τους φίλους στην αληθινή Καπουθενή, σας ζητώ συγγνώμη που έκλεψα τα ονόματά σας για να 'βαφτίσω' τους τελείως φανταστικούς χαρακτήρες μου.

Trans: Thanks and love to all my friends on the real 'Kapotheni', with apologies for stealing your names and attaching them to wholly imaginary characters.

Much gratitude to Dimiter Stamatov (author of *The Soul Doctor*) for laughter, generous criticism, encouragement and an invaluable cultural perspective. Ongoing thanks to Chrysanthos, my Greek teacher, for his patience, humour and profound knowledge. Grateful thanks to Celia J. Anderson (*Living the Dream* and many others) for her generous support and to James Collins (*Remotely* and many more) for his editorial help and reliable ability to reduce me to helpless giggles.

Many thanks to the Exeter Story Prize, the Earlyworks Press Competition, the Fish Short Story Prize and the Bath Short Story Award, for their encouragement.

I have hubristically attempted my own free translations of C. P. Cavafy's poems, in order to draw out the resonances of his lyrical, ironic and sexually truthful voice. I was introduced to Cavafy in the lovely and scholarly Rae Dalven translations, which include some of the 'repudiated' and 'unpublished' poems, in *The Complete Poems of C. P. Cavafy*, Chatto and Windus 1968 (still to be found in good second-hand bookshops).

I would like to thank Daniel Mendelsohn (translator of the beautiful *C. P. Cavafy Complete Poems*) and Nikos Argyris of the Ikaros Publishing Company, for their help in the labyrinth of the Cavafy canon.

The original Greek is given, to pay respect to the nuances and rhythms of this extraordinary poet.

Permission: The Greek text of *In the House of the Soul* is published courtesy of the Cavafy Archive/Onassis Foundation. All rights reserved.

ABR

Contents

The Beautiful Journey

Η Ιθάκη σ'έδωσε τ' ωραίο ταξείδι.

Ithaca brought you the beautiful journey.
Ithaca C. P. Cavafy

'I think it's time to jump ship,' Tim said, staring over his coffee cup apparently into the future rather than the cheerful yellow of the spring garden. 'It's the best thing to do. I feel it in my water. I was expecting to jog on to sixty-five but something's brewing. I don't like the look of what's going on in the States.'

'Oh?' she said, preoccupied with one of her lists.

Dry cleaning

Screws cupboard

Ring Pete for light

Butcher

MOT

'And the rich-boy wreckers are hovering over us and this time I think Tristram's going to cave in. We've discussed. No point in staying while Rome burns.'

'Oh,' she looked up at his face to check if he was feeling as sanguine as he sounded. He was twiddling his hair.

'Don't twiddle.'

'Plenty to do,' he said. 'I was thinking of building a shed.'

'Please don't,' she leaned across and lightly stopped his hand, 'and don't twiddle.'

'Would you be alright with it?'

'Not with a shed. Why do you want a shed?'

'I mean having me lounging around here, while you work your little fingers to the bone hammering away at the craptop?'

She worked from home as an editor and had no plans to stop, but they both hated technology which had forced them to learn not just one set of new tricks but a seemingly endless succession of them over the past twenty years, which, for old dogs, had caused considerable brain ache. They had been happy with Ms Dos but apparently no-one else had been.

He put his lips to the cup and twinkled at her over the rim, 'Of course, I will need more sex to brighten up my empty days. I read somewhere that the trauma of retirement is greatly alleviated by extra special blow-jobs punctuated by extremely lengthy cunnilingus with a good deal of cardio-vascular screwing. It'll be like when Jake went to Uni and we got the house to ourselves. Imagine. Listening to *Woman's Hour* while you wank me off. Or I could watch porn in my shed, of course.'

'Who listens to *Woman's Hour*?'

'Or turn up the heating and have *The Afternoon Play*, naked with a bottle of vodka?'

'Well,' she said, grinning. 'In that case Yes to jump ship and definitely No to shed. As long as we can still do Kapotheni? If you're going to turn into an old shed person and there's no Kapotheni, I'll divorce you. And I will anyway, if you fart like that. Stop it. You'll kill the cat . . . How's your back this morning?'

'Not me,' he said. 'Cuddles! You're disgusting. Leave the room . . . Yeh, back's OK. Must have been the gardening.'

'Oh, Tim. Look at him. He thinks you mean it. Give him a stroke . . . Don't you think you ought to see the doctor?'

'About the farting?'

'About the back.'

'Doctors? Nothing but lackeys for the NHS actuaries . . . We could do a few months on Kapotheni, if you can swing it? May to July. Nice. Before the August hordes. Christ, love, if it's just us, we can live on Kapotheni for what it costs to pay the bloody council tax. When we were all going out mob-handed with the kids, that was ridiculous. The kids were great but then there was Dilly and her fine dining at swanky Vassili's or . . . what was it called? The one with the two gay guys? And dear departed Martin needing ouzo for breakfast, poor sod, and Bill querying every bill and always managing not to pay his whack.'

They laughed and intoned together, 'When I tip people it's because they've kissed my arse, not because they've done their fucking job.'

'Lovely old Bill,' Tim said. 'Eleven at the table. Remember?'

'I do,' she said. 'And I remember Lefteri sweeping up enough splattered food from the kids to feed a small African country and mopping up a river of Fanta which always got knocked onto the floor. He had the patience of a saint . . . *Aristeros* – that's what the boys' place was called. We've got one of their posters on the second landing.'

'What happened to them? Those boys?'

'The boys went back to Liverpool when the blond one's mother died . . . We don't really need *Athene*, you know, if you're going to be a poor old pensioner. It's a bit palatial for the two of us. Sevasti could find us something smaller. Well, palatial isn't quite the word, what with the funny toilet and the water pump and Mrs Sam.'

'Nothing like that view, though,' said Tim, twiddling again. 'Nothing like that balcony. What's the odds? Sevasti gets her money and Mrs Sam has hardly anything to do if it's just us. She likes a chat and a nose through your perfume and nail varnish. And Dilly can swan out and drag us off to eat posh, as long as we give her the nice toilet. She seems to have got over poor old Martin, doesn't she? And Fiona and Bill still pitch up sometimes.'

'Dilly is amazing. I think she went to Al Anon. The one for people who can't stop loving people who can't stop drinking. Same sort of problem really . . . I don't think Bill's coming out again. His asthma was awful last year in the heat.'

'Was it?'

'God, Tim. He could hardly breathe. Do you ever notice anything that's going on?'

'Oh,' he said. Tim hated the illness and debilitation which were slowly causing friends to fade and fall away.

Jump ship. At the time she had thought that it was clever and typical of him to be able to see the writing on the wall. When it became clear that the boy-wreckers wanted him to stay on for two years, Tristram urged him and rang her to urge him, to take the offer, 'Enough for a Ferrari, Jane, and the running costs for Christ sake,' he said to her, then remembered their incomprehensibly ramshackle life and amended it to, 'or maybe a nice little cottage in the country or some place on that bloody awful island.' Tristram had sailed grandly into Kapotheni one summer in a shiny white sea-monster, sleek with chrome and black glass. He had not taken to the unservile Greek attitude.

Tim would not budge and took his money and ran. They had two good years, for which she felt she should be grateful, but she was not. She was very angry and she wondered always whether somehow his brain had known about another impending catastrophe and that was what he had felt in his water.

She *was* grateful that the children were away. Jake was on a Scottish island looking after birds and Amanda was in Australia. They did not see the rages. They did not go through the bewildering year when he put the groceries in the pond, forgot where he was going or where he was, boarded trains with no money, stowed her iPad in the freezer and put her iPhone in the bathroom cabinet, and, with pitiable lack of concern, began to urinate in the bed. She hid car keys and credit cards. That year, for the first time, they did not go to Kapotheni. He said nothing about it and she felt too sad and too tired to make any arrangements. He had no insight and could not see that there was anything wrong. She was sure it was a brain tumour, but he would not hear of a doctor.

Eventually she told Dr Shah everything. He said, 'Bladder problems are not uncommon in old age. Get him to come in.'

'I can't,' she repeated wearily. Old age? Were they really old? Tim was as fit as a flea and as readily priapic as a goat. 'He won't. He thinks there's nothing wrong.'

'Difficult to adjust to having someone home all day?' he conjectured, making it plain in his bored tone that, in his opinion, her husband was probably right. 'Perhaps you're both finding it annoying? You want to get on with the housework and he is under your feet?'

'I do not spend my day in a pinny with a hoover,' she said, wanting to say 'in purdah' but knowing that this would be very rude and probably get her kicked off the list. 'I work on academic typescripts and have done for many years. He is . . . was perfectly capable of finding things to do, including the housework, a year ago.'

'You say these things irritate you?' he retorted edgily, looking at his notes. Unfortunately in spilling it all out to Dr Shah, she had been more open than she should have been. He looked as if he thought that a man doing the housework was in itself evidence of a disordered household. 'I'm afraid that irritating one's partner is not grounds for a section under the Mental Health Act.' He laughed a dry laugh to himself.

'I am aware of that,' she said to the chauvinist pig in his nicely laundered shirt. It flashed through her mind that she did not dislike Dr Shah because he was not of her tribe, but because he was a smug, inattentive little prick and that she was feeling not racism but personism and so should not berate herself. '. . . but putting expensive equipment in the freezer not only irritates, it calls into question the state of his mind, in my opinion,' she said, trying hard to breathe normally. She could feel herself being pushed into pigeon holes labelled *Over Anxious, Old* and *Annoying*. '. . . as does ordering meals in the Savoy with no money. As does ringing me up and asking if he is on the pier at Brighton or Llandudno. As does trying to find the clutch in an automatic car and the shoelaces on a velcro trainer.'

'You're shaking. You're very anxious,' he said, as if light were dawning on the problem. 'Are you always so anxious?'

'This is not anxiety,' she said, getting up to leave before she committed an offence, 'this is anger. This is what anger looks like, doctor.'

Then Tim disappeared and after three days a policeman was summoned by a Hampstead resident who could see 'something' in the alley at the end of her garden. Hampstead was thirty miles away. Tim had no coat, no money, no shoes but he did have hypothermia. Jane had tried to report him missing but no-one would listen. Luckily a few weeks earlier, she had found a paper bag with all the old unused name tapes bought for the children years before. Jake Timothy Crashaw. She had cut off the 'Jake' and sewn a label covertly into every garment, trying to find places Tim would not notice.

When she got to his hospital bed he burst into tears and flung his arms round her waist, terrified, 'Don't leave me, Mummy.'

They scanned and a doctor told her it was very bad, very advanced damage, surprised he could even walk, very bad luck at his age but sometimes happened. Not a tumour. His brain was shrivelling up and dying. He needed twenty-four-hour care.

It was like a death. She was so busy with all the arrangements that there was no time to attend to the pain which lurked in her stomach and her head and her heart. Like morphine, the phone calls and visits to nursing homes and frequent conversations with the two shocked children, dulled the anguish which she knew she was feeling but she could not quite feel.

Dilly and Fiona visited and vetted homes with her, took fruit and bewildered gentleness to Tim in hospital, insisted on putting homemade frozen meals in her freezer, endured her furious critical ranting about everything, and cried and talked to each other privately at the end of each day. Amanda rang Fiona from Australia in the middle of the night with a guilty conscience, needing to be convinced that Fiona understood that it was impossible for Amanda to come back right then. Fiona was annoyed. Dilly commiserated with Fiona, 'Children are always selfish. It's not their fault. Probably ours. But they really should learn to live with it, without needing to be absolved, particularly at times like this.' Jake rang Dilly and said he wanted to come down and see Dad but his mother kept telling him not to. Dilly said, 'He's ga-ga, Jake. It's really quite awful to see him. I'm sorry. I'm afraid you will find it very painful.' Fiona said Dilly should not have said this, which made Dilly cry and drink too much and have to have a cab home.

They found a place which catered for EMIs, the elderly mentally infirm, none of which sounded anything like Tim, who only a few weeks before had been pruning the wisteria, admittedly with Jane's best dressmaking scissors. The Home did not smell too bad. It had a beautiful garden and the Matron gallantly rode out Jane's hostile and weary list of questions.

'If it is a consolation,' Matron said, 'from what you tell me, this is far worse for you than him. I'm afraid you will feel very upset for a while.'

Jane burst into tears and Dilly got her into the car.

He forgot who she was, almost from the day they moved him into the Home. She had packed the clothes that suited him best and the shoes he liked. She had collected photographs and put them into an ingenious flip-over holder. Sitting on the sofa going through the old family albums, she had to bend over periodically, her face to her knees in a dry, tearless agony. 'This is the pain of my heart breaking,' she said aloud, into the empty room. The cat started to live in the garden, wary of the sound of her crashing about swearing and crying and then the silence.

Jake came down. Tim smiled and stroked his face. Jane was anxiously convinced that Tim thought Jake was his brother, who had died in a crash before Jake was born. She dug her nails into her hand hoping Tim would not call Jake 'Andrew'. He did not. Jake cried and she took him out to dinner because cooking felt too complicated. She packed him off the next morning, glad that his Land Rover was clearly so old that it could not possibly go over the speed limit.

Amanda emailed complicated questions about Tim's condition, littered with incomprehensible medical terms. She urged Jane to read various clinical papers and sent the links. After some weeks of trying to sound interested, Jane lost patience and wrote, 'They say it's hopeless. I don't want to read about the fascinating hopelessness of it all. Sorry. Love Mum.' Amanda rang Dilly and bored her with how worried she was about her mother's irrational state of mind. Dilly lost patience and said, 'Your mother's struggling to get through the day without strangling the cat, the milkman or anyone else. This is a perfectly reasonable reaction to what has happened to her and your dad. Fiona or I go in every day and force soup down her, if we can. She's a very lucky woman. When I'm miserable I eat like a horse and put on stones. She's nearly a size ten. For the sake of our friendship, I won't let her get to an eight, I can promise you.'

Three months later, a routine had developed. The children established weekly contact of the *How r u? Hows Dad?* variety and stopped feeling bad when they had a laugh or felt good about something. Jane visited Tim every day for twenty minutes and held his hand. Sometimes she kissed it and he looked at her in surprise, but smiled.

They had had sex until the day he disappeared. She wished she could talk to someone about that, but it was too embarrassing. It seemed ghoulish. Even Amanda with her wonderful doctor's detachment might be somewhat disconcerted by the information that her father, with hardly any functioning brain cells, had still been able to get an erection and never forgot how to make her mother come.

Matron was a kind woman, who always seemed to be adjusting flowers in the hall or popping into the lounge when Jane was leaving. She would walk with her to the door, sometimes gently putting her hand on Jane's arm, asking after her, 'How are you managing? If you need a bit of an offload, my door's always open.' But however solicitous, Jane did not think that Matron would react positively to being asked if Jane could just sneak in one night and get into bed with Tim and see if he would take her, under the imperative of whatever bit of his brain had stayed alive and ready for her through the past year.

What would Matron say? 'I'm sorry my dear, but I don't think that would be appropriate on the grounds of health and safety.' If she allowed Jane access again, she would hover all the more solicitously in case of elder sexual abuse.

Jane tried to masturbate but always ended up crying, so that was no good. She was astonished at the mindlessness of her envy. She envied Fiona, who had fat breathless Bill to curl up with, and Dilly, who was being seduced by another alcoholic.

In order to knock all this out at night, she took a mixture of Night Nurse and valerian and painkiller. She lived on the occasional boiled egg; anything else made her want to vomit. There was something too physical and hopeful about putting food in her mouth. Fiona and Dilly tried to take her out for meals, but the sight of happy couples, or even just couples, made her want to weep and scream. She did not tell them this, but said that a stupendous amount of money was pouring out of the account into that of the neat, polite, extremely wealthy Mr Savanandijam, who owned the Home and, when she was up to it, she was going to have to talk to someone about money. Until then she felt she should keep expenditure basic. The next day Bill rang her up wheezily and said he would happily go through the books with her, if it would help. It would not. She knew he was itching to find out exactly how much Tim was worth. After several false starts, talking on the phone to men who either patronised her into a carpet-biting frenzy or urged her to call them by their Christian name, which made her distrust them, she located someone who asked useful questions, was polite, said he was Mr So and So, called her Mrs Crashaw and was able to locate his diary. Mr So and So eventually told her that she could maintain the status quo, house, Nursing Home fees, lifestyle, for about seven years, if the economic situation remained stable. This was a very big If. After that? 'I'm afraid it would be family silver time,' he said.

Dilly and Fiona proposed that the three of them go to Kapotheni in the summer, to have a break.

'I don't think I could go without him,' she said, but they went.

At the Rhodes hotel where they always stayed to get the morning ferry, Fiona dashed ahead and said things to Niko.

'I very sorry to hear this, Madam Crasho,' Niko said to Jane, when he had noted her passport number. Discreetly out of his sight and hearing, they used to crack up about being called Sir and Madam Crasho. This time there was nothing funny about it at all.

'*What* did he hear?' Jane asked Fiona in the lift.

'I told him Tim was . . . ill,' Fiona said.

A surge of bile welled up in Jane, 'So what am I doing jaunting off on fucking holiday with a sick husband at home?'

'Oh, oh, I'm sorry love,' said Fiona, stroking her arm, 'I'll explain it more.'

'Well good luck. His English goes as far as saying how the key works and the time of breakfast. Do you know the Greek for Advanced Alzheimer's?'

When she had calmed down, they talked about what to say about Tim. They decided to tell Sevasti the facts. She could relay the information to everyone on the island who knew them.

She slept in the large courtyard bedroom, where they had billeted all the kids together until puberty dictated separation.

Dilly bagged the beautiful bay-facing front bedroom with its three tall windows. Jane could not tell if Dilly did this from empathic intuition or long-frustrated desire. Jane and Tim had always used it. She tried hard to avoid even looking through the open door.

Much of the holiday hurt. She had only just started to wake up into an immediate knowledge of what had happened. For months previously, when she woke, there had been a few terrible seconds of illusory contentment, before her brain whacked her into reality. On Kapotheni she had to see everything in this new way. Without Tim.

At Mr Tavrakis's crammed grocery, Mr Tavrakis was not there. His son was at the till. He was distant and quick. The young ones did not believe in making friends with tourists.

Mr Tavrakis had a standing joke with them. Hearing the five year old Amanda called Darling by her mother, this became his name for her. Amanda would firmly tell him that she was called Amanda, but he took no notice. When Jake and Amanda stopped coming out, he would say 'How Darling?' and it would be 'Darling's going to university', then 'Darling's getting married', then 'Darling's gone to Australia'. His face had dropped at that for an unguarded second. Many of the islanders had lost children and siblings, uncles and aunts to Australia. 'No,' they had assured him, 'not for ever.' But it had been. He knew more than they. Amanda and her husband liked it and they stayed. Australia wanted them.

In Mr Tavrakis's grocery, Dilly wandered up and down, squeezing with difficulty between the shelves and piled-up boxes and local shoppers who, quite rightly in Jane's view, were always served before the tourists on account of the fact that they were living real lives. Dilly held up tins and bottles plaintively asking tired Greek wives whether this was shower cream or hair conditioner, mayonnaise or mustard? The wives nodded and smiled noncommittally. Fiona went round methodically with her basket and list. Mr Tavrakis's son packed it all into plastic bags and shoved the bill under their noses, which he had obviously decided was easier than trying to get these idiots to understand a verbal request.

Sevasti had done a good job with the island version of instant messaging. When they went to expensive Vassili's restaurant, he held Jane's hand and stroked her back in the comforting way which expresses commiseration, sympathy or simply good fellowship. Everyone who knew Tim, was kind and concerned, but as the islanders keep their demented elders at home, slumped in armchairs outside their doors being greeted by all passers-by, Jane was not convinced that they would understand the concept of Mr Savanandijam's Nursing Home, the annual fees for which would keep a frugal island family for eight years. The resident English were naturally far more English about it and contented themselves with a muttered 'Frightfully sorry about Tim' before launching into a grumble about the xenophobic Town Council or the erratic electricity supply, to improve which they knew, for a fact, the Council had received EU money five years ago.

Dilly and Fiona cried off the usual trip to the monastery, shrine of Archangel Michael. Dilly, on the grounds that the taverna was very basic Greek and the lavatories unspeakably splattered. Fiona, on the grounds that the bus was stifling and last time she had had to sit next to the old priest, who stank of body odour and donkey. Jane went on her own, with a fragrant mother and child on the seat next to her. She lit her candles and contemplated Michael with his great sword. She ate houmous and drank ouzo and water. She felt that she was doing the trip for Tim, with Tim and without Tim.

It was agony, but when she arrived home, the hours in the sun, Lefteri's tomato feta salads and his wife's sad embrace, as gentle as the warm sea, had relaxed and nourished her neglected body. She gathered and sorted Tim's remaining clothes. She consulted the children about any of his possessions they might like to have. There was a muted argument about his trumpet which he could never really play, but his version of *Lights Out* had annoyed the neighbours, to the children's delight.

She decorated and moved into Amanda's old bedroom, finding, during this process, a very revealing diary, detailing incidents which she was glad not to have known about at the time. She found a reliable, if opinionated, gardener and a willing handyman called Pete who could turn his hand to most things, if they sat down and thought it through together. After six months Pete told her that he had just come out of nick, for not knowing that the boxes his mate had asked him to store were stolen computers. By that time she was as sure as she could be that he was a good lad. She kept him on. The house and the garden had to be maintained. They were her family silver. Her supply of editorial work, while never recovering completely from the months of total indifference and unreturned phone calls, provided spasms of concentrated thought.

The pain of the black hole in her heart was less viciously gnawing and became more of an ache. She visited Tim late every afternoon and came away with tears in her eyes, then she made tea and checked the television pages. She knew she had lost who she was. She had been the woman Tim knew for so many years and now she was someone else, whom the crotchety gardener and gullible Pete knew. She met Dilly and Fiona every Friday night and they claimed listening time for their own lives and grumbles and dilemmas. She tried once to talk about missing the sex, but Fiona 'had given up on it years ago' and Dilly had been disappointed to discover, again, that long term drinking and sexual performance are not compatible. They both intimated that she should be jolly grateful for what she had had. They no longer came round on a rota to force her to eat soup.

The next year the daffodils and the forsythia outdid themselves. Grumbleguts the gardener put it down to his manure: 'Terrible weak soil you had.'

The colour often reminded her of the jump ship conversation. That clean fresh yellow had been the colour of their life, buoyant and full of growth, newness.

The ravening sexual hunger for Tim's practised understanding of her body, had had to be dealt with by her own version of Cognitive Behavioural Therapy. Every time she felt the dark empty despair of Never Again, she forced herself into an action. Add more logs to the stack by the door. Bring in more logs. Clean the bath. Prune something, whether it needed it or not. Clean the oven. Something vigorous and finite followed by coffee and toast and Marmite. At night she eked out a small bag of green cannabis, making a toke at eleven, which blessedly never failed to put her slightly above wherever she was and lowered her into sleep.

Fiona had confiscated a stash belonging to her visiting and wayward son. Fiona used it for her back pain and swore by it.

In the winter Jane holed up with piles of box set DVDs and decided that, in the summer, she must go and say goodbye to the island and their golden time. Then she must come back and put the house on the market, so that the buyers could see the garden in June and July, its best months. Mr So and So approved her prudence.

When she arrives at *Athene*, exhausted by the heat and noise of travelling, she lies on the cool white bed in the beautiful bay-gazing bedroom. The high painted ceiling with its primitive trompe l'oeil caryatids, repeated cornucopia and scenes of churches and fishing boats, floats above her, uncaring of the indifference she and Tim had shown it, as they ran in and out gathering clothes and beach stuff or lay entwined.

Now she wants to remember in detail what they did together in this room, but it saddens her that all the times have run together and there are just little flashes like film clips. Their sex life would appear to have been a comedy.

Scene One: Tim kneeling on the wooden floor with her legs over his shoulders sucking her like a fig, until one year he gets cramp and leaps from foot to foot howling 'Ow!' bringing Fiona and Bill to the door, where Fiona screams with laughter and Bill looks as if he might vomit.

Scene Two: Here is Tim pretending to decline Fuck in Greek while he slowly moves all the way in and all the way out: Fucko fuckis fucki . . .

Question: Which one of them will hit their head on the sturdy wooden bedstead this year? At home there is padded leather.

Scene Three: At the window they watch the headlights of the old bus trundling up the mountain road, while she feels his penis expectantly nudging the small of her back.

They are not as bad as she feared, these memories. They do not burn and lacerate. She remembers him standing naked at the window, with his hands on the sill, staring out at the sparkling lights of the little port, 'Heaven,' he says. 'It's heaven.'

At home she does not have a full length mirror in her room. He no longer sees her. She has nothing to look at. In the great tarnished mirror at *Athene*, she sees how puckered and thin she has become. Her skin has shrivelled like Tim's brain. She does not have the body he kissed.

When she gets up in the early evening to do the shopping, there are thick white clouds on the horizon and wispy threads of organza floating in the sky. She buys the basics, packed brusquely by Mr Tavrakis's son, but this time with a small indifferent smile of recognition. She walks slowly back through the narrow alleys, pressing herself against the walls when a motorbike buzzes or roars up behind her. There is something odd. There is no defined shady side on which to walk and, when she reaches the high open space of the village square, she is surprised by a grey heavy sky, not at all right for late May. The breeze is cool. She has never once needed anything more than thin cotton or silk. She considers the very surprising notion that she might need a sweater.

When the shopping is stowed safely away from the ants and she has showered, she walks down to the little bay, to Kris's taverna to have his mother's special stuffed vine leaves. She will sit on the platform roofed in vines, which juts out over the sea, offering a mooring to the diminutive fishing boats, bobbing like charms on a bracelet. The cicadas rattle their inexhaustible chorus and the donkeys provide a descant across the olive groves, but the barren rock slopes of the mountain are not turning pink in the sunset. The grey clouds have leached the tint up into themselves, like a spreading water colour.

At Kris's there are no stuffed vine leaves. The old lady has been ill in the winter. Kris, her white-haired son, mimes a paralysed side, a stroke.

She touches his arm and says slowly, 'I am sad for you,' hoping he will understand.

She has homemade meat balls and Greek salad and beer. The little boats are mute and still, the sea flat and leaden, sulky like a disgruntled child, slapping the beach half-heartedly. She throws a piece of bread into the sea to watch the little fish wrestle it down, but nothing happens.

The water-taxi brothers sit in a corner and raise their hands and glasses in greeting. Stamati, one of the brothers, comes over, 'How you family?' he asks.

'The children are good,' she says.

'You boy, son. He OK?'

'He's in Scotland looking after birds,' she says, wondering what on earth he would make of that.

'Scotland very cold,' he says, grinning. Stamati lived in Newcastle for many years with an English wife, then he came back.

'How you husband now?' he asks.

'He's very ill,' she taps her head. 'His brain is sick, you know.'

'Is very sad,' he says. 'I think is lot of this thing.' He rubs her back. 'Is difficult for you. Is good you come here. You very thin. Kapotheni make you better.' She feels tears and sees that he notices. He pats her and kindly walks away.

Giorgio with the round-the-island boat comes in with Mr Tavrakis, whom he has brought on his motorbike. They join the brothers and start their loud, jossing conversations, which always made her think they were angry with each other, until she heard the brutal tones of a real argument. Giorgio comes over and shakes her hand. He is a breathtakingly beautiful man, much courted by generations of tourists. Like many of the islanders he never seems to look older, just larger but with hard flesh. She doesn't think she has seen any islander with flab apart from Pangelis with the water cart. The perspiring shoals of wobbling tourists, who trail off the day boats, seem like another species.

Mr Tavrakis waves, 'You back. Is good,' he shouts. 'How Darling?'

'She's good,' she shouts back.

Kris comes over to take the dishes and she asks for yoghourt and another beer. The bay is dark and the houses which perch round its edge offer their lights onto still black water. There is a strange noise. She thinks it is fish. An intermittent plopping sound. The vines start to rustle, as if birds are rootling in them. A sudden yellow flash illuminates the bay, the houses, the boats, the tables on the platform and their upturned faces, followed by a crack and long rumble of thunder. A corresponding roar comes from the men who clap their hands laughing. Another flash shows the sea like a boiling pot, pitted with perpendicular rain which now drives its way through the vines and smacks onto plates and into glasses. A wind howls violently through the boxes of geraniums round the edge of the platform. One of the boxes smashes over.

Kris comes out in a flap, waving his arms and beckoning them into the house. He picks up her yoghourt and beer, 'You come. You come,' he yells above the sudden spattering din of the rain.

The bay is illuminated again and another long deep drumming roll of thunder races around the enclosing hills. By the time they have run into the house, all of them have been stung by the deluge, which pours in fierce hard lines through the vines. Thunder bounces from mountain to hill and back. Kris drags chairs to a table by the door and everyone sits down laughing and shaking out their T-shirts and their hair. More geranium pots fall over and slide across the floor. A branch of vine starts to swing and tear. Chairs crash backward and forward. Table cloths flap angrily and rip away, twisting recklessly out to sea. Windows can be heard crashing in and out. From the nearby houses there are cries and exhortations, as they struggle with the shutters. The sea seems to have risen two feet and is slopping menacingly over the platform. The moored boats buck and rear on their anchors, flashing white in the lightning, rolling and yawing in the sudden swells.

A stream of rain is sluicing down from the hill road catching on debris and piling it against the creaking cradles of the dry docked boats. The motorcycle crashes onto its side. Giorgio swears. The storm is so loud that no-one can hear what anyone is saying. It subdues and overpowers. They sit and drink and smile at each other.

Then it moves on. They hear it rumbling over the main port. The lightning becomes a regular flowering glow in the sky, but the rain falls with relentless steadiness and the wind jags around capriciously. Stamati orders more beer for them all. Jane looks at her watch and wonders about the last bus. As an answer the phone rings. It is the hotel. A tree has come down on the hill road. Miki has rung to tell them that the bus will not be coming any further. He will stop at the tree with his passengers. Kris announces the news. She wonders what the passengers are going to do about the tree. Perhaps the hotel, where most of them belong, will organise a rescue party.

Everyone lives on the other side of the tree, apart from Kris, so they will have to make the journey. She wonders about checking into the hotel, which will not be full at this time of year.

Silently all the lights go out. Something has happened at the rusty old generating plant, which hums and clanks at the bottom of the hill. The phone rings. It is the hotel. Their lights have gone. Has Kris got light? She wonders why they don't just look out of the window. The whole bay is black.

Kris rummages about and finds candles. With difficulty against the wind, he shuts the double doors. The rain is pelting down, bouncing pellets of mud at the walls. By the uncertain light of the candles, she hunches forward and peers at her phone to see if she has the hotel number. They have so many island phone numbers for ordering tables in the days when they were a crowd.

'You ring boyfriend?' asks Stamatis, clearly thinking this very funny.

Stamati's brother gives him a bit of a stern look. She smiles at Stamati. She can see he meant no harm. 'The hotel,' she says.

'No stay there with all the fat Germans,' says Stamati. 'You OK. We get up the hill OK.'

Giorgio is worrying about his bike. A torrent of debris is rushing down the hill, smashing into everything in its path. There is a discussion with Kris, who rummages again in the murky kitchen passageway and comes back with two old waterproofs. Giorgio takes one and wrestles with the doors, which the wind is determined to smash against the wall. The candles blow out. Everyone groans impatiently. Kris lights them. Over the noise of the rain and the wind Giorgio can be heard growling viciously as he tries to secure his bike. The men laugh. Stamati puts his hands briefly over her ears, 'Bad words,' he says.

The phone rings. It is Miki the bus driver, saying he is about to descend from the village and he will have to stop at the road fork before the tree, so that he can turn round.

'You go,' says Kris, holding out the other coat to her. 'Take.'

It envelops her and they laugh. One of them pulls the hood over her head. It sinks over her eyes. Someone pulls up the heavy duty zip. Kris strains with the door and they tumble out into the angry wind, which howls through the pines. She cannot see anything and her sandals threaten to come off in the fast-flowing flood water. Someone takes her hand, for which she is very grateful. The men are shouting and laughing like boys. She clings on to the hand with both of hers and begins to feel very frightened. Something large crashes past them, half-flying, half-floating, bouncing off tree trunks. Something else surfs down the hill, a crate of bottles or cans. She is dragged out of its path. The trudging up the hill through the streaming rubbish-laden flood seems endless. Her legs feel like rubber and her breathing is tight and shallow. The stricken tree bulks up solidly in the dark and they all stop.

The headlights of the bus show that it is completely blocking the road, its roots torn out of the steep hillside and its branched head hanging over the precipitous other side. She is pushed up, grazing her hands, shins and knees. Someone drags her over and someone catches her legs and bundles her over his shoulder in a fireman's lift and they stagger toward the lights of the bus. She is placed upright. Giorgio has been her fireman. She wonders how many women would have paid good money for that thirty-yard trip. Her sandals have gone and her legs are so shaky that they have to push her up the steps of the bus, like they do with the very old ladies. She is winded, scratched, bruised, wet and cold. She slumps in her seat and starts to cry with relief and exhaustion. Someone slams down next to her amidst the noise. He pulls her hood back and peers into her face laughing.

'OK? OK? You cry? No, is OK.' It is Mr Tavrakis. He pats her cheek gently, 'No cry.'

The bus contains a number of white-faced hotel guests who seem to have decided to stay on it and return to the port. Miki is happy to spend any amount of time smoking and exchanging stories of the devastation with the men, but eventually he starts up the engine and turns the bus round and climbs the hill, going slowly through the torrent on the road, so as not to raise too much of a wave, watching out for large flotsam. What looks like a dead donkey forlornly ripples past them and an old fridge threatens to stop the bus, but veers off over the side of the road. Vicious buffeting gusts of wind rock the vehicle and the men all roar with delight, slapping the handrails on the seats. The hotel guests sit in a huddle with their iPhones and iPads, furiously stabbing fingers at screens and muttering about insurance.

She is frightened of what it will be like up in the village on the crest of the hill. At the bus stop she has to walk a little way further up and then down an alley to the square. She sees herself sucked off the open square and smashed down the precipitous hillside to the port. At the village stop, Miki says it is too bad to go on, the even steeper road down to the port will be impossible. He will wait till the storm subsides. The brothers make him give them cigarettes and Giorgio stretches out on the back seat and puts his feet up. The Greeks get their phones out and begin to ring whoever might be expecting them, or anyone else who might like a chat and a meteorological update. The hotel guests shoot disbelieving looks at everyone. A man tries to ask Miki how long this will be. Miki suddenly does not understand English. He leans back in his seat and puts on his iPod.

She feels sorry for them, 'He'll go down as soon as he can. There's a place next to the bank at the port called *Ariadne*,' she says. 'It won't be full. I'm sure you could put up there.' They stare at her in outrage and surprise. She realises that her arrival slung over Giorgio's shoulder may have been open to interesting interpretations. They do not seem to have expected her to be an old Englishwoman. 'What did they think we were going to do?' says a woman, 'climb over that tree? My husband's got emphysema.' She tuts, 'These people . . .'

Mr Tavrakis stands up and politely indicates that Jane should go down the steps first. The English stare with scandalised interest, like the old colonials watching a woman who has gone to the dogs. 'You come,' he says. He makes her walk behind him and they battle up the hill, through buffeting wind and rain, to the alley where he opens the shop. He gestures for her to take off the coat and sit on the old chair which they keep for frail or infirm customers. She sits down trembling. He brings a towel for her hair and pours two ouzos. She does not want it, but feels it would be remarkably rude to refuse.

'You good now,' he says, patting her shoulder. 'Is good storm, eh? Strong. Very strong storm.'

He sits on a box packed with washing powder and raises his glass, '*Yeia mas.*'

'*Yeia mas.*' She takes a sip and puts down her glass and begins to examine the grazes on her legs and knees and arms. Mr Tavrakis finds cotton wool and disinfectant and she manages to explain it has to be diluted, so he pours some water into a cup. She dabs the grazes and a cut on her ankle. The storm is still raging around, rattling everything it can find, hurling rain like gravel against the shutters. It is warm in the shop, the thick walls of the houses, squashed together in the warren of the village, soak up the sun from March onward, like medieval radiators.

As she dabs, she thinks how alone and weak she is and that it will be like this for ever. She wants to weep and howl with the storm.

'What you think?' asks Mr Tavrakis, his dark eyes smiling at her in the dusty gloom.

She thought, well you asked and I'll tell you. 'I'm thinking,' she says, not making any effort to speak slowly or use simple words, 'I'm thinking that I have lost everything that really kept me going and made me who I was. My children are grown and I have become just someone for them to worry about. Tim has gone and all the time I have to fight the fucking loneliness and missing him. I can't bear for it to be over and it is over and I've got to go on living for years. Years of it going on fucking hurting and I don't want to do it and I feel I can't do it but I have to, there's no choice. It's such a price to pay for being fucking happy. I'm not brave. I wish I was out of it like him. There's nothing ahead. Nothing good. A broken heart just keeps fucking breaking, Mr Tav. It just keeps breaking over and over.'

He sits back and stares at her. There is no expression in his face, no tension of laughter or sadness, and yet it is not blank or withdrawn. His eyes seem to open wider, but there is no sense of challenge, as there might be if this were some sort of staring match like the ones she played as a child. She looks at him. She sees the white and black hairs in his eyebrows and his stiff wiry hair and the white stubble on his cheeks. She sees a scar on his forehead and a mole on his chin. She feels no need to smile or look away.

He puts his index finger up to the middle of her forehead and presses it lightly, 'You want sex?' he asks, as if it might be in a tin or a bottle on one of his shelves.

She pulls back from him in alarm and surprise. 'No. Oh sorry. No,' she says, appalled that she has made him think this. Perhaps it was because she swore? 'I'm too old to . . .' She thought, what am I saying, it's nothing to do with being old and now very ugly, it's because he isn't Tim. 'I love Tim,' she says, not caring whether he can understand her. 'Sex with Tim was so lovely and it won't happen again.'

'I too am old,' he says, either not understanding or not taking any notice of this last pronouncement. 'How many years you come here and I am always old man?'

This is true and it makes her smile.

'Come,' he says, 'I show you.'

He takes her hand. She does not snatch it away or say 'Stop' or get up and march to the door. He threads her through the winding paths between the boxes and shelves. In a little room are more boxes and a narrow space between.

'See,' he says laughing, 'no mirror. No see how old we are.' From a shelf he takes brightly coloured blankets and puts them on the floor in their polythene covers.

'You take off your clothes,' he says and pulls his shirt over his head, takes off his trainers, and pulls off his jeans. Mr Tavrakis is wearing a rather snazzy pair of striped boxers, which she could have sworn were Marks & Sparks.

Oh Christ, she thinks. Beam me up, Scottie. How the hell could I have got myself into such a fine mess as this one? She thinks of Tim, two hours behind but still doubtless in bed and probably drugged to sleep. Tim, come here, she orders him in her head. Come here and get me through this. I've royally fucked up. You always wanted a threesome (I trust not seriously). Well, here you are and it's Mr Tav. Not quite what you meant, I think. I'm afraid it's a case of having to follow through, like it or not. There's been some serious miscommunication and it must be mine.

She takes off her clothes in the coffin-like space and they lie down with some difficulty. When he puts his hand on her, she flinches. She is dry and, when he comes into her, she remembers how it was with men before Tim, when she could not connect and just waited for it to be over.

Mr Tavrakis pulls out of her and sits back contemplatively between her legs. 'Wait,' he says, as if she is showing signs of making a naked dash for the door and the alley. She is so embarrassed that she cannot imagine herself doing anything but getting this over with and going to bed in *Athene* and staying there behind the great double doors, for the rest of her life. He walks back into the shop with his cock jutting out over the spaghetti and rice. He comes back with a pot of butter substitute, no doubt stocked for the English. That's quite clever of him, she thinks, because it will be soft, or is this his usual lubricant for rogering the tourists? She feels sorry for misleading him. He seems quite sincerely to believe that he is doing what is required and she wants to get it over with, so she opens the pot and smears the stuff over his penis and she takes him in her mouth. He crashes back against the boxes groaning and pulls her away, 'No, not yet,' he says, gripping his cock with an agonised grimace. Bugger, she thinks. Then she thinks about STIs or whatever VD is called now, not something that she has ever had to think about, being of the blessed generation who did their casual sex after penicillin, with the pill and before Aids. The possible damage-limitation consultation, with prissy, male chauvinist Dr Shah, would be a blinder.

He lays her back and comes into her again. The low fat cholesterol-busting spread (oh dear) makes it better or should she say butter? She starts to shiver with laughter. He stops and looks down at her, 'I'm sorry. *Sygnomi,*' she says. 'It's the butter.'

He grins at her, 'I like you laugh,' he says. 'I always like you laugh.'

He plunges his fingers into the pot and puts his hand down to find her cunt. He grasps her thighs, which are so thin that his hands almost enclose them. He pulls her toward him, putting her legs over his shoulders and gets on his knees, raising her into a position for which she should have prepared with at least two years of Pilates. He pulls her arms round his neck and holds her and stays still inside her. An odour of donkey comes off his skin, but clean donkey. She has always liked donkeys ever since she rode them at Whitby beach.

'I like,' he says.

'Good,' she says, in an incongruously English matter-of-fact way, as if he were commenting on a cup of tea.

'Now more butter,' he says.

'More?'

'Yes, I go there,' he slides his hand down her back to her buttocks.

'Oh no,' she wriggles away from him as far as this is possible in the confined space.

'Why no?'

'It hurts.'

Tim had wanted to do this sometimes but she could not. One of the Before-Tims had done it to her viciously, when he realised she wanted to leave him. He tore her and terrified her and the medical treatment afterwards was almost as humiliating.

'Not hurt,' Mr Tavrakis firmly contradicts her. 'When I inside there, you come. Is very good. You not do before?'

She shakes her head, wishing she had been more serious about learning Greek, but if someone had told her she would need it for this eventuality she would have thought they were barking.

'I first then. Is nice. I be first one.'

'No.'

'Oh,' he says, 'Look. I put here plenty butter and be very soft. You shout, bite me if it hurt and I stop. Is old man cock anyway. Very small.'

Not so, she thinks. I'm going to have great difficulty with the spaghetti and rice shelf, now that I've watched your prick hovering over it like some kind of bald feather duster. She can't help laughing. He tousles her hair. She really wishes she could ask him if he has seen *Last Tango in Paris*. There is no cinema on the island but perhaps they have ferry expeditions to watch porn in Rhodes.

She lets him do it, because she wants it over and why should she care? There's so much pain anyway. He does not hurt her. He is gentle and slow and then he finds her and she comes for a long time and pulls him into her, to feel him come. He makes a noise like a donkey, a whistling hoarse cry, and although it's funny she does not laugh because she feels the surge of pleasure racing through him and it is good to make him happy.

She is crying because it is not Tim and she is laughing because it is Mr Tavrakis in the back of his shop. They sit up and look at each other smiling.

'Is heaven,' he says, between breaths, 'is heaven.'

They get dressed and he puts the blankets back on the shelf. She hopes he is going to check for butter. She wonders what he will do with the ravaged pot. Something for his toast in the morning? She reckons that Mr Tavrakis is not a waster.

They walk through the shop and he opens the door a crack. It is quieter and the rain is a hesitant scatter, apologetically drifting onto the walls and cobbles. She puts on the coat and he zips her up and pulls on the hood. He steps out a little way and looks up and down carefully.

'Is good now,' he says. 'You go.'

At *Athene* she lets herself in and goes peacefully to bed without thought. In the morning she wakes when the sun tops the hillside and flashes its heat through any crack in the shutters it can find. She wonders if she suffered a prolonged hallucination, but on her fingers there is a donkey buttery smell which makes her laugh.

In the shower she discovers again all the grazes and bruises and cuts.

She had decided to go to the monastery that day and light candles for Tim and the children. She cannot imagine what it will be like getting the groceries. There is only one shop in the village. Perhaps Mr Tavrakis's son has taken over completely, leaving Mr Tavrakis free to indulge in geriatric buggery with any deranged tourist he can find.

At the monastery in the little jewel-coloured golden chapel, she stands before the flashy silver portrait of the Archangel and asks him to take care of Tim and watch over the children. She has always liked the Archangel, in his armour and sword. The one who threw Satan and his crew out of heaven and pursued them to the depths. His expression says, 'Don't mess with me. None of your mealy-mouthed excuses. Just fuck off.' Strangely, too, this particular Archangel Michael has a reputation for being good at helping ladies who badly want to be pregnant. The rail is adorned with little dolls and bootees, bracelets and watches. *This is something precious of mine but nothing could be more precious than a baby. My time is running out. Help me.* She thought how easily she had conceived her children and of the searing unfairness of it all. Tears for these empty mothers stood in her eyes. Their hearts, too, must break every day.

'Give me some strength,' she begs the icon. 'I've lost my mooring line and I'm drifting. Help me to hold on, until it's time to let go.'

The Archangel stares back with his resolute calm expression. She steps up and kisses the glass which protects his silvered portrait from countless supplicant lips. She crosses herself and leaves through the narrow door out into the great heat and the milling press of tourists. The candles have been put in a shelter nearby, to protect the newly cleaned frescoes and the arching pictures of the saints, which glow on the ceiling of the chapel. She weaves slowly through the day trippers and lights her candles. She puts a large amount of money into the alms box.

She has lost Tim. She has lost the containment and safety of their merged understanding. They had found a safe harbour, as beautiful as the huge natural oval of peaceful water at the head of which the monastery raises its bell tower, where last night the sea crashed contemptuously over the broad stone flags and the wind howled round the chapel and maybe even rocked the icon on the wall, until the storm moved up the island to the little bay where she sat.

She was waiting for the bus, when her phone beeped, it was Jake texting: *This is an official announcement. Hav met someone I want u 2 meet when u get bak. Wil bring her down. Sat 3/6 b OK? Sheilagh. Islander. Shepherdess. I may b here 4 life. Hope so. Bit scary this.*

She texts, *Don't be scared of love.*

Where u?

I'm visiting Archangel Michael.

That old tinman! Want u 2 do yr special steak thing & one of yr trifles. Can we hav u & Dad's rm? No dble bed in my shack. Luv u, J xx

She does not tell anyone it is her last time. She will talk to Sevasti on the phone from England. She leaves Mrs Sam so much money that she will probably retire or probably not. No-one seems to stop working on the island.

One time Mr Tavrakis is at the till. Her body becomes flustered, when she sees him and her hands shake. He puts her groceries in a bag and tells her how much. Then he picks up an apple from the box next to him and gives it to her smiling, 'Heaven,' he says. 'I no forget.'

When she gets home, she goes to see Tim, who smiles politely and mutely allows her to sit down and hold his hand. She wheels him into the garden. He can only stay out there for a short while, before he becomes anxious and starts to shout. Taking advantage of the privacy, she tells him about what happened with Mr Tav and says how sorry she is she would never let Tim do it, because it would have been lovely, she's learned that, but he knows why she was frightened and she is grateful to him for always being kind. He smiles at her with his puzzled gentleness.

She takes him back into the lounge, where he nods happily at Shaun the Sheep on the television. She kisses his forehead.

In the hall Matron waves cheerily.

'You were having a good chat,' says Matron.

'Yes,' she says, trying not to laugh, 'I was telling him about heaven.'

A Feeling World

Οικίας περιβάλλον, κέντπων, συνικίάς...
Κ'αισθηματοποιήθηκες ολόκληρο, γιά μένα.

The ambience of the house, the meeting places, the district
. . . You have become my feeling world.

In the Same Space C. P. Cavafy

B
ill sat down heavily on Helen's new silk dress.

'Those bloody squirrels have dug out three of the pots,'
he grumbled, picking at a piece of dried mud on his trousers.

'Excuse me, could you move, Bill?' she said, raising her
eyebrows at the crushed dress.

'What? Oh,' he raised his bottom half an inch. She gently
withdrew the delicate material.

'Whoops, bad boy,' he said, smacking his hand, 'silly me.'

Her suitcase was laid on the bed packed with layers of
tissue paper between the light silk and cotton garments that
she liked to wear on the island. In his suitcase Bill would
throw four T-shirts, two pairs of enormous khaki shorts and,
if she reminded him, some pants. She had to go through it
surreptitiously to make sure he was not taking his gardening
clothes. The rest of his suitcase was crammed with the
techno-gadgets he could not be without, many of which
were also strewn about his body in pockets or hanging round
his neck. Bill could and did tell you wind speed, atmospheric
pressure, temperature, light reading, phase of the moon,

position of any nearby satellites, and what the pilot had for lunch on any passing plane. He could also see in the dark through a sinister apparatus which fitted onto his head and take photographs under water and make very jerky movies of the walk down to the beach from the little camera he strapped round his execrable floppy hat.

'Have you asked next door to pop in and made sure he has a key?' she asked.

'What?'

'Next door. Pop in. Key?'

'Don't get ratty. All in good time,' he said.

She went to her list on the dressing table and wrote down *Next door Key*, to remind herself to do it.

'Have you ordered the taxi?'

'Oh for Christ sake, stop nagging.'

'Is that a yes?'

'Don't get in such a bloody panic.'

She wrote down *Taxi*.

He wandered out, shedding mud from his shoes. She stood very still and reflected. *Had she raised her voice? Tutted? Allowed even a small amount of exasperation to creep into her tone? No, to all three. She was not in a panic, nor had she nagged. Are we agreed on that?* she asked her other self. *We are,* the other self replied. The internal dialogue between Helen One, who was a cheery, equable and kindly soul, and Helen Two, who was an angry, irritable person with a sadistic sense of humour, had developed considerably since Bill retired. She diagnosed that it was a kind of safety valve, rather than incipient insanity.

In the early hours of the morning, as she waited for the lights of the taxi, there was a rumbling crash and a cacophony of swearing on the stairs and she went out to find the contents of her suitcase cascaded down the stairs.

'Not me, guv,' he said, holding up the empty suitcase in triumph. 'You didn't zip it up.' He was standing on the pale blue dress, which was her favourite. She came up the stairs, gathering garments and tissue paper and squeezed passed him.

'Just mind the dress,' she said, fearful that he would grind it even further into the carpet.

'Keep your hair on,' he said. 'You're always in such a tizz about travelling.'

I'm in a tizz because you have just thrown all my clothes down the stairs, she thought, repacking the case with brutal, methodical care. *Breathe. Breathe and think of the island.*

She zipped the case firmly. She was sure she had closed it, but she had been sure she had locked the car two nights before and had found it open. They were both getting old and senile. She must have left the case half zipped for the last minute items. However, didn't everybody check when they picked up a suitcase?

No, not butterfuckingfingers, said Helen Two.

Not fair, could happen to any of us, said Helen One.

Oh sod it, you're always so reasonable, you make me sick, replied Helen Two.

In the taxi, she felt him step on one of her new white sandals as he got in. He was wearing his hiking boots. There was an ominously dark scratch across her soft white leather toe. She dug her fingernails into the palm of her hand, but he felt the stiffening of her anger.

'Whoops,' he said, looking down. 'I didn't tread on you, did I?'

'Looks like it,' she said, forcing herself to speak quietly.

'Women and their shoes, eh?' he said to the driver. The driver laughed.

At Rhodes airport he joined the competitive ring of husbands and fathers, tense and determined as if they were at a school sports day, anxious to be the first to haul their luggage away. In doing so Bill almost knocked over a small child. A skinny blonde mother with tattoos called him a 'fucking twat' and looked as if she were about to punch him. Helen apologised profusely.

'The *VARKA* HOTEL,' he shouted at the taxi driver. 'The coast road. None of this zigzagging about. It's eight miles. Twenty-five euros and a rip-off at that.'

When they got out she said *Euharisto* a lot of times and gave the driver a big tip. He grinned at her and shook her hand.

In *Varka*, Niko looked at them over his glasses and riffled through his printouts, 'There is nothing here,' he said, shrugging his shoulders in commiseration. 'No reservation.'

Bill started to huff and swear, so she leaned toward Niko, 'Is there room? Can you squeeze us in?'

'Of course,' he said. 'You are in Greece, Madam. Here we will do anything for a smile.'

With a lot more *Euharistos* and smiling from her, they received a key. In the lift, Bill stared at the ceiling and drummed his fingers on his thigh, all his little gizmos clanking together on his chest.

'Whoops,' he said, without a trace of regret, 'suppose that was my fault was it?'

'No harm done,' she lied. The harm it did to her blood pressure was probably catastrophic.

She went out to the balcony and welcomed the night heat. The masts of the pleasure boats and the palms at the harbour swayed gently in photogenic glimpses between the buildings and over the rooftops. The buzz of traffic and people was muted, smothered by the warmth.

Even the urban sprawl of Rhodes lifted her heart, with its rows of crammed shops, tattooists, henna painters, child beggars mournfully playing flutes off-key, the unstoppable stream of tourists pouring from planes and boats into the alleys and streets, the waiters accosting all of them with mechanical multi-lingual patter. She looked out across the sky where the stars were obliterated by the city glow, where the island waited.

'Shut the bloody door,' Bill growled, sitting on the bed in his pants, ferociously poking the air con remote.

On the ferry Bill declared that he had the squits because of the pizza the night before. She found the medicine in her carry-on and gave it to him. Helen Two could not have cared less. *I ate the pizza as well*, muttered Helen Two, *and my internal arrangements appear to be normal.* Now she would have to listen to graphic descriptions of bowel movements for the next twenty-four hours.

She left him in the lounge and went upstairs to watch the exciting familiar coastline, round which the ferry scurried like a robin flying officiously between nest and food table. The other ferries were big and important and their sirens blasted round the port majestically. This little one gave a short beep saying *Hurry up. I'm here* and if you were not quick, she bustled off again, like the White Rabbit checking his watch, leaving you dumbfounded on the quay.

When the ferry entered the port she could see Theo, on the harbour road, leaning against the four wheel drive, smoking grumpily, staring down at the paving stones as if he were about to be executed. One of the tasks on her bucket list was to get a smile out of Theo. She went down to the lounge and chivvied Bill to join the press of passengers gathering for the scrum of bag snatching, shoving and shouting, aided by the irritable harassment of the crew, which passed for orderly disembarkation.

As they bumped over the cobbles in the car, she sat in the back while Bill and Theo enjoyed a moan about the heat and the European Union. It was possible that these two issues were connected in some way, but she was not really listening. The conversation was punctuated by Theo yelling out of the window in Greek, either at his friends in greeting, or at tourists trailing along from the boat, who were advised to get the fuck out of it, which resulted in most of them smiling weakly and falling over their luggage. Helen Two found this funny, which was really too bad of her.

Theo panted up the steep path to the house with their bags, dumped them at the door and handed Bill the keys. Damn, she thought as he stumped off without the trace of a smile, another task not yet accomplished.

Bill said he had heartburn and indigestion and lay down on the sofa, while she hauled the bags into their bedroom. She found the medicine and put it on the table beside him.

Outside the glorious sea spread out in a deep blue shimmer, littered with the white hulls and gleaming chrome of the billionaires' cruisers. Below on the harbour path, people wandered along with bags and towels, or, if they were German, American or mad, jogged grimly in their small worlds of iPod, pony tails, straight backs, sharp elbows, tight arses and special sunglasses which did not fall off.

She decided to shop and then to have her first *himos portokali*.

The old man shook her hand, smiling under his crinkled eyelids. His son gave her a welcoming pat. Nothing had changed in the shop. She was careful to remember that she did not have the car and must only buy what she could carry. Sevasti, Theo's thoroughly different wife, who was extremely efficient and charming, had supplied the villa with water, bread, milk and ouzo.

She walked to the bar, reminding herself to go slowly in the heat, and there was Young Thano rising from his chair, unusually tall for the island, still not showing any sign of middle-aged spread or receding hair, kissing her on both cheeks, smiling and going off to get her orange juice. She had known him from the time when he was beautiful and young, with one baby daughter and a shy wife.

He sat beside her for a while. She tried out her Greek. How were his children? The youngest had gone to the university. His wife? Her asthma was much improved due to some new treatment. His mother? Very good. Very strong. And she? He asked. How was she? Yes, all good but much better now that she was here again. Her children? Patrick in London, very busy. Diana in Liverpool, and now another grandchild.

'Bravo,' he said, patting her on the back, 'that is three you have now and your Greek is better and better.'

He went off to replenish some beers and on his way back, he said, 'Bill is not with you?'

'No,' she said. 'He's lying down. He has stomach ache.'

'Ah,' he said and returned with an ashtray, which made them both laugh. 'While the cat is away, eh?'

She pulled out her cigarettes, which had lain patiently in wait for almost forty hours. She inhaled blissfully, luxuriating in the absence of surrounding disapproval, particularly Bill's. God what a hole of petty-minded, fascist hypocrisy England had become, grinding its people into poverty and haranguing them constantly about the expense they caused with their miserable attempts to enliven their existence. Workhouse UK. You want *more* gruel? Christ, when was there going to be a revolution? She had been waiting all her life. Even Helen One agreed with this.

She sat for a while listening to the chat amongst the Greeks, now able to understand some of it. She had been working at her Greek for four years. Bill scoffed. 'They just want our money,' he said. 'They don't care if we speak Chinese as long as the euros keep coming. You think you have friends out there? As soon as you and your wallet have gone, they've forgotten you.'

Why not? She thought. They have their own lives to lead and manage. But who comes up to me in Sainsbury's to shake my hand? And who kisses me on both cheeks and asks how I am, when I go into Starbucks? Such small things, but how much they nourish me.

Bill did not feel well enough to go out and eat, so she cooked spaghetti, while he groaned on the sofa, just loudly enough for her to hear.

Fucking indigestion, Helen Two muttered, shaking the spaghetti vigorously in olive oil. Helen One poured him a glass of water and took it to him.

From the sofa he watched while she laid the table and brought out the food.

'It's the bloody heat,' he said. 'We'll have to stop coming here. It's too hot.'

He ate a mouthful, made horrible spluttering noises, announced that there was too much garlic and eased himself back on the sofa. Later she sat on the balcony with a glass of wine. He had the air con turned to arctic, which would make her wake in the night with dry sinuses. She looked at her book, picked it up and put it down. On the harbour road a family with two small children trudged back to the town. The father carried his son on his shoulders holding his two chubby legs. The mother walked hand in hand with the little girl. The boy was laughing and pulling his father's hair. Up on her peaceful balcony she smiled, but felt sad.

'What do you do?' someone had asked her recently at a meeting of the Residents' Association. 'I don't "do", I just am,' she wanted to say but, of course, had not. She felt that you could say that sort of thing in French, perhaps, but not in English. What she had 'done' was far away now. She had been cut. The prison service did not need expensive psychologists, with years of deepened learning. They could train young graduates in six months to advise the inadequate and mentally ill to count their blessings. She might have said, 'I take photographs in the woods. I crochet. I listen to opera. I do my Greek homework. I try to keep up with Windows and Apple and smart phones. I keep in touch with friends who are now, like me, sinking into indoor lives of safe routine, talking at the radio, scared of driving in the dark.'

When the poor dog died she missed him terribly, but Bill became seriously angry at the idea of another one.

If anyone asked Bill what he did, he said, 'Scientist.' He had been retired for five years.

She decided to walk to the Port Beach, which would be deserted until later in the night when the motorbike boys and their girlfriends would colonise the loungers, leaving the evidence of their thoroughly disreputable behaviour to disgust the elderly early-morning swimmers. At this time of the evening the grisly manager of the beach would also be absent, shouting in some bar on the harbour.

Bill moaned slightly on the sofa as she passed him. She paused, waiting for another request for pills or potions, but he sighed and stayed silent, his eyes closed.

She did not return until midnight. Lulled by the soft silence of the sea, she had slept over her book on one of the loungers. The great chapel bell was hammering out the hour above her, as she trudged up the path.

Sevasti sat with her on the balcony and rubbed her back. Inside Theo was discussing matters with the doctor and the police. They had taken the passports and asked her questions, which she had great trouble answering. What was Bill's grandfather's name? Slater, yes, but she had no idea of his first name. And her grandfather? Her mind was blank. Perhaps it was Percival or Peregrine. He had died before she was born. Why on earth did they want to know? Thank God, she kept thinking, I renewed the travel insurance and did not leave it to Bill.

Bill had been so dead, when she returned to the villa, that she saw how it was immediately. His mouth was open and his eyes wide. She had made a little muted scream and stepped back, her hand over her mouth. She had said, 'Oh,' several times. Finally she had sat down and rung Sevasti.

'Sevasti? Hi. It's Helen. I . . . um . . . I'm afraid I think Bill has died. I think he's died on the sofa. I'm sure he's dead.'

While she was waiting for them to come, she had touched him gingerly, but the unnatural stillness of his body shocked her backwards again.

'I'm so sorry,' she said to Sevasti on the balcony.

'No. No,' said Sevasti. 'Do you have English friends out here? Is there someone?'

Bill had made it impossible to be friends with anyone. The resident English were, she agreed with him, a pompous bunch smugly asserting their superior knowledge of all things Greek, but left on her own she would have smiled and listened and fostered a greeting acquaintance. Bill had sighed and drummed the table and stared into space, while they rattled on about their intimate relationship with the island. She was fairly sure that there were some interesting English who stayed away from the bars and the tourists. There was an old couple who lived on a tiny island and came over each day in their inflatable. She had met the old lady in the shop and they had had a fascinating conversation about *Captain Corelli's Mandolin*.

'I should ring the children,' she said to Sevasti.

'Yes,' said Sevasti. 'Is good thing. They will come out to be with you.'

Fat chance, she thought. Patrick stuck in his 24/7 stock market job, with all the money in the world and no time to spend it, and Diana with a four month baby and two little ones.

The voices were louder and more decided in the room. The doctor came out. The body would be taken to the police station. There would need to be a post mortem. She stood up and Sevasti put her arm around her, as if she were an invalid who needed support. The men moved away from the sofa and the body. Clearly they felt she should make some gesture of farewell, but Bill was a gaping staring corpse, not Bill. She stood helplessly at the sofa, amazed by the totality of its emptiness.

The men cleared their throats and someone moved her gently aside. Sevasti sat her down at the table.

When they were gone, Theo and Sevasti stayed with her. They drank small glasses of ouzo. She knew they must leave her. They had work in the morning and it was deep night.

'You must go,' she said.

'No,' they said. 'You must not be alone.'

'Come, Theo,' she said. 'Take Sevasti home. You have to be at work in two hours.'

He put his hand on hers and patted it, 'Death is more important than work,' he said and he smiled.

'Oh Theo,' she said. 'You smiled.'

Sevasti tried to smother a giggle, 'He has the face of stone,' she said, 'but a good man,' and she rubbed his arm.

They stayed until dawn and Sevasti arranged to return later. There would be many formalities.

Helen One thought there was an issue of culpability. I *should have seen that he was really ill. I should have called the doctor. I should have cared. Instead, I sat on the Port Beach smoking, listening to the sea, thinking about sealing wax and string, while Bill died.*

Helen Two said, *Nonsense.*

The silent interior argument continued at home, through the long months of arrangements, decisions, meetings and form-filling, which follow death.

In March, in the dripping London cemetery, where the grouped benches seemed to be waiting for the dead to rise at night and chat together, she helped the gangly deerhound puppy out of the car and walked to Bill's grave. Rufus wiggled and trembled in his tartan jacket, half afraid and half desperate to be free. It was forbidden to bring dogs, but there was a heavy mist and she would not be long. Something stirred in the bushes far across the silent necropolis and he stiffened for the chase, but he was too young to be allowed his head and must walk with her, strengthening his limbs. When she moved to the island he would be old enough to run on the headland, although there would have to be some serious discipline regarding the goats and sheep.

Bill lay between a *Dearly Missed Mother* and *Thomas Brownlow RIP*, who apparently had not been missed. Piles of brown mud in various places drew attention to the prosaic work of burial.

She wanted to see the headstone. She had already checked it at the masons, but she wanted to see it *in situ.*

William Slater, she read, *1940 – 2011. Loved and Missed.*

She had thought about this and had decided against giving any precise information about who had loved and missed him. The children had been very shocked and sombre for a while, and she was grateful to them for remembering good times and holidays.

She placed a bunch of daffodils in a glass pot and squatted down to scrutinise the stone. It was very unorthodox and probably contrary to the bye-laws, said the mason. Nevertheless he was young and could be won over. On the right hand lower corner of the stone, in very small letters, he had carved

Whoops

One Candle

Ενα κερί αρκεί. Η κάμαρη απόψι
νά μύ έχει φώς πολύ.

One candle suffices. The room tonight
must not be too well lit.

For Them to Come C. P. Cavafy

At dawn Tom was at the laptop, downloading onto his Kindle. Below his apartment, fortuitously, Petro's bar had WiFi. Caroline was coming in on the nine-twenty ferry. The calendar had eighty days neatly ruled out. Eighty days since she left last time. He ate breakfast on the balcony. This was the only time he sat in the sun in the summer, even so his face and forearms were a startling mahogany colour which he never quite recognised as his own.

He wanted to meet the ferry. He wanted to stand on the quay and watch while the boat rounded the headland, but he had never done this. They always met at the bar.

Since childhood Tom had warned himself about excitement and schooled himself to put it firmly to one side. His wife had been the same. A quiet-faced Thai woman, they had met at work, not, as everyone assumed, on some website. She, like him, had wanted order and safety. Her depression had not been discussed between them. He always accompanied her to the doctors, made sure she took her pills and visited her in hospital. When the two policewomen came, it was their subdued excitement which he found disturbing. They expected him to be shocked, but he had known for years that her illness could not be cured by pills or visiting nurses taking her out for a walk. He had known that it could kill her.

He had been ten years older than his wife. He could retire, so he sold up and bought *Sophia* apartment on Kapotheni, the island they had visited every year in July. In the final years there were times when she had smiled, when they sat together at the taverna on the Port Beach.

At six he settled himself in his usual chair and Petro brought him a beer.

'It's very hot,' said Petro unnecessarily.

'Yes. It is a wave of hot,' he said.

'What?'

'In English we say wave of hot,' he said.

'Oh,' said Petro.

They spoke in Greek. Tom had worked hard with his textbooks and dictionaries.

Tom opened his Kindle. He did not like the novel about a gay professor; the sexual detail was unpleasant, but once started he did not stop. If he looked up, he could see down the alley where Caroline would appear.

But she surprised him and suddenly she was sitting down at his table, her shopping bags spilling out at his feet, fanning herself with a coaster.

'Bloody hell,' she said. 'This is a bit much. What is it? Forty?'

'Thirty-eight at midday,' he said. 'Hello Caroline.' They shook hands but she pulled him forward and kissed his cheek.

'How are you Tom? Been keeping busy?'

Petro appeared, put a small beer on the table and shook Caroline's hand.

'*Yeia sou* Petro, I've been looking forward to this all day,' said Caroline. She turned to Tom, 'Gotta tell you, Tom, I met Dawn in London. Complete chance. Did you know she'd left thingy?'

'No,' said Tom.

'Trust you,' she laughed. 'Yes, about a month ago. She's living with her mother. Can you believe it? Mother's about a hundred. Dawn must be seventy.'

'He never said anything,' said Tom.

'Really, Tom. I do expect you to keep your ears open for the scandal. Where are you eating?'

'*Clocktower.*'

'Oh great. I'll tag along then, if that's OK?'

While they sat next to each other in the bar he did not look at her, but her perfume floated around him and the colour of her dress glowed in the corner of his eye. She touched him frequently, little strokes of his arm, if she took one of his cigarettes or thought he had said something funny or wanted him to call to Petro for another drink. People came up to greet her and shake her hand. Vassili the florist (to distinguish him from Vassili at the *Daphne*) and Dimitri the boat (not Dimitri the goats, who rarely appeared and smelled hideous). Tom tentatively allowed himself to enjoy the feeling that Caroline was with him, while the men came and went.

At *Clocktower*, he sat next to her again. Sitting opposite her would have made them seem too much like a couple, which was presumptuous. He would ask her, when she was recovered from the journey.

She wanted to know what he had been doing. He found he was busy now, on the island. The women's group had needed a pianist for their folk-dancing evenings. The new English couple had been glad of his help decorating and advising them on how to get deliveries from Amazon and IKEA. He was renovating an old Lambretta for the Samagdios's youngest next door. With some amusement, he told her about Mrs Samagdios's alarming habit of smashing the plates she could not be bothered to wash at the celebrations for her monastery's name day, but Caroline did not seem to be listening.

'Oh God,' she said. 'Three weeks off. Bliss.'

He did not know what her work was. Perhaps she had told him. Anyway, she must be fifty and coming up to an age when retirement would be possible.

'Look,' she said gripping his arm, 'there's thingy.'

Dawn's husband, Paul, was wandering along the quay.

'Hey,' she called.

Paul wavered over. He had a kitten in his hand, 'Hi,' he said. 'What d'you think of this little sweetie?'

'Adorable,' she said, but did not make a move to stroke it. Tom was glad. The island cats had fleas.

'How's Dawn?' she asked, which made Tom shift nervously in his chair.

Paul stared out at the harbour with a small frown, as if he were trying to remember who Dawn was. 'Oh,' he said slowly, 'yes. She's OK. Anyway, we'll be off. Gotta date with a saucer of milk, haven't we pussy?' He ambled away.

'What's he on?' she said. 'Spaced out. Dawn said he was doing an awful lot of weed.'

'I wouldn't know about that,' said Tom, laughing so that it did not sound pompous.

'Pot not your thing, then?' she asked. 'What *is* your thing, Tom?'

He laughed again, embarrassed, 'I don't think I've got one.'

'You mean you're not telling,' she said.

He carefully split the bill, but Caroline would have none of it, 'My treat,' she said. 'Go on, bite the bullet. I won't do this again.'

They stopped for a drink at Petro's bar.

'Did you eat well with this beautiful lady?' Petro asked. 'Food tastes better with company.'

'Yes, I bite on myself very often and it is not joyful,' agreed Tom.

Petro turned away hurriedly.

'Blimey, your Greek is coming on,' said Caroline. 'What's Petrodollar laughing about? Petro baby, what's the joke?'

'Is nothing, Karolina,' he spluttered, waving a hand and holding on to a chair with the other.

'He's really got the giggles,' she said. 'You must have said something hilarious.'

'I don't think so,' said Tom.

They stayed at the bar watching the parade of tourists meandering round the harbour and the locals roaring about on their bikes. The ranks of boats rocked gently.

Rigging tinkled, while the hills above the town turned from grey to pink to black. A large Englishwoman, her breasts haphazardly contained in a sequinned sundress, bustled up attended by two embarrassed daughters, 'Oh there you are,' she bellowed at Tom. 'Now, where should we eat? You've got the local knowledge.'

'Well . . . *Clocktower*. *The Schooner*. *The Captain*. I eat in all of them.'

'Ranking?' she demanded. 'On a scale of one to ten?'

Tom looked uneasily at the table of islanders nearby, who were all listening.

'They're all good in their different ways,' he said.

'Not like home, then?' she said, laughing.

'*This* is my home,' he said.

'Well, thanks,' she said. 'We'll try *The Captain*. Come on girls.'

The islanders grinned.

'Let's hope they don't get food poisoning,' said Caroline, 'or she'll be after you.'

'They won't. Eva is very careful about hygiene,' he said.

'Joke,' said Caroline. 'Where did you pick sparkly up?'

'They were trying to find the bus stop,' he said. 'One has to be polite.'

He walked her up the alley. At her doorway she pointed out the huge moon which hung over the rooftops. He told her about the size of the moon being due to the position of the sun and the earth.

'Thanks Tom,' she said, yawning. 'See you at Petro's tomorrow.'

He went to the church with its cobbled courtyard and sat on the wall talking to his wife, wondering if she minded, wondering what she thought. But she had never told him what she thought in life, so he was not surprised that she did not answer. He did not like to smoke in the church grounds, so he walked back to Petro for a last drink.

Petro put a beer on the table, 'You like Karolina, don't you?' he said.

Tom smiled, 'Oh, maybe.'

'I see how you look at her,' Petro persisted. 'Do you want to marry her?'

'What?' said Tom, his Greek deserting him in his panic.

'Marry,' repeated Petro sitting down. 'I think you would like to marry Karolina.'

'I don't know,' said Tom, laughing in extreme discomfort. 'I don't know.'

'Anyway,' said Petro, 'Will you take this to her? She left it.' He took an iPhone from his pocket. Tom remembered her checking her emails.

'She is in the bed,' he demurred.

'She will want it. I won't open in the morning, my son and the children have come to see my mother.'

Reluctantly Tom took it.

He was expecting the outer door to be locked, in which case, he would have to take the phone home and return in the morning, but, at his tentative push, the door swung open. The enormous moon illuminated the courtyard and showed everything carved in stillness, the umbrella, the lounger, the table and chairs. There was a bottle of wine on the table and two glasses. He went over this a hundred times for many nights. Two glasses. He could have put the phone down on the table. He could have put the phone down and left.

He stood by the inner door, 'Caroline?' he said and he pushed the door. It opened and suddenly, as if all three of them had been holding their breath, there were gasps and noise and rapid movements and Caroline was coming toward him very fast, like a ghost in a horror film, pushing him backwards with one hand, holding some flimsy white thing to her breasts, and the man was standing motionless in the corner by the window, as if, by standing still, he would not be seen.

Abruptly Tom was in the courtyard and the door slammed shut. He put the phone down on the table very quietly.

He could not sleep. His mind was stuck, like a damaged DVD, on the scene in Caroline's room. Downstairs he heard Petro opening up, which bewildered him. He must have lost a day, yet every minute ached. He kept away from the balcony, heartsick at the thought of seeing Caroline fluttering nonchalantly down the alley.

He did not go out for two days. He told Mrs Samagdios he had a headache. She brought him some *stifado* and said he must eat and go to the doctor. He managed to get a night flight to Bournemouth and hurried to the ferry, stumbling through all the back alleys. At his sister's in Nottingham he tried to appear normal. By the end of two weeks his sister was very alarmed about him, but he could not begin to tell her anything. He could not begin to tell himself anything, except why had he not just put the phone down on the table?

Eventually he returned, heavy with the grey skies and long days of television. Petro gave him a beer and sat down beside him, 'How is your sister?' he asked.

'She is hairy,' said Tom.

'You mean happy,' corrected Petro, without a smile. 'I think you are not happy?'

Tom was silent. He had no words in Greek or English to describe how he was.

'Karolina is lovely, but she would not make a good wife,' said Petro. He patted Tom gently on his back, 'Maybe you will find one. But you are home now. Eh, my friend?'

A Kind of Solution

Οἱ ἄνθρωποι αυτοί ἦσαν μιά κάποια λύσις.

Those people were a kind of solution.
Expecting the Barbarians C. P. Cavafy

It's extraordinary how faces are unforgettable, but names, at my age, simply do not get filed in the database. In any case, I am sure we did not exchange names in the deserted theatre bar. She was at least two inches taller than him in her gold heels; he was built like a small orangutan, but his suit was impressively cut to suggest grace and subtlety. You would have said prosperous gangster and moll, but she belied this impression, at a second glance. She was his age if not a tad older, but the wrinkles on her face were still at the stage of proclaiming experience rather than decrepitude. Her legs were fabulous, hence the beautiful shoes and the short, slightly above the knee, skirt.

'Sorry, darling, couldn't hear a fucking thing,' I heard him say to her.

'I know,' she said. 'Awful wasn't it? Such a shame.'

'He's forgotten how to open his gob.'

'Yes,' she said, 'no projection. I expect it's all the film work.'

'You sound as if you've been disappointed,' I remarked. Clem and I had also retired to the bar, having given up on trying to decipher the mumbling from the stage.

He was standing further away from me and she was turned to him. I noticed that she did not move, but he bent round her slightly enough to smile at me and in that smile was contained an early life of beauty and the adoration of others. He had been a heavenly youth and the charm of the blessed still shone in his eyes, despite a spectacularly broken nose. I wondered if her stillness was defensive. Perhaps she had seen too many women glowing in his winning smile. I thought it was delightful of him to offer it to me.

'Couldn't hear a thing,' he repeated politely.

'I'm glad it wasn't just us,' I said. 'I was beginning to think I needed a hearing aid.'

She then turned and smiled. I think we discussed the weather and the nuisance of having travelled up to London for nothing. He frequently called her 'darling', as if he needed us to know that she belonged to him. I thought it was sweet.

'I'm annoyed,' she complained without rancour. 'I really wanted to see that guy. I love his films.'

'Never mind, darling,' he said, smiling at me again. It was clear he liked women. At my age, to be given the eye, is a novel and delightful pleasure. 'She's giving me an education,' he explained. 'She took me to see . . . what was it, darling?'

'*Macbeth*,' she said, giving me the wisp of a conspiratorial smile.

'At the National?' we asked. She nodded.

'Yes,' he said. 'Have you seen it? The old bird was totally starkers sometimes. That was a bit of a facer. I didn't expect that.' Clem and I had to smile at the idea of the beautiful Kristen being called 'the old bird'.

'He went to sleep,' she said laughing.

'I woke up for that bit,' he said, winking at Clem.

My second idea, that he was one of the new breed of cockney intelligentsia, had faded, but she was unclassifiable except that there was a good private school in the background, judging by the rounded vowels and the open-faced assurance. I faintly envied her. His sexual charisma came over in waves, but I could never have coped with the roughness of the diamond. We left them debating on which pub to patronise because, he declared, the prices in the bar took the fucking Mick.

'Very odd people,' said Clem, waving his umbrella at a taxi. 'The last time I saw someone like that man, he was appealing against a perfectly sound sentence for armed robbery.'

'Interesting,' I said.

'You find everything interesting,' he said. 'I'm too old to be interested.'

Two months later, I nudged Clem who was snoring in his seat as the ferry bumped through the Aegean. 'Look who's over there,' I said. He didn't remember them of course. Clem never does remember people, other than his cases. I have actually heard him having difficulty remembering the names of his grandchildren.

I saw the gangster first. He was weaving his way back to the seats with two paper cups. This time he was in the ubiquitous English holiday garb of T-shirt and jeans which, luckily for him, accentuated powerful shoulders and slim hips, rather than the more usual surplus of fat. His face, without its startling smile, was decidedly forbidding. I assumed it was the same woman, but she was obscured by the seat. He sat down beside her and leant toward her solicitously. I thought she might be seasick. He seemed to be ministering to an invalid. I was apparently correct for, not long after, she made a wobbly dash for the loos. When she returned, the skin of her face, which was patchily visible behind large sunglasses, hair and hat, was white with the drained pallor of illness.

I made a mental note to force Clem to get to the front of the queue for our bags, when we arrived. Sick people irritate me and I always find it vaguely annoying that anyone else comes to the island, which is ridiculous of me, as thousands of us come every year. Clem always laughs about the 'Secret Paradise' articles, which regularly appear in the Sundays. 'Not so secret now,' he snorts. But the island has to make a living, I suppose.

We can walk to the *Napoli* from the ferry and there we stay, rooted to the seats under the umbrellas by the water's edge, reading our Kindles and feeling righteous about how much salad we are consuming. The old hotel is dark and spacious with wood panelled floors and walls, cool with fans and air conditioning, quiet with self-contained Europeans who do not need any more friends. Occasionally a rich young honeymoon couple might make us smile appreciatively at their polished beauty, but generally we murmur to each other politely and pass on. Clem and I have done the sights and visited beaches, but now we content ourselves each evening with a stroll round the port, or a taxi to one of three restaurants which do not disappoint. When it is time for the day trippers to come in and slouch round the harbour in herded groups, we retire to our room for a shower and a nap. Generally, we have discovered it is best to avoid the ex-pats. There is always a reason why someone has decided that they cannot tolerate their own kind. Largely it will be because their own kind have stopped tolerating them. There is a particularly dreadful Professor of something, whom Clem seems to think was at his old college, who has tried to engage us in fey conversation. Very bright people are so difficult to manage, I find. Give me a well-educated dullard with manners any day.

Clem and I may appear to be, indeed we may actually be, smug, complaisant and detached, but, to borrow my youngest's sailing language, we are both bricking it. We have reached the age when illness in all its trumpeted, grisly detail, is hovering like a vulture above us. It is not death which frightens us, it is the over-advertised, documented, earnestly discussed terrors of stroke, heart attack and dementia. We constantly watch each other and ourselves for signs of confusion and paralysis, sudden shooting pains in chest or arm, or bizarre placement of household objects, all of which happen from time to time because we are far too sedentary, eat too much and drink a bottle of Waitrose *Shiraz* every evening to dull the anxiety of being in our perilous seventies. Both of us belong to *Dignitas* and place our trust in the airlines and the final cup of poison. The children are embarrassed about this and think we should pretend to be immortal.

We were at breakfast. We have a rule not to read newspapers when we are on holiday. I had my much acclaimed, awfully boring novel and Clem was doing his crossword.

'What's that thing horses have?' he asked.

'Saddle,' I said.

'No. On them. On their legs. *A mad old equine*? Walnut?'

'Chestnut,' I said, remembering my pony club days and, as I looked up, I saw her walking purposefully away toward the Port Beach. She must have appeared from one of the flights of narrow steps down to the road, because she had not passed us. I was annoyed that they were living nearby, but then I realised that they would not remember us. For the relatively young, people of our age are ghosts, fading into oblivion.

To my great irritation, she turned up an hour or so later and flopped down at a table near us. I raised my Kindle. Clem had his back to her, but he would not have noticed unless she had sat on his lap. She ordered orange juice. She took off her sunglasses to rummage in her bag and she must have known that she was being watched. She looked directly at me and there was a moment when both of us knew that the other was wishing our recognition had not happened. I was slightly disconcerted. In my experience, people usually wish to know me.

'Hello?' I said. 'How strange. We met at the theatre, didn't we?'

She pretended to be surprised, 'Oh,' she said, 'how weird.'

Clem looked up, flustered by the prospect of social interaction. 'This is the lady we met at the theatre, Clem,' I said. 'When we couldn't hear anything.'

He twisted round and smiled at her, like the trooper he is, 'Been for a swim?' he said. Her cotton dress was plastered to a wet bikini.

'No,' I said, 'she's been skiing.'

We laughed. The tone was set. Light polite conversation, followed by a graceful retreat.

'Do you stay here?' she asked. 'It's very lovely.'

'We like it,' said Clem.

'Lucky you. Gloria Porter, the model, stays in the house next door, doesn't she? Have you ever seen her?'

'Hardly ever,' said Clem, because we do our best to stay out of Gloria's way, if she is staggering about the island behaving badly. Gloria Porter is a sad case of someone who has not handled celebrity well.

'We're staying with Giorgio who has the boat,' she said, rather stupidly because almost everyone has a boat here.

'Is this your first visit?' I asked, it was very unoriginal but what everyone says.

'Yes. Well no, not really? I came out with a couple of friends in the eighties? We ran out of money and slept on a beach? Port Beach?' Somehow she turned every sentence into a question. We all laughed gently at the escapades of youth.

'It's a beautiful island,' I said.

To my surprise she did not take the cue, 'Actually, it's a brutal place,' she said, staring out across the gleaming sea. All the bouncy, nice-girl, savoir-faire seemed to have instantly evaporated. I remembered her pale, stricken face on the ferry.

'Oh,' I said. I felt quite defensive of our little haven. 'Why do you say that?'

'Years of sadistic colonisation,' she said, as if she were giving us a tutorial, 'and an island? Close knit, self-protective, riddled with secrecy and corruption? A Mediterranean island? Primitively misogynistic? Used to feuds and vengeance. All islands are the same.'

Afterwards, Clem and I agreed that neither of us had any idea what we should say to this comprehensive damning of our favourite holiday retreat. I blame the television and the radio, on which everyone is encouraged to blurt out their opinions on all occasions, regardless of the context.

Finally Clem said, 'Oh dear,' as if he had just spilled some coffee on his trousers. 'Are we safe in our beds?'

I was a bit cross and took a more pragmatic stance, 'So why have you come back?'

She stubbed out her cigarette and started to fiddle around in her bag again, 'It was a friend of mine? A neighbour. She comes here every year? She writes poetry? She loves it here.'

'That's not Sylvia, is it?' I asked. 'Sylvia Glasgow, the poet?'

She lit another cigarette and shot me a glance which was almost unfriendly.

Despite the woman's rudeness, in abruptly turning a safely predictable conversation into a polemic, she was beginning to be interesting. There has been talk of Sylvia being the next poet laureate, which, as she is black and a woman, would fit well with the times. Clem and I have been tax efficiently charitable for some years and Sylvia's community arts centre has benefitted.

'We know Sylvia,' I said. Clem looked perplexed, 'Sylvia Glasgow, Clem. The poet. Immensely tall woman with kaftans. You know. At the *Rainbow Place*. I do like her work. Apart from anything else, I can sometimes understand it.'

The woman laughed, suddenly back in her sociable persona, 'Yes,' she said, 'I know. I'm not really a poetry person. We've got a whole list of people she wants us to look up? I'm loaded down with presents. She's always knitting, you know. We've got to find all sorts of people? I've just been to see her son's father to give him an Aran sweater. In this heat, for God's sake? And there's a decaying aristocrat lurking somewhere, one of Sylvia's old boyfriends. Giorgio knows him?'

She rose and paid her bill and trotted away. Clem returned to his crossword, while I digested the information about Sylvia. I like her because she is successful. I have never seen much point in spending time with people who are not. I'm sure unsuccessful people are very nice but, frankly, what is to be gained? Successful people are like us. Industrious, thoughtful, intelligent and determined, whatever they may look like on the surface. Some of the wildest-looking pop stars I have met, at charity events, can have a thoroughly competent conversation about asset management. Sylvia is not rich. That would be extremely status incongruent for a poet, but she has a wonderful nose for contacts and networking and she is well known. That is our world. Sylvia writes poetry about the island and visits every year, but I had no idea that her son was some holiday romance by-blow. He is a bit dark, but Sylvia is black, so it's to be expected. He was at Westminster a few years after our youngest and is a rising star in Mither and Bluett, who happen to be our brokers. He is a frightfully sweet young man. Sylvia has done a good job with him.

We both agreed that it would be as well if we did not go out of our way to cultivate our acquaintance with the odd couple any further. It had been interesting to hear about Sylvia but, other than that, the woman did not offer much, with her disconcertingly critical views, her rising inflections and breathless admiration for the appalling Gloria, who may look very pretty in the magazines, but is a nightmare socially. My ears had pricked minimally at the mention of a 'decaying aristocrat', which sounded promising, but I was on holiday and needed to turn off my radar for a while. I was a teeny bit curious to see her sexy but grim consort again, but not curious enough to do anything about it.

A few days later we were dining at *Daphne,* where Vassili anxiously oversees a very competent French chef, who could manage perfectly well without interference. The restaurant is built out above the hillside, providing a platform from which a few sought-after tables enjoy a sweeping view of the bowl of olive groves between the mountains and the little bay beyond. Clem was enthusing over his scallops, when I heard English laughter and, looking over the low wall, I saw that there was a small courtyard below us and that the couple were standing alone near a table. It was clear that they had no idea of being overseen. Their behaviour indicated that coitus was imminent, at least it would have been if Clem and I had ever behaved like that, which we might have done a hundred years ago. I retreated behind my wall. I calculated that the courtyard belonged to a dark bar, which was one of the few places that did not welcome tourists. Unsmiling young men slouch in plastic chairs in the lane outside and grim-faced young women glare from the counter inside. There is no attempt to translate the faded menu on the wall and aggressive Greek pop music blares out from the gloomy depths.

More laughter incited me to peer over the wall again. The couple had been joined by the barman, towel in hand, who indicated the table and sat down with them jovially, clapping them on the shoulders and raising a glass. I attended to my *stifado* and when I glanced over a little later, the woman was alone with the barman and something surprising was going on. I did not dare say anything to Clem, who is slightly deaf now and would have yelled at me to explain, which, even at this height above them, would have alerted all concerned to my spying.

The barman was urging his suit upon the woman, his hand on her knee and his arm around her shoulders. She leant toward him, smiling and laughing. I was riveted to my seat and Clem had to touch my arm to draw my attention to Vassili, who was hovering beside us enquiring whether we were enjoying our meal. When Vassili had dashed away to bother another table, I was quite anxious to see whether broken-nose had returned. It seemed to me that the consequences, should he discover this dalliance, would be noisy and violent, but he was back at the table with a proprietorial arm around the woman and all three were gaily raising glasses and being the best of friends.

You hear that people do some very strange things when they are on holiday, so I could only imagine that this was one of them and did not allow myself to speculate further.

We did not see anything more of them and our holiday passed quietly and without any medical emergencies, although on the grapevine they say that Rhodes hospital is better than anywhere in England for the catastrophes of age. Certainly the hotel receptionist's father had a stroke and I saw him positively bounding up the steps this year.

It was about two weeks after we returned that I got wind of the news, when I was catching up at lunch with Judith, who also, unfortunately, sojourns on the island. This is particularly annoying because I told her about the place and it is not *comme il faut* to follow friends about the world like sheep.

'And what about the murder?' she asked.

'What murder?'

'On the island,' she said. 'Really, Parthi, you were out there at the time.'

'No idea.'

'It's in the papers. Well, the international bit anyway, which I never usually bother with, but Mark saw it.'

'Who was murdered?'

'Only some Greek. They found him on the Port Beach, Parthi. They're talking about a gangland execution. Won't do the tourist trade much good. All the *Guardian* readers will hightail it to Kos. Puts you off, doesn't it?'

'Not if the *Guardian* readers stop going, it won't.'

I put it all together triumphantly in the taxi going home and I'm sure I'm right. Dementia be damned.

I had seen something seriously brutal in that man, despite the wonderful smile. I can't believe she actually fired the shot, but, then again, private schools aren't what they were. She probably did all the tidying up afterwards, like women always do. I did ponder on how much willowy Sylvia knew, but it's not the kind of thing one can ask directly. Sylvia is a bit scatty anyway, all artists are. She is always spouting psychobabble. I'm surprised her son is as sane as he is. I could imagine Sylvia advising that a return to the island would bring 'closure' on whatever brutal interlude there had been. Well it certainly did, for the Greek.

I probed gently, when I saw Sylvia at a fund-raiser, towering above us all in silver lamé. 'We met a friend of yours on Kapotheni this year,' I said, watching her closely.

'Oh?' she said, popping a canapé into her large mouth.

'Never got her name,' I said. 'She said you had given her some commissions. She had just been to see Hermes's father.' This was a bit naughty of me because Sylvia has never said a word about her son's parentage, but I calculated that the element of surprise might just catch her off guard and lead to indiscreet revelations.

Sylvia stared blankly over my head through her pink spectacles, then light appeared to dawn, 'Oh, yes,' she said. 'Hermes is a quarter Greek and a quarter Armenian, that's his father. We met on the island.'

'How exotic. Such a sweet boy,' I said. 'And is there any news of the murder out there?'

'Murder?' she said, peering at the tray of sushi which a waitress was offering us.

'You're so well connected there,' I said, 'I was rather hoping you might have inside knowledge. They don't seem to have got very far finding the culprit.'

Sylvia blinked down at me, chose something green from the tray and chewed thoughtfully, 'It's an island, Lady Carson,' she said. 'Unless you're born there, you're always an outsider. On the island you have to live in peaceful ignorance. The desire to know can be very destructive.'

'Do you think it's safe?' I asked hastily, pretending to be silly and anxious, Sylvia sounded as if she were becoming mystical and I have a very low tolerance for mysticism.

'Safe?' she said. 'Is anywhere? Oh, there's Tony. So sorry, must do the rounds,' and she swayed away, like a silver giraffe.

I have always felt that I missed out, really. They *were* an interesting couple after all, and, judging by the apparent lack of any suspects, because I check up quite a bit on the Googly thing, not only interesting but also very successful. As we always said to the children, it doesn't matter what you do, as long as you do it very well. That applies to gangsters just as much as anyone else, in my opinion.

Another Sea

... θά πάγω σ'άλλη θάλασσα.

I will go to another sea.
The City C. P. Cavafy

Sevasti was up just before the red disc of the sun began to appear above the ridge. She opened the front door into the alley, wedging it so that any slight breeze from the bay might cool the house. She rolled down the curtain, to thwart the fierce heat which would be hammering at the door by ten. Theo liked the old ways. The air con gave him sinusitis, he said. The doctor said it was the cigarettes. At the little stone wash-house opposite, Sevasti drew a bucket of water and sluiced and swept the paving.

When she went in, Theo was at the kitchen table in his vest, smoking. The schedule and keys lay before him. Theo was trying to ignore them. He did not like tourists and their heavy luggage, before a morning of his proper job. She put on the television to cheer him up because he liked the blonde newsreader.

It was Wednesday, mainly an English arrival day at this time of the summer. Two regular couples, two new ones and Galia. Sevasti was always slightly nervous about new visitors, especially the English or German ones. The Italians and Scandinavians were more understanding of old buildings and odd plumbing. She had fifteen apartments to manage and the *Sea Captain's House*, a grand building on the edge of the bay. It had been a ruin when Sevasti was a child, but it belonged to a Greek American woman who renovated it. The frail old lady sailed in every year and was helped up the steps by her crew. When she died, the mayor asked Sevasti to let the house.

Galia had been staying regularly in the *Sea Captain's House* for a long time.

'Galia,' Sevasti said to Theo across the table, pointing at the name on the list.

Theo sniffed and made a rude noise.

You forget, she thought. I remember Galia surrounded by you boys, doing tricks on your bicycles, diving, running to get her cigarettes, calling from the steps. 'Galia. *Bella*'.

Her real name was Gloria, but no-one could get their mouths round the 'gl' sound, so she was always Galia.

Galia had first come on a rich man's boat, more than thirty years ago. The person who was supposed to deal with strange arrivals was asleep in his house. The fishermen stood and gawped as the yacht slid in, the Athenian crew yelling obscenities. The Greek man with Galia spoke English to his friends and he lived in London. That night they ate fish at Costa's, with the boys all sitting in a row on the sea wall, watching and giggling. Sevasti was helping in the kitchen. Galia was her own age, but Sevasti could see nothing to connect her to this smooth slim creature, who revealed tanned skin at every long-limbed movement, her blonde hair pinned up in artful curls, her eyes wide and blue and painted black, and, as the boys whispered and pointed, her unrestrained breasts moving gently under her clothes.

Sevasti grinned at these memories, as she picked up the bag of rubbish for the skips by the bus stop. Now the tourists amble through the streets clad in bulging bikinis and there is not a soul who would bother to notice or think to complain.

All those years ago, Galia did not want to sail on in the morning. She wanted to stay. Her Greek Englishman made enquiries and hurriedly Yanni and Kyriaki moved out of their harbour home.

The boat sailed away with the other rich men and the rude Athenian crew. They would return in four days.

The women shook their heads. Galia is a child, they said, you can see she is hardly grown. She has no ring. He is at least forty. He will be married. What does he do with her?

The men were less concerned and more imaginative.

The next day the English Greek gave the boys drachmas and told them to show her the best place to swim. In a tight gabbling group they swarmed around her and took her to what is now the Port Beach, with its taverna and bar and boy waiters running back and forth and landscaped rock garden with waterfalls and floodlights. Then it was a boulder strewn strip of stones, with lurking sea anemones and sea urchins waiting to shoot agonising poison into an unwary foot.

Galia spread her white towel on a Galia-sized boulder and took off her crimson kimono. She was wearing the smallest garment ever seen on the island. It was two pieces of gold cloth. She proceeded to take the top one off. The boys stepped back. One Mummy's boy, set on being a priest, pedalled off to raise the alarm.

The donkey team went by twice. Women wandered by with shopping bags on a track which led to a deserted hamlet five miles away. The fishing boats waived their territorial rights and bobbed about within keen-eyed sight of the boulder. Sevasti and the other girls sneaked away from chores and peeped round the clumps of wild herbs.

Galia lay in the sun for a while then clambered across the boulders to plunge into the sea. The boys joined her like dolphins, diving down to touch her legs. She played like a child, splashing them back and screaming with laughter.

The mayor visited the English Greek as he sat in the fishermen's bar. The mayor had intercepted an old priest who was marching toward the bar with an entourage of black widows. The mayor took the view that they were seeing the island's future. The English Greek had been astonishingly munificent with his drachmas. If rich people want to lie in the sun, let them do it and charge them for it. The confrontation, which quickly became a council meeting, was carried by the mayor.

He sat down with the English Greek and discussed the absence of the top half of the gold bikini in the friendliest of terms. Perhaps Madam Galia might sunbathe in this way upon her balcony? The English Greek understood perfectly and apologised. The mayor begged him not to disturb her immediately, mainly because the mayor had not yet taken a walk by the beach.

Sevasti walked home with the bread, enjoying these memories. Now breasts of every shape and size wobble on the beaches; even the downward pointing flaps of the old are roasted into brown purses. Galia's small russet-brown apples of breasts were an adornment to any boulder.

Sevasti had been proud to be detailed to clean the house where Galia stayed. She stared in wonder at the clothes and jewellery. She watched in horror the first time she saw Galia curl her eyelashes with the little machine. Galia showed her how to do it and carefully applied unnecessary mascara to Sevasti's black lashes.

'Look how pretty you are,' said Galia. 'Such long lashes.'

Galia never treated her like a servant.

'In England girls like you go to university,' said Galia. 'You're clever. They wanted me to go, but some bum took pictures of me on the Kings Road and one thing led to another.'

Galia tried on this or that and asked her, 'What do you think? Does it fit here? Can you see my arse when I bend down? The trouble with this one is my boobs keep slipping out.' Although the words were certainly not anything taught in school, where they were fortunate to have Kirios Katrios who had lived in London after the war, Sevasti understood and was entranced by Galia prancing about the room swinging her kaftans around.

The night before the boat was due to return, Sevasti found Galia weeping. Sevasti sat next to her and stroked her arm.

'What is problem?'

'I don't know. I'm stupid. I want to go home, Sevasti. Or stay here. That would be fab.'

Sevasti grinned, 'Is lot of work here. Must get water, cook, clean.'

'You're so lucky,' said Galia. 'You've got a dad and mum and your brothers. You are really safe here, aren't you?'

'Yes,' said Sevasti, having never thought about this at all.

'I'm not safe on that boat,' said Galia.

'Why not safe?'

'Oh,' said Galia, sitting up straighter and giving her a little pat, 'nothing really.'

'But Kirios Mikos look after you,' said Sevasti.

'Yes, well, not really. It was sweet of Miki to stay here but I'm what you might call the entertainment, Sevasti. It seemed like a brilliant idea in London, but,' she shuddered, 'I don't like that boat.'

'You not go then,' said Sevasti firmly. 'You get ferryboat to Rodos and airplane to Athina.'

'No money,' said Galia.

'You have gold,' said Sevasti. 'Kirios Dimitrios the mayor is rich. He will buy.'

'It's not *real*,' laughed Galia.

'You get Kirios Mikos to give.'

'Miki is more likely to give me a black eye,' said Galia. 'Well, my fault for being a dumb blonde. I'll have to take it on the chin or in the butt more like.' She pulled a face.

'What is butt?'

'Nothing, darling. Nothing. Would you like this perfume? It's called Chanel Number Five. *Très chic*. Take it.'

Sevasti spoke to her mother, 'I think they do bad things to Galia on the boat,' she said. Her father overheard and laid his hand on her mother's arm to silence her, 'Galia is an Englishwoman,' he said. 'England, France, Germany, the women do what they like. Bad things happen to them because they take no notice of their men. It is what happens. They are stupid.'

But Sevasti thought Galia was lovely and, if Sevasti was not a woman neither was Galia, even if she might have to do bad things with men.

In the February of the following year a heavily stamped, much examined, ragged parcel arrived on the ferry addressed to *Sevasti, Kapotheni, Greece*. It contained some of the silken kaftans and a letter from Galia. She said she was modelling and sent a magazine in which you could hardly tell it was her, wearing glittering clothes in twilight settings. Galia's huge blue eyes looked out into Sevasti's heart, in a way which made her sad. Galia wrote that things were mega fab and sent kisses to everyone. Sevasti guarded the magazine. She was afraid that the pictures would end up with the boys.

Sevasti was the first girl on the island to go to the university in Rodos. Kirios Katrios spoke for a long time with her father, who sighed a lot, but the boys were already out with the boats and did not want to go away. Sevasti was carefully lodged with one of the mayor's aunts, who locked the doors at nine and went to church every day.

When Galia came again, Sevasti was married to Theo and working for the mayor, but Galia had regularly sent parcels and letters and a delicate shawl for Sevasti's first born. The mayor had been working hard. Visiting yachts were starting to come into the harbour. Little Niko was appointed harbour master and rushed about with a piercing whistle. Panteli manned a water cart which trundled constantly round the quay. Theo was kept busy maintaining the perilous cables which snaked everywhere offering a precarious supply of electricity. Bars and tavernas began to be established around the harbour.

Galia leaped about the quay hugging and kissing everyone she recognised, including the mayor, which caused a stir. The first thing she did was to find Sevasti. They needed a house for the summer. This was the start of Sevasti's business. Another crop of boys became Galia's entourage and her previous protectors suffered some marital discord if they were seen looking at her. Galia had come with a photographer who took pictures everywhere. Still Galia had no ring. Sevasti was reticent, when asked about the sleeping arrangements. The mayor invited Galia and the photographer into his house, where his wife gave them coffee and cakes with a gritty smile. The mayor's wife had heard more than she wished about the wonderful Galia.

When she left the island, Galia merrily announced to everyone that she was pregnant. In the shops and alleys, the old black widows received this information with bewildered horror, but many people just hugged and kissed her, as if she were married.

The photographs appeared in *Vogue* all over the world. Galia sent a copy. The mayor sat in the fishermen's bar and toasted her with metaxa.

When she next arrived she had a sturdy blond son who came with a servant. They arrived on an imposing motor cruiser. A smoothly tanned older man sat on the shaded deck making phone calls on a bricklike piece of equipment which excited Theo. They dined in the Italian *ristorante* and the new one on the headland, opened by two Englishmen who were lovers.

The older man sat patiently in his silk suit and sunglasses, while Galia greeted people and flitted about buying jewellery and clothes in the little shops, which some islanders had established in Rodos but now had brought to Kapotheni. He bought her a diamond necklace from the one serious local jeweller, who ran up the thousand steps to tell his wife that they could now have the air conditioning she had wanted.

Galia came every year like an exotic migrating bird, her silk kaftans billowing in the hot wind. She remembered everyone's names and asked after their families. She brought presents for Sevasti and the children, huge silk scarves from somewhere called Liberty, boxes of Lego, dolls which cried and peed. The mayor regularly received, with formal gratitude, a bottle of very important whisky. It was as if Kapotheni were Galia's family. Sometimes she brought her son and his servant, sometimes she came without him because he was at school. He lived there, she explained. Always there was a man, but never the same one and always, Sevasti saw, these men were old in spirit or years and Galia was young.

The mayor, who was getting very old, always found himself entranced into a much younger state of mind by Galia's smiles and gentle stroking of his arm. His wife had abandoned her raging jealousy and now hugged her warmly like a mother.

One year, Galia explained that even on Kapotheni she had been followed by photographers with long lenses. She needed somewhere with privacy. The *Sea Captain's House* had a luxurious walled garden, extravagantly watered, bringing the council a handsome rate. It was discreetly lit by night with lights installed by Theo. A Rodos gardener brought shrubs and flowers to replace any which were lost over winter. A widow nearby devoted herself to its maintenance.

When Sevasti showed the house to Galia, she flew about in delight. She loved the marble bathroom and the elegant salon. She adored the high ceilinged bedrooms with their great wide windows. She was amazed at the painted wooden floors. She was astonished by the gleaming kitchen fitted out with expensive German equipment. Her man followed her about, talking on his phone, and her servant busily wrote lists.

When they were alone, she said to Sevasti, 'The sun does me no favours now, darling. You should see some of the stuff they've published. Tits like handbags and my arse like a couple of pears. *Dégoutante*.' Sevasti tried to look sympathetic but, to her, Galia seemed as lovely as always. Theo said, 'She's a rich woman. Why should she want to be photographed all the time?'

Then, one year, Galia was alone. No man, no son, no maid, no secretary. She came in by helicopter and Stefano drove her to the house. She was wrapped in a dark silk cloak and hid behind great black sunglasses, saying nothing. When Sevasti came, Galia said she needed someone to cook for her. She did not want to go out. Sevasti was worried because the few good restaurants were too busy to lose a cook. Finally the English boys agreed to provide whatever Galia wanted and to get someone to bring it to her. Georgina, at her clever supermarket which catered for the yachts and even had Marmite and Russian caviar, sent over her entire stock of

Lanson champagne. The cigarette kiosk had to give up all its *Marlboro,* ask the other two for theirs and order some more for the next ferry delivery. Galia seemed to be preparing for a siege.

A few days later one of the English boys called to Sevasti from his kitchen. His delivery boy had stumbled back two hours later than expected, in a state of disorientation so severe that they had kept him in the back and walked him home, when the last customers left. 'She'd been giving him weed, Sevasti, probably the weird stuff they smoke in England. Have a word. Tell her to pick on the motorbike boys, not little fellas like Dimi.'

Galia lay on the wide sofa with a half empty *Lanson* bottle and an overflowing ashtray, her flawless arms outstretched as if she were crucified.

'Sorry sorry sorry, darling. *Je m'excuse. Sygnomi. Bolli. Bolli.* Won't do again. Just needed a bit of company, you know.'

'I will come, Galia,' Sevasti said. 'In the evening, after you have eaten.'

When she did, it felt as if she had raced back through the years and was standing amazed at Galia's table of makeup and jewellery, but now it was a strange little pipe and lumps of brown sandy stuff, which Galia burned with her gold lighter, and white powder which Galia sniffed up her nose. Galia talked a lot, while Sevasti sipped the *Lanson* and watched the lights of the boats in the bay. Finally Galia produced a pill from a small porcelain box, took it and fell flat backward across her bed, her wonderful face as peaceful as a saint's. Sevasti sat on the bed and stroked Galia's hair away from her face. There were fine red lines running neatly down the skin from her temples, round her ears and under her chin. Sevasti drew back in empathic shock at the thought of the operation which had lifted Galia's face. It made Sevasti feel sick to think of the way they must have cut and pulled and stretched the skin over the fragile beautiful bones.

The next day the helicopter clattered and roared overhead and Galia had gone. She left everything, her clothes and shoes and drugs and a handbag, which looked completely ordinary, but may have been worth even more than the three thousand pounds sterling with which it was stuffed. Sevasti boxed everything up and made sure everyone was paid. The cleaner pulled a face when she came for her money. The bathroom had been as bad as the latrines at the monastery, she said.

Galia rang Sevasti. She was in New York. She was sorry not to have said goodbye, '*Yeia sou*, Sevvi. See you next year. I love you.'

Managing Galia's visits became increasingly demanding. Sometimes she holed up and lay in the salon smoking and watching DVDs on the television. Sevasti had to call in twice a day, trying to persuade Galia to send out for something to eat, gathering empty champagne bottles and tidying away pills and bags of powder and anything else that might scandalise the cleaner, who was a religious woman. This became so difficult that Sevasti took to doing the cleaning herself. Theo protested because it was not commensurate with her status on the island.

Other years Galia appeared in restaurants and bars, dressed wonderfully. Euro notes seemed to fall about her in a trail like handkerchiefs. She left bags and shoes wherever she went, which were always carefully returned the next day. The motorbike boys and those of their older antecedents who had married but not settled, hung about waiting to see if she would choose to ride to the other bay for a drink or take one of the boats out to the chapel island, where they smoked their home-grown weed or shared her stash of powder and laughed when she shed her silk clothes and wandered backwards into the dark moonlit sea, waving her arms above her head like a reversed Venus. Theo heard about all this in the fishermen's bar and came home growling.

So this year, thought Sevasti, which will it be? Hermit Galia or Galia the dazzling star? Theo had trundled grimly off to get the four wheel drive. Galia would come in on the helicopter. Sevasti was always glad that Galia was not subjected to Theo's silent contempt. Stefano, Galia's loyal taxi driver, was contentedly married with four children and dismissed all the bar stories with a wave of his hand, 'Wanking dreams,' he declared.

While Sevasti was explaining the power switches to newly arrived Mr and Mrs Peabody, she heard Galia's helicopter buzzing overhead like an angry mechanical hornet.

Galia flung her arms round her. When they drew back, Sevasti saw how thin she looked and something worse, how old.

'Have you been ill?' she asked.

'Ill?' laughed Galia.

'You've lost so much weight. Kilos. Galia, you have no flesh.'

'Size six,' said Galia, with a triumphant toss of her gleaming hair. 'Even the little bitches can't get there. Not all of them, anyway.'

A glowing opal necklace circled her neck. Sevasti stared at the sinews of skin which disfigured the throat, beneath the ironed-out face. Galia fingered the necklace, 'Pretty, isn't it?' Sevasti nodded mutely. Galia was looking as old as Sevasti's mother or, at least, Galia's neck was.

'I had another face job,' said Galia. 'Great isn't it? Got the arms done too. They're good but the scars are a bitch. Tummy took a hell of a tuck, but hey ho Sav, what's to be done? Gotta stay young and beautiful.'

Sevasti smiled at her, 'You have always been beautiful, Galia. You will always be.'

'Poof, Sav. Tell that to my fucking agent.'

She wandered through the salon and sat on the deep sofa, 'Have we got any fizzy? Break it out then, Sav. Tonight I shall go and see my lovely boys.'

'Oh they've gone home,' said Sevasti. 'To England. Harry's mother died and, you know, she was the one who could not accept that they were . . . together. So they decided they would go back now. Go to Vassili, Galia. He now has a French chef.'

'Vassili is such an obsequious prick,' said Galia.

'The new place? *The Paradise*. George Clooney was in there last month. And Penelope Cruz.'

'With George Clooney? That *is* news.'

'No, she stayed at the *Napoli*.'

'Bloody hell, this island,' said Galia, laughing, 'I suppose the fishermen's bar is now a lap dancing club.'

'No, no,' said Sevasti, 'it is still the same.'

She wished she had not said this.

Galia appeared at the fishermen's bar at ten o'clock that night, carrying two bottles of *Lanson* in a supermarket bag. She was dressed in a transparent silver shift, very simple and scattered with what turned out to be real diamonds. As ever there were no undergarments and, in a certain light, it was clear that Galia was shaved from neck to toe.

The fishermen's bar had devoted years to tourist watching and was quite blasé about bodies, only pausing to raise eyebrows at the near perfect or the grotesque beyond imagining, but the fishermen's bar now froze in stunned delight.

Galia slapped a wodge of brown fifties on the counter and ordered Alexo to fill everyone up because they were all going to get rat-arsed tonight. Some football-watching English and Germans stared offensively and made remarks about 'the rich tart' but Alexo, who had been one of her first adolescent fans, quietly told them that, 'If she buy you drink, you drink and like. Yes? If no, you fuck off. Yes?'

Galia requisitioned two chairs, one for her bottom and one for her feet, and ordered someone to open the champagne. Those men who were expected at home, happily toasted Galia and left, to relay the news that Galia was back and very happy this time, very beautiful. Galia kissed all of them. A priest, who had been enjoying a quiet beer with his brother, managed to slip out of the back door unnoticed.

Getting rat-arsed is not a sport enthusiastically pursued on the island. The English and the Germans readily joined in, but the islanders' response was muted. They sat and listened and smiled and laughed at Galia's glamorous declamations about New York and *fuckingVogue* and darling Mick whoever he thinks he is the little prick and where is she to get the gold *Louboutins* that bloody Cressida got in Paris and says they only made fifty pairs and who cares about the base rate does Gloria fucking Porter? does she hell and who on this wonderful island who has the coke or the Es or fuckit just a bit of the green stuff? Who? someone must know because she has flown out leaving her stash in the pink *Zagliani* so that at this minute she has nothing to ease her pain and boy oh fucking boy my friends my great good only friends my wonderful wonderful friends does she have pain to ease.

The older Greeks melted away, visually sated and happy to have been part of this event, until it was only the English, the Germans, Alexo and a gang of motorbike boys. At two o'clock Alexo thankfully closed the shutters and pointed the swaying tourists up the thousand steps. Galia roared off on the back of a motorbike, in a cavalcade like a police escort.

Where did they take her and what did they do?

The new mayor was very angry about what happened. It was very bad for the image, he said. The new mayor, who had been in post for ten years but was always called the new mayor, was an accountant who proudly spoke of 'Kapotheni plc' and loved spread sheets. He had negotiated EU loans for great improvements. The harbour now had a separate water and electricity supply at each mooring and there were wooden tubs with flowering shrubs. The harbour master wore a white shirt with epaulettes and gave instructions on an iPhone. The fishermen no longer pounded octopus on the quayside to make it tender: the visitors on their yachts, being served their breakfast in the cool of their canopied dining areas, did not like the sight or the sound of it.

Kapotheni sold itself as a sophisticated place. Quiet and untouched but discreetly cosmopolitan. A famous model floating dead off the Port Beach was not helpful. Journalists started arriving, but the islanders were used to spotting the annual tax inspectors and most of them smiled at the journalists and knew nothing.

But not all of them and the newspapers with their headlines, *Naked Gloria drowns in paradise*, *Sex romps and drugs on Gloria's last night*, caused the mayor to grind his teeth and make a surreptitious deal with the bar which stocked this garbage and somehow the European newspapers did not reach the island for a few days.

The police stamped about angrily, frightening the hell out of the motorbike boys, but she had gone with them willingly and there was no sign of violence on her drowned body. Some said she took all her clothes off and made love to the statue of the old mayor. Some said she pole-danced round an umbrella outside Vassili's restaurant. Some said she took the boys back to the villa and offered one thousand euro to the one who could last longest. Some said she crawled from one to the next, giving each fellatio of such phenomenal power and efficiency that they were ruined for normal family life. Some said they did things to her with courgettes and empty champagne bottles. These were bar stories, but one way or another, Sevasti heard them all.

They found her magical dress folded carefully on one of the loungers at the Port Beach. This was the detail which made Sevasti cry.

They said that Alexo should have stopped it. Alexo spread his arms, 'Galia? Who stops Galia?' he exclaimed.

Galia's son politely emailed Sevasti saying his mother had loved the island and could she be buried there? He would gladly take care of the cost.

They buried her in the cemetery just past the Port Beach where she had first entranced the island with her innocent body and her open heart. There was an argument about this in the Town Hall. Some priests, old enough to remember her first scandalous arrival, querulously objected that she did not belong to the island, but the new mayor, nephew of the old mayor, maintained that Galia had put Kapotheni on the map. She had done the island an immeasurable service, despite her unfortunate end, and even that seemed to have drawn in the rich and curious. The son obediently sent a lot of money, some of which was used to erect an imposing memorial. There was much discussion of what should be inscribed on the marble stone. Even the resident English, who had largely ignored her as an embarrassment in the later years, put forward haughty suggestions. The new mayor, being an accountant, freely admitted he had no idea, so Vassili and Alexo and Stefano argued it out and, borrowing shamelessly from the great Kazantzakis, decided on *Eimai elefteri*, I am free.

Sevasti visited the *Sea Captain's House* every day, unable to get to work cleaning and preparing it for new tenants. She wandered around, holding and stroking the beautiful dress.

She stood at the high windows at dusk and stared out at the great stretch of peaceful sapphire sea, the pink-grey distant mountains and the cupola of turquoise sky in which the stars began to shimmer, seeing, as all the islanders do from time to time, the infinite beauty of the place.

Nothing in excess

Μηδέν άγαν...

Nothing in excess . . .
Julian Seeing Indifference C. P. Cavafy

Aristides Papazian, known as Ari, and The Right Honourable the Earl of Palsy, Lord Westavon, known as Reg, had been sitting in Alexo's bar on the memorable night when the famous model drowned. Naturally there had been many discussions of her heavenly body, which had arrived on the island every year to entrance and enchant and had decorated expensive magazines around the world. But, when she began to come alone, she had contented herself with the motorbike boys and treated Ari and Reg, as she did all the local men, with alcoholic affection and not a second glance.

The news of her drowning flew around the island as soon as her body was found by the fishermen the next day and there was a sombre tone to the evening conversation.

'Fucking beautiful woman,' said Reg, sighing.

'Drinking. Smoking. English,' said Ari. 'Rich woman. Too much ganga.'

'Fucking beautiful,' repeated Reg.

'Beautiful and mad,' said Ari screwing his finger into his head. 'Like The Mother. Yes?'

'The Mother' was Ari's invariable name for Sylvia, who had arrived on the island thirty years before. The result had been Hermes, Sylvia's son, with whom two years later she returned to England.

Ari was outraged at this desertion, which he explained as a prime example of the madness of English women, but he quickly found someone else to share his bed, run the bar and manage the taverna on the Port Beach. Reg had also suffered the early loss of love but he retreated into stoical solitude and remained alone through the years, reading and sleeping, attending a frigid English Christmas gathering in winter and working on the round-the-island-boat in the summer, making up outrageous stories about his non-existent seafaring life, to entertain the tourists. Reg and Ari agreed that women were creatures of incomprehensible uncertainty. Ari continued to pin the butterflies down whenever he could; Reg became content to watch them fluttering about the summer port.

They sat in amiable silence watching the ambling crowds of holiday makers and the scurrying locals. Two middle-aged tourists in unbecoming sunhats and flowery kaftans wandered by, clutching sheaves of Google information about tavernas and boat trips.

'Old hens,' said Ari, nodding at them, 'stringy but grateful. Very grateful. Better than the sweet little chickens who think you should pay for them to eat and drink before they go to bed with you. But I think in England you stop fucking when you have the babies and then everyone gets fat. It's not pleasant when they are fat like whales. You feel you might be squeezed and die, like with a big snake.'

Reg snorted and lit a cigarette. Ari's indefatigable appetite for tourists was not news.

'And,' continued Ari, 'they do not want much. English, you see. Bang bang bang they want, then they are tired. You have to kiss them first though and afterwards. If not they get angry and talk with their friends and won't speak to you.'

'Shut up,' said Reg. 'You're making me feel ill . . . Hey, Jimmy.' He jumped up from the table and waved at a passing Lambretta. Jimmy, red faced and blue bodied with tattoos, parked and joined them.

'When did you get in?' Reg asked. 'How's Ange?'

'Saturday,' said Jimmy. 'She's knackered but she'll be alright in a few days.'

Slapping the table, Ari continued, oblivious to this hiatus, 'Is English. You not like sex. An old woman in the dark can be very good, as long as she is not fat. Many of the young ones are fat too, aren't they? Is alright. Big belly, big tits, but not when it all rolls around like dough at the baker's.'

'Christ, Ari,' said Reg. 'Give over.'

'Yeh, give it a rest,' said Jimmy, waving at Alexo for a beer.

'Also,' said Ari, 'I think you must do nothing but make babies in England because the women do not allow anything else. This can be boring.' He nudged Reg, 'Aha, the Madonna arrives.'

Next to Alexo's bar was Nasso's bar. The red-cushioned cane chairs of Nasso's bar sat under an expensive white canvas roof which could be moved in and out at the press of a button. Alexo provided battered metal tables and wooden chairs, which had to be moved into the shade when the sun came round.

Reg, Ari and Jimmy watched idly as Nasso, having kissed her hand, escorted a woman to a chair with elaborate courtesy. Once she was settled, he gestured briskly to a boy and ordered a drink which was brought with uncharacteristic rapidity. Replacing the drink on its coaster with obsessive solicitude, Nasso retired to his dark corner at the back and lit a cigarette.

'She comes to the taverna on my beach,' Ari commentated. 'Her friends lie in the sun. They come two . . . three years.'

'Don't tell me he's banging her,' said Reg. 'She's as old as my mother.'

'I say nothing of your mother, my friend. Your mother is ninety, I think. Look again. This one is not young, you are right, but for Nasso she is very beautiful. I have said, Speak to her Nasso, she comes always to your bar. But he just sits there in his chair like a dolt. He likes her shoes and her red hair.'

Reg squinted through the low sunlight at the shaded figure leaning back in her chair, 'OK. Sixty,' he conceded. 'Bog standard English middle class. Home Counties edition, I bet. Two a penny in Waitrose. Can't see the shoes.'

'Always high heels. Nice legs. Pretty hands. What is Waitro?' asked Ari.

'Posh supermarket, but in England supermarkets are as fucking big as Rhodes airport, not like here,' said Jimmy.

Ari thought about this, 'Maybe this is why the English get fat,' he said. 'Watch! Watch.' He gripped Reg's arm.

The woman was searching in her bag and brought out a packet of cigarettes. Nasso snaked between the tables with his lighter like a darting lizard and arrived beside her just as she fished out her own. She bent forward toward the flame. She smiled.

'A plentiful bosom,' said Reg. 'That Nasso's thing?'

'You have to be careful what you say to Nasso,' said Ari. 'For him she is an icon. And here are her friends.'

Two women carrying shopping bags bounced down cheerfully at the woman's table, talking and laughing.

'Oh, I know them,' said Reg. 'The tall one often comes on the boat. The other one came once and was sick.'

'Yeh, we know them,' said Jimmy. 'Angela and them rabbit on about arty farty films. Fucking awful boring things they are, them films.'

'Oh, not football?' said Reg, grinning. Jimmy punched him on the arm.

'I like tall women,' said Ari. 'The Mother was very tall.'

'She was,' agreed Reg. 'She seems to have got shorter in the last few years. When is she coming out?'

'Next Wednesday,' said Jimmy.

'Hermes is coming with his fiancée,' said Ari. 'The Mother is telling me that someone must come and clean my house so that the fiancée is happy.'

'Probably a good idea,' said Reg. Although Ari now lived in a stone built house in place of his shacks, his sheep and various goats had not entirely grasped the new domestic arrangement.

'Tchah! Hermes must make her happy. If she wants to clean, she can get busy in the day.'

'Not how it works, Ari. Not in the UK, anyway,' said Jimmy.

'The Mother is bringing jerseys for us,' Ari announced.

'Bugger,' said Reg. 'I've got three I've never even worn. The bloody woman does nothing but knit.'

'I like the tall one,' repeated Ari, appraising the group again. 'She laughs a lot. The blonde one is serious. A woman with a face like a goat is not sexy.'

'Leave off with that lot, Ari. I bet they're all grandmothers,' said Reg.

'So?' said Ari. 'My *yiayia* married again when she was seventy-five.'

The following evening they were joined by Vangeli from the supermarket in the village, Teri from the fruit stall and Stamati the jeweller. They endured an hour of repetitious grumbling from Ari about the town council's attitude to his plans for an outdoor cinema near the beach, which would guarantee custom at the bar in the evening.

The three women had sat for a while in Nasso's bar and then set off toward the bus stop. The tall one smiled at Vangeli, who gave her a wave. Jimmy got up and walked after them, 'Evening ladies,' they heard him saying. The women turned and smiled.

'Ha,' said Ari to Vangeli. 'Nice woman, yes?'

'Very nice,' said Vangeli, 'she comes to my shop.'

'She eats a lot of bananas, doesn't like them brown like yours, Vangeli,' said Teri.

'She'll get belly ache,' said Vangeli.

'She'll like my banana,' said Ari.

'For God's sake, Ari,' said Reg.

'She bought my moonstone necklace this year,' said Stamati. 'Every year she buys.'

'Rich old hen,' said Ari, clucking and waggling his elbows. They laughed.

Jimmy returned and settled on his creaking chair.

'I'm having the tall one,' said Ari, waving a warning finger at him. 'Or perhaps the red hair. If Nasso does nothing it's his problem.'

'Fuck off, I was asking them if they want to come to our gaff for some nosh,' said Jimmy. 'Angela's enough for me.'

'Ha, English,' said Ari. 'No fun.'

A few days later, when Reg arrived at the boat, Giorgio was busy with the tourists and it was not until they were going through the straits with their cargo of legs dangling over the side and bodies stretched on the cushioned deck, that Giorgio nonchalantly handed Reg his iPhone. At first Reg did not know what he was looking at on the little screen. Giorgio was giggling and slapping his leg with one hand, while keeping the other on the wheel. It was dark in the fo'c'sle and Reg went out onto the deck and tilted the phone about in the glare.

'Where did this come from?' he yelled, but Giorgio was speechless by this time and hanging onto the wheel, convulsing with laughter that was becoming painful, 'Water,' he gasped trying to stand upright and compose himself. Reg gave him water with a shaking hand, sat down on the bench seat and rolled sideways, clutching his stomach in a paroxysm of astonished delight. For the rest of the day it was impossible for them to discuss the images. Every time they looked at each other they started to laugh.

In the evening Alexo's bar was unusually crowded. Iphones littered the tables, beside the small cups of coffee and the ashtrays. Ari roared past in his enormous four wheel drive, scowling and almost knocking over a tourist, but that was all they saw of him that night.

The three women sat together in Nasso's bar and then set off for the bus stop. The tall one waved.

No-one could work out quite where the video came from. It had flashed round the island from phone to phone and it seemed not to have an identifiable sender. The opening sequence, strangely domestic, in a dim moonlit bedroom, revealed Ari methodically taking off his shoes and T-shirt, undoing his belt, pulling off his jeans and sitting on a bed, sliding off his pants. He placed the clothes neatly on a chair. His socks remained on his feet. He might have been alone during these business-like proceedings, but occasionally he looked up, grinning, and there was a long wisp of something white and unfocussed at the side of the screen, which was possibly a person. With a magnificent flourish of his hand and a commanding expression, he displayed his considerable erection to the white wisp and, now, to a large proportion of the island's population. At this point there was some amateurish camera shake as it moved toward him past the wisp, with the accompaniment of a burst of explosive feminine snorting and giggling. Ari's panic stricken face, naked body shrinking backward in horror and inadequately shielding hands, were firmly ensconced in a thousand memories, never to be erased.

Angela and Jimmy sat outside their house by the water's edge, playing chess by the light of the moon in the enveloping dark warmth of the night.

'That was you, wasn't it?' she said. 'You put them up to it.'

Jimmy grinned, 'Clever old hens, aren't they?'

He placed his queen, 'Checkmate, darling.'

A **Fabulous Caparison**

μιά εξαίρετη θά κάμω πανοπλία...
...Αλλά δέν θά ξέρει...
...που κείνται ή πληγές μου...

I shall make myself a fabulous caparison . . .
. . . no-one will know
. . . where I am wounded . . .

Aemilianus Monae Alexandrian AD 628-655 C. P. Cavafy

People say I look like Daddy. They say I 'take after him' and they're wrong because I was adopted as a baby. Nobody knows this in the whole world apart from Daddy, Mother and Andrea. Mother says I can look at all the papers she has kept and find out things about my real parents but I never want to. They aren't 'real'.

People think I'm like Daddy because we both have dark blonde hair and skin which tans so when we are on the island we have sun streaks in our hair and our skin goes really brown. I have long hair. When I was a toddler my hair was white. Flaxen they call it. The Greek people used to come and touch it and smile.

My favourite meal is lunch. I want to go to St Nick's every day because the beach is flat and there is some sand so you don't have to walk out into the sea over pebbles and Lefti in the taverna gives me a lot of chips. They are really nice. Almost as good as McDonald's. Mother wants to go shopping or to other beaches or the boring old monastery and Daddy is always moaning that he should be doing some writing but usually one or other of them takes me to the beach for the morning or the afternoon. Stamati lets me hold the tiller on his water taxi and gives me his hat and wears mine which makes him look really uncool.

I spend a lot of time in the sea. I look for crabs and try to catch fish and row about in our blow-up boat and moor it up at the rocks and pretend I'm a pirate coming ashore or an explorer. I put all my shells in the boat and row it back to the beach and put them in a bag to show Petro. I swim well, so nobody worries.

Daddy can swim very well and he taught me. We have a sailing cruiser at home and he says I'm a really useful crew now. Mother doesn't like sailing as much as I do but she comes anyway.

A lot of people like Daddy. My friends like him too. He doesn't look weird for a start. My best friend's father is as thin as a skeleton. Really creepy. Daddy doesn't wear embarrassing clothes. There's a father at school who wears shorts even in the winter. Daddy doesn't start dancing with my friends when we have a party and he doesn't show-off telling them about stuff he knows or how great he was when he was young. Sometimes he's on television but it's really boring stuff about war and the government so I never tell anyone.

The lady in the OMG shop is very pretty. We call it that because Mother goes round looking at things and then she looks at the prices and says Oh-my-God. She thinks it's terrible that all these posh shops have opened on the island for the people who come in on their 'stinky gin palaces'.

That's what Daddy calls them. Mother says 'Who needs a three hundred pound bikini on this island?' and the pretty lady laughs. She's English but she has lived here for years and years. She must have been very young when she came because she still looks twenty-one. That's what Daddy said. Her name is Sandy. She wears heels four inches high. Mother said she'd break her ankle immediately if she even walked a step in them. Sandy says it is because she is so short and has to look taller.

There's an ace thing we do, Daddy and me. We go down to Petro while Mother is having her shower and putting on all her makeup and we pretend to be posh and that we're having cocktails at the Ritz. The Ritz is a really top hotel not a biscuit thing and a cocktail is like a fruity drink with stuff in it like leaves and orange peel and you drink it through a straw even if you are a grown-up. Petro always pretends he's a proper waiter and gives me a special little round mat thing and calls me Madam which makes me laugh so much sometimes I wet myself a little bit. Daddy says 'Don't make her laugh' but he never tells him why which is good because I would just die.

A few times Daddy has made me laugh so much I really wet myself. I tried to stop it but there is a moment when there is no point in trying and out it all comes down your legs. He makes up names for people we know and they are really rude. There's a man called Charles who's mega old and always drunk and falling over and farting loudly so you hear. Daddy calls him *Trumper*. He says 'Here comes *Trumper*' and I have to cross my legs really hard in case I wee. There's a lady called Teresa, who works for a travel company. She's always shouting. Daddy calls her Misty Bin (Miss T Bin –

gedit?), because he says she is like the toilet bins which open if you wave your hand over them, which is quite cool but she isn't cool. Her titties are all wrinkled and she calls me 'Dear'.

He says 'Keep talking, cookie. Misty Bin's on her way over. Look serious and she might keep going. Imagine they've just nuked McDonald's. No more Happy Meals. Boo hoo.'

Sometimes Sandy comes past on her four inch heels on her way to work. Daddy calls her *Twinkle* which isn't rude because he likes her. Mother says that's because he's always twinkling at Sandy and they laugh as if it's a joke.

Mother says I will stop nearly wetting myself when I am grown up but there are loads of adverts for ladies who wet themselves and have to have special pants so I'm not sure about that.

Daddy smiles with his eyes not with his mouth. He still holds my hand, if I want to. He tells me about everything I want to know. Not like Mother. When I wanted to know how to make a bow we went into the woods and found some straight ash branches which were just right then we had to make notches and knot string in them. He let me make the notches with his really sharp knife. The string wasn't much good so we used fishing line. Ash is really bendy.

Daddy and Mother got me because the police took me away. Mother says they were very lucky to get me because babies are in short supply. It doesn't look like that to me. Babies are everywhere. Mother's always trying to tell me things and I try not to listen. When I was ten, four weeks ago, she told me that there are men who put their dongles into children's bottoms and mouths and minnies. That's boys and girls though boys don't have minnies so I don't know where they put them with boys apart from their bottoms and mouths. She said that's why I must never talk to strangers which is ridiculous because she does it all the time but I suppose if anyone tried to put their dongle into Mother she would go ape like she does when the computer won't work.

Then she said that was what happened to me when I was a baby. She said I mustn't tell anyone because it would frighten them. I said it must have been a very small dongle like Jackson's in Year Two. He was always getting it out but you could hardly see it. She said that's why I have the funny bumpy mark on my minnie but soon I would grow hair there and nobody would be able to see it. I can't think of anything more disgusting than having hair there so I told her I had to do homework and went upstairs. I wish she wouldn't tell me things. I don't remember any of it because I was a baby.

I don't know how they do it. It must be like trying to put a sausage into a keyhole. Daddy's dongle is all wobbly like one of those long balloons when they're old. I saw it once when I went into their bedroom to find a hanky. He was hopping about putting his pants on. It had hair on too. I thought that only happened to Daddies so it was a shock to find out it would happen to me. Gross or what?

I don't talk to Daddy about the things Mother tells me. He just thinks I'm brilliant. He says so. I wonder why he married Mother though. When I asked him he said, 'Because she is the most beautiful woman in the world.' It was kind of a nice thing to say but it is definitely not true. Miss Hopwood who teaches Year Four is prettier than Mother. I expect he said it because you have to say that kind of thing about your wife otherwise you look a bit of a div for marrying her. I won't marry anyone and I certainly won't have babies. There are plenty of them around. I want to join the Navy and be a Captain. Daddy says I have to work hard at Maths if I want to do that. I can't see why. I could sail our boat on my own now if he let me.

I wonder what these strangers say when they want to put their dongle into you? Mother says they often ask you if you want to get into their car and I must never say Yes but I got into May's dad's car the other day after school to go to her house and he's almost a stranger because he's her new dad. The old one went away. He didn't say anything about his dongle. I'm dying to ask my friend Suzie because she always knows but Mother says it's a secret and I mustn't talk about it. Anyway they can't ask a baby. Babies are really boring. I really don't want this hair you know but I don't care about the bumpy mark and no-one is going to see it anyway.

Andrea says the nightmares are about bad things which are worrying me and sometimes we don't know what is worrying us because we are so worried. Sounds a bit mad to me but I like going to Andrea. She's got a room full of stuff you can use like paints and a sand tray and lots of little dolls' house people except they have dongles and minnies like real people which is a bit rude but I don't say anything. I tell her stories. She likes my stories.

I've always had nightmares. I have them almost every week. That's why I can't go to sleepovers with my friends. I wake up screaming and Mother has to come in and hug me and give me a drink of milk. I don't tell anyone about that because it is really babyish. Sometimes I wet the bed because I am so frightened. Often the nightmare is a lion which is roaring at me and opening his mouth so wide I think he will bite my head off. Sometimes it is about this thing that comes in the room and I can't stop it and I know it will go right through me and kill me. You probably think I'm mad. When they wanted me to go and see Andrea they said I could talk to her and I said that I talked to them so why did I have to go? I can't think what there is to talk about anyway other than whether Miss Hopwood wears French knickers like Suzie's mother does or if the travellers really eat hedgehogs and badgers. The kind of stuff we talk about at school. They said perhaps it would help with the nightmares so I went because I'm too old to wet the bed and it has to stop. I can't wee the bed when I'm a Captain. I don't know why they think it will help because Andrea never answers my questions. I asked her why she thought Daddy married Mother and she said 'What do you think about it?' She always says that. It's really annoying.

I don't get many nightmares when I'm here on the island with Daddy and Mother. I haven't had one this holiday so far. Daddy says it's our treasure island and I'm his treasure. There's nothing wrong with Mother of course. Some of my friends say she's cool because she talks to them as if they are people not children but I'd quite like it if it was just Daddy and me. Mother worries about me. Daddy said 'She loves you, honeypot, and she wants the best for you.' And I said 'But you're not worried about me, are you Daddy?' And he said 'Worried about you? You're a pirate and you're going to be a Captain. What's to worry about?'

Lovely Corpses

Σάν σώματα ώραια νεκρών που δέν εγέρασαν
....έτσ' ή επιθυμίες μοιάζουν που επέρασαν
χωρίς νά εκπληρωθουν...

Like the lovely corpses of the young
. . . that is how desires are which have been
denied . . .

Desires C. P. Cavafy

Linda Swayne's estimate of herself was low. She was not pretty, graceful or charming and she was not exceptionally clever. She considered herself, instead, very lucky. She seemed to have met so many people who were ready to support, help and encourage her. Added to this, when she was young, there had been no particular shortage of men interested in talking to her, asking her out. There had even been more than one proposal. Her mother had consistently pointed out her faults and predicted a rather miserable adult life, so it came as a slow and pleasant surprise to discover that her mother might have been wrong.

The commonplace and appalling stress of bearing and rearing children, consumed her energies for many years and she joined that group of women who quietly give up on passion or adornment and only go to the gym in order to be able to be a suitably active example and parent. She did not have a husband who subtly or otherwise demanded dinner party skills and she and her friends were content with fund-raising school dances as their major social outings.

Thus, at sixty-three, Linda Swayne found herself with a comfortable part-time job as secretary/receptionist to a sole practitioner GP, a house which felt shiftily quiet with too few people to use the rooms, the sustaining accompaniment of Radio Four through the creation of quilts and embroidery, and a relationship with her husband which was similar to that with the doctor. Both men were organisationally challenged and drifted through the logistics of time management in a haze of fascinating data associated with their work.

Each year, Linda steadily read through the short list for the various novel prizes, quietly astounded by the demands upon the reader, which always included up to fifty pages of incomprehension before the actual story began to be apparent. With friends, she went to the local cinema to see opera and stage plays. She came to the conclusion that later life was undoubtedly the time to appreciate the wild agonies of Carmen or Hamlet. With less experience, such extreme responses to the vagaries of life would appear to be quite unusual, but Linda's job and her ability to be a good listener had taught her that people could and did behave in astonishing ways. She saw nothing wrong in this, although of course terrible consequences often occurred, but she was glad that as far as she was concerned, she had never been called upon to contemplate drastic measures or formidable risks in a quest for happiness. The happiest she had been was the day her mother was solemnly declared dead by a kind young doctor, who looked a little startled when Linda immediately packed up her knitting, shook his hand and left. She had been very happy at the birth of her children, but nothing compared to the burst of joy which exploded in her mind on that morning, as she walked toward her car in the sunlight.

This year, like every other, she had spent patient months trying to negotiate an agreement with her husband as to when exactly he would take time off for a holiday. At last two weeks were found which were free from conferences, grant applications, interviews or necessary seminars. Linda obtained his secretary's assurance that the weeks were in the diary and picked up the telephone to make the arrangements for the house in Cornwall and then she paused, with the receiver in her hand, and stared into the garden, where her roses were preparing, slowly this year, to put spring to rout. It had been a long wet winter, and spring had only faintly been present. She put down the phone, went to the laptop and started to Google.

When her husband was eating his dinner, a very moveable feast which meant that she always ate regularly at seven and made meals which could be reheated for him, she informed him that they would be going to a Greek island, small but supposedly very beautiful. He said, 'Very nice,' shovelled the last of the shepherd's pie into his mouth and set off for his study, then 'We aren't going to Cornwall?' from the stairs.

'No,' she said.

'Right,' and the study door closed for the remainder of the evening.

The furnace blast of heat which hit them as they came down the plane stairway told her that her packing had been stupidly inappropriate. The thin cotton jerseys for the evenings and the jeans and skirts suitable for a tramp through English summer woods would broil her alive, but she supposed that people on the island wore and bought clothes, so she would have to do some shopping.

The ferry deposited them on the quay in the early evening where a glowing array of kaftans, jewellery, sandals were displayed in profusion along the harbour road in the myriad of little shops. She had booked them into a 'boutique hotel'. This had not seemed quite right for a Greek island, but it looked quiet and peaceful and the owners were English, which meant that there would be none of the stress of trying to ask how the shower worked, etc.

They had both travelled, but he was always chaperoned by assistants and embedded in conversations about work and she had been led around ruins and art galleries with eager friends. Cornwall demanded boot-cleaning and hot baths to counter the chill. This was the first time they had sat in the sun, with nothing to do.

Her first discovery was that he was inclined to drink a great quantity of beer both before and after the healthy Mediterranean meals, enjoying the extraordinary prospect of assured warmth. Her next discovery was that this meant he did not wake until the sun was hammering at their shutters and three hours of useable day had streamed by.

She decided to go to the harbour beach, where it seemed almost possible she might swim, even though it would be seven in the morning.

She had guessed that the beach would be quiet, but she was reduced to a mesmerised knee-hugging state of gratitude and wonder by the huge calm of the dark sea, which stretched away to the mountains of Turkey, and the expectant growing light of the dawn, while the sun crept up and over a barren hill top steadily illuminating more and more of the mountainside behind her.

Two or three purposeful Greek ladies of her own age walked past her and *kali mera*'d politely, before swiftly undressing and plunging in, wearing swimsuits and flowery hats. Thus encouraged, she stepped into the welcoming, buoyant Greek sea. She swam out a few metres and lay luxuriantly on her back, but, as she turned, something gleamed below her and she was astonished to see white sand and rocks seemingly miles beneath her feet and, in the huge depth, fish swimming purposefully about their business. The mountainside, she realised, continued on its dive below the surface of the tideless unassuming water.

On the third morning, her peace was disturbed. A tall elderly man was obviously accustomed to joining the ladies and long conversations ensued as they bobbed in the water. She swam carefully along the line of the beach, turning discreetly before she reached the group, but on this morning, as she was sitting on her lounger, he came out of the water directly in front of her and said, '*Kali mera*'. Politely she responded with the flat intonation and averted eyes which, in England, means, 'Please don't pursue this conversation'. Ignoring these behavioural signals, he sat on the lounger next to her.

'You are Swedish?' he asked in surprisingly unaccented English. No she wasn't.

'German?' Not a possibility which the English of a certain age find very appetising. No she wasn't.

'English,' he said triumphantly. 'It is very beautiful here in the morning. Are you alone?'

Oh God, she thought, just the kind of thing which always

seems to happen to me on the tube or the train, weirdos attracted by some unerring radar, probably because I look as if I won't hit them.

'I am married,' she said, in icy hostile tones. She stood up and gathered her things.

'This is good,' he said. 'You should be. I am sorry, perhaps you are offended. We are very direct in Greece. I am married a long time. A good marriage. It is nice that you come to the beach. Will you come again and perhaps you will not think I am a strange person?'

Bewildered and embarrassed by his intuition, she left. Bugger, she thought, I have made a wrong assumption and been rude. Now I won't know whether I should go to the beach and show that I accept his apology, or stay away.

She decided, after a great deal of anxiety, that it would be ungracious and nastily English not to accept his apology. She went to the beach in one of her new cotton kaftans in brilliant shades of blue and green.

On this meeting they exchanged their names, how many children they both had, three for her and four for him, how many grandchildren, two and eight, what he had done for work, something on ships, and what she did. He informed her that he had seen her shopping but where was her husband? She told him her husband was very tired and worked very hard and needed his sleep.

The next morning she found herself telling him about her son being deaf from birth and how well he had done in his obstacled life.

'This is because he has had a good mother,' he said, and told her that one of his daughters had polio as a child and it was very sad for all of them, but she was very clever and now lived in Athens and was a lawyer and married.

'Oh bravo,' she said with complete sincerity and then felt horribly self-conscious because it was not at all an English thing to say.

'My wife cried so much,' he said.

'So did I,' she said.

'But not now,' he said smiling and reaching out his hand.

'No,' she said, holding his warm fingers, 'not now.'

'Bravo for both of you,' he said.

The next morning he said, 'Does your husband sleep all day? You were buying strawberries from Teri, alone again. You must come to the *Orange and Lemon* bar and have a coffee with me. It is next to the ferry kiosk. People will say to me, who is this lovely woman?'

She laughed with all her English deadening irony.

'Why do you laugh?' he said. 'I am not making a joke.'

'Of course you are,' she said, but that seemed a little too close to flirting. 'Don't say things like that.'

'Sorry,' he said. 'You are angry?'

'Oh, no, not angry,' she never admitted to anger, 'but I'm an old woman.'

He became very stern and stared at her, 'Look at me,' he said. 'I am seventy-five, it is true,' he said, 'but I see a lovely woman. Do you say I am blind or I am mad?'

'I'm sorry,' she said. 'It was rude of me.'

He laughed, 'The English are always trying not to be rude, but you are very rude people. You never believe anyone. You do not understand honesty. I think you are a very suspicious race.'

She thought he was probably right.

She took the trouble to locate the *Orange and Lemon* bar and made plans to avoid it on her wanderings and to steer her husband away from it on their evening perambulations. She was alarmed. She played and replayed a nightmare scenario of this man informing her husband that she was lovely and, possibly, that he should not spend so much time sleeping. She blushed as she thought of the social bewilderment which would ensue. Her husband would not think of creating any kind of scene, but he would find it incomprehensible and vaguely concerning and certainly would question how it was that she was conversing on a daily basis with this delusional and impertinent old man.

But no such scenario occurred. The conversations on the beach ranged over issues of family, houses, his travels, her hobbies. He was very surprised to discover that she did not have a dog which he seemed to think was an essential component of an English family. He taught her a little Greek and made her say *Hello* and *How are you*, when they met. She became used to his ubiquitous knowledge of where she had been and where she ate and they exchanged estimates of the various restaurants the island offered. But she was unable to countenance his continued commentary on her appearance without suppressing a smirking laugh, until the last morning.

'Goodbye,' she said, holding out her hand.

He held it, 'Goodbye,' he said. 'Will you come back? The sun loves you. Your skin is shining. I like our conversations.'

'So do I,' she said.

He kissed her hand, 'You looked very beautiful in your pink dress last night.'

'Thank you,' she said. 'Thank you, that is so lovely of you.'

It was the first time in her life that she had ever accepted a compliment and the grace of the exchange stayed with her all the way home.

Misguidedly she tried to speak about the man on the beach with her friends.

'Well,' said Charlotte, 'I suppose they're all on the lookout for the Shirley Valentines. You're very brown, you should see the doctor and get your moles checked.' Charlotte disapproved of the sun.

Edna in the sewing group shrieked with laughter and gripped her arm, 'Linda. How could you? At your age? I mean. We're all dried up and past it.'

Mary, who organised the archaeological expeditions, assumed a very grim expression, 'And what was his poor wife doing while he dallied around on the beach with you?' she asked. 'You've astonished me, Linda.'

Linda opened her wardrobe and stared at the beige and navy clothes. When the next dollop of catalogues thumped through the letter box, she systematically listed a number of brightly coloured garments, pink being the dominant hue. In measuring herself for the sizing she discovered that she was rather smaller than she had thought and, one morning, unable not to admire her tan before it faded, she saw for the first time that, although she was not a beach nymph with long hair and a body so thin that it could not possibly contain all the necessary organs, there was little sign of the cellulite, the flat breasts or drooping bottom, the varicose veins or pneumatic bulges, which lay under most umbrellas.

One night she masturbated, a little tentatively, to see if, according to Edna's belief, everything had withered into obsolescence. She did not think of the man on the beach, because he seemed too nice and too real to be used in this way. She remembered a very bad boy she occasionally met in the woods, when they were all teenagers loafing about with nothing to do, and with whom she had had a surprisingly nice time.

Everything seemed to be in working order, despite her vagina being, no doubt, very surprised.

She considered his wife. Well, his wife had been at home making breakfast by the sound of it, and he seemed to have been a rather good husband on the whole, probably the long absences had helped.

Wearing a pink silk shirt, she was wrestling with the appointments spreadsheet, which the doctor had comprehensively dismantled in her absence, 'What have you done?' he asked, suddenly stopping his disruption of her filing cabinet.

'Nothing,' she said, indicating the screen, 'you did it.'

'You look fabulous,' he said, 'have you dyed your hair or something?'

'It's the sun,' she said smiling. 'And thank you, that's really made my morning.'

'Oh well,' he said, 'happy to cheer you up.'

'I'm not miserable, am I?' she asked in surprise.

'Oh God, foot in mouth,' he said. 'Not miserable, just . . . quiet. Sorry about the spreadsheet.'

The man in the dry cleaners, with whom she always enjoyed a brief pessimistic overview of the political situation, sifted through the bundle of extravagant silk purchases, which had made themselves irresistible on the island.

'Looks like you've had a good holiday,' he said.

'I did,' she said.

'If that's what Greece does to you, I'd better get off there and I shouldn't say that, being Turkish.' He winked at her, 'I know those islands. Did someone fall for you?'

'I don't think so,' she said.

'Hm,' he said smiling at her, 'I wouldn't be surprised.'

She smiled back.

Linda was going to her new pottery class on the train. Her pottery teacher was as abrupt as the man on the beach and would not have any truck with Linda's childish ideas of plunging her hands into a large dollop of warm wet clay. Linda was being educated in the complexities of the bowl.

Opposite her at the table seat was a man with a white beard and very tousled grey hair. His shirt had something green staining the collar. Just my type, she thought, probably can't even knot his own tie. He was marking a sheet of print with a green biro. She tried to read it upside down, then gave up and produced her knitting. She glanced at him. He looked as grim as Mary. But our faces all set into these fixed lines, she thought, whether they are laughter lines or lines of anguish, eventually we all look grim until we smile.

He looked up and caught her stare, 'Love the hat,' he said.

'Yes, it's great isn't it?' she said. The hat was purple. His eyes crinkled up in a smile. When our eyes cease to twinkle, that's when we should give up, she thought.

'Where are you off to?' he asked.

'I wonder,' she said.

Perhaps

Ίσως αυτήν ώρα...
...μραίνει-
... ο Θεόδοτος,
Φέρνοντας τέτοιο ένα φρικτό κεφάλι.

Perhaps, at this very time . . .
Theodotus is creeping in
carrying the frightful severed head.
Theodotus C. P. Cavafy

The postman left the letter on the courtyard step, where I found it late in the morning. The locals get their mail delivered personally, with conversation. We ex-pats must find it as and when. The letter made me very cross.

Dear Harold it began. Only my parents had called me Harold. The letter was written in a tone which suggested that the writer knew me, but a glance at the name gave no clues. *Liz Caldwell.* No bells rang.

Liz Caldwell asked me how I was. She said she had *some things* which her mother had wanted me to have. *Sadly,* her mother had died. Did one report that *happily* one's mother had died?

She continued that her mother had insisted that she give these things to me personally. She revealed the information that her mother had been my father's cousin,

Dora. Apparently the old woman had felt that she was in possession of family memorabilia which must be passed to me as I was *head of the family*. I immediately started to think of ways to decline this importunate and bewildering request.

Then I remembered. The cousin was a stringy fussy woman whom my mother detested. She had lived nearby for a few years before we moved to the Chilterns. There had been two children. Both the children were adopted and so, of course, nothing to do with us at all. We are a successful family, starting with coal mines, sending sons to university to branch into medicine and literature. We have a best-selling novelist and a knighted surgeon amongst us. Our forebears were Victorian philanthropists. There are still institutions which bear our name. The two little waifs were of no genetic significance.

Furthermore, this one had turned out to be a thief.

Liz Caldwell wanted to know if it would be possible for her to visit in the next few weeks. No, I thought, it would most certainly not be. Whatever delusions her mother harboured, I was not interested in junk. I placed the letter in the bin.

I came to this island thinking that I could subside slowly and pleasantly toward death. I had no patience left for the arrogance of the young. Too many of them do not want to know what has gone before, so cannot build their knowledge on solid ground.

All my life it had been necessary for me to have a formulation, a way of thinking. I used it in my work to good effect. As long as there was a way of thinking about what I was doing, I was content. This applied to my work, my marriage, my love affairs and my relationships with my children.

And now this process has failed me. I can find no way of thinking about what my life appears to be. I packed my notes, intending to work quietly on the Rhetoric book, but the laptop remains closed. I find it difficult to believe that two years ago I would wait impatiently for the students to shuffle out of my room, so that I could hurriedly record a new idea or jot down a reference, which had swum into my thoughts as I listened to them babbling.

I wake when the sun rises over the mountain. I sit on the balcony, drinking coffee and smoking. I read thrillers which, if they are good enough, give me a reason to read a little more. I carefully drink at least two litres of water each day. I make plans to go to this or that restaurant, if it is the holiday season, but rarely do. I eat meals for which I am not hungry, from incongruous remnants of food in the fridge. Sometimes I find myself drunk when I get up from my chair in the evening, and must use the table and chairs to assist me to my bed. All sense of what will or should or must happen next, has disappeared. I am old so I expected something of this, but not this existence without thought, without a centring focus for my mind.

But what focus could there be? It is seven years since my last affair and I have grown used to the tranquillity of life without sexual tension. A last book would do nothing to propel me toward any form of advancement.

My wife lives apparently contentedly in the UK, busying herself with village committees and visits from the grandchildren. When I return at Christmas, we have no cause for argument. The bitterness has faded. Perhaps we have become too old to taste it. Her mind is still sharp. It seems to me that we quite like each other now.

People ask me why I came to the island. I say I like the heat, which I do. I wanted the quiet. I was tired of a constant stream of communication, most of it irrelevant and commercial. I felt that increasingly I was battling with noise, through which my thoughts were forced to squeeze themselves like unconsidered strangers at a party. Now, at low times, I wonder if strangers are not, perhaps, given life at a party.

I am not depressed. I have given this thought. I know that people become depressed in old age but this is surely a failure of intelligence. It is inevitably a time of loss. I do not yearn for my young body. I used it at every opportunity. Now it is worn out and what else does one expect? I manage the problem of my antiquated bladder. We have good doctors here. I keep active. I take out my little boat and fish off *Agios Nikolaos* beach. I am on cordial drinking terms with Tom, my neighbour, although he has no conversation of any merit. I enjoy an occasional sharp duel with Paul, who has a first class mind, despite his tiresome drug addiction.

In a way you could say I have lost my mind. My mind was always my entertaining, stimulating companion, sometimes to my shame I even became irritated by its inexhaustible capacity to find something new to work on, to research, to develop. These fits of irritation were only fleeting. I came to love my mind and to rely on it. It could be trusted to find a way of thinking about anything which crashed into us as we were carried through time. It was a marriage which worked. There is no disease, no Alzheimer's, no Parkinson's, but my partner is silent and the quality of this silence is not angry, not sad, not exhausted, it is the silence of the island at night. Even in the high season this silence settles on us all in the deep night, as if it came from the sea.

Out here, time has changed. In the UK I was beginning to be aware of the curious illusion of time speeding up, which begins to happen to people in their sixth decade. I wonder if the apparently dozing nonagenarians in nursing home lounges are actually experiencing an alarming sense of hurtling through each day at breakneck speed. Certainly I was finding that months and weeks, if not yet days or hours, seemed to flash past, rather like those times when one is driving a familiar route and realises that nothing of the journey has been registered in the conscious mind and yet hazards and road junctions have been successfully negotiated.

Time stretches or shrivels according to whim. I sit on the balcony for my morning coffee and when I get up it could be eight-thirty or half past twelve. I have stopped taking notice of the bells and the summer ferries which register time.

I completely forgot about the letter. So I was stupidly taken aback when the second one arrived. This one announced that she had been assured by my wife that I lived at the address she had used and she was sorry if it inconvenienced me in any way, but she had a duty to fulfil her mother's wishes and would be coming on the *Blue Star*. She had booked herself a room at the *Ariadne*.

I resigned myself to the arrival of this unwanted visitor and found that, not surprisingly, I was looking at my mother's netsuke, a collection of exquisite Japanese ivory figures housed in a glass-fronted cabinet, which the carpenters made when I first arrived. My local char, a Mrs Samagdios believe it or not, reveres the netsuke almost as much as I do. I think her reverence is prompted by the fact that she knows these artefacts are valuable, rather than an appreciation of the craftsmanship. Her favourite is the monkey with the ruby eyes. It was little Lizzy's favourite, too, I remembered with foreboding.

I did not want the woman in my house. It seemed to me that I could easily appear to be courteous if I asked the *Ariadne* to tell me when she arrived and to give her a message that I would visit her there. I could always show her that my house is up a precipitate hillside accessed by hazardous flights of steps, although in fact there is a serviceable road circling round the back.

I really did not want to see her. I was a child at the time and the upset caused by her misdemeanour made a deep impression on me. I had never heard my mother weeping before and I can still hear my father's tone on the phone, cool, measured, but vibrating with rage. I lay upstairs in bed while, downstairs, unusual sounds of muffled perturbation penetrated my dark room.

No-one spoke to me directly. I think my parents were obscurely ashamed to tell me that a theft had taken place, as if this were a reflection on their ability to provide a safe home. There was also the embarrassing fact that the theft had been perpetrated by a relative, if only a relative in name.

I had lain awake, trembling with the anxiety which permeated the house. The phone rang and I heard my father answer, his voice now more measured but still stern, using his cousin's name in the way he used mine when he was displeased.

'Well you must search her room, Dora,' he said. 'Yes, a monkey. Dora, understand, this is an extremely valuable piece. It must be found, tonight. Of course she must have done. Harold does not *play* with the netsuke. He knows better. I told you, Eve saw her pick it up. Of course she never imagined she would take it.'

I got out of bed and stood at the top of the stairs, propelled by the urgency and distress in my parents' voices in the drawing room. Eventually my father came out and saw me and called my mother to deal with my unauthorised appearance. She would not answer my questions other than to say, 'Elizabeth has been very naughty,' in her most unforthcoming voice.

I returned to bed shivering with the thought that the chubby little girl had stolen the monkey.

I never saw her again or any of the family and then we moved. Father received apologetic letters from the cousin which were disapprovingly discussed at breakfast. The monkey appeared, but a new cabinet arrived, with several keys, which my father pointedly said were to be kept in his safe.

Many years later at some family occasion, perhaps mother's eightieth, my children were being given father's lecture on the netsuke. As a great concession he produced the keys and opened the cabinet. Mother immediately became flustered, her mind was becoming unsteady. 'No need to worry dear,' he said. 'These are Harold's children. No little thieves here.'

On the day before her arrival, I went to the hotel and informed Yanni that a relative was arriving on the *Blue Star* and wrote a message for her.

Then I went to Nasso's where I chatted with Tom for a while, mainly about his water pump. It was irritatingly windy. The shutters were banging and cigarette packets were sliding off tables. When a table toppled over and crashed down the steps, I left.

The wind was howling around the house. I made sure of the shutters and windows and went to bed.

It was the banging on the courtyard door which woke me, even though the thunder and lightning were rolling around the port as if unable to find a way out. Rain was lashing down and the courtyard was awash. I tried shouting, but there was no response so I had to paddle through and struggle with the wind and the door. A woman came forcefully through the doorway and went straight into the house.

I tried to turn on the light but the electricity had failed. She was standing in the gloom of the shuttered room.

'Well . . . excuse me, Madam,' I said. 'Can I help?'

'I'm Liz Caldwell. Little cousin Lizzie,' she said. 'Yes, you most certainly can, even though I have to do it this way.'

'What way?' I said. I was completely astonished and had no time to think about ferry times or whether I had somehow slept into the next day with the ubiquitous storm.

'I want the netsuke,' she said. 'You promised me the netsuke.'

I sat down. It felt as if I were forced down by the woman's intensity.

'No,' I said.

She took a step toward me and I shrank back.

'You nasty little prick,' she said. 'I was four. You promised me if I took my knickers down and showed you my cunt, I could have the monkey.'

'I'm sure . . . I wouldn't . . . I didn't know the word.'

'For fuck's sake,' she hissed, 'I can't remember what fucking word you used, you bastard. You got me branded a thief and it wasn't true. They sent me to a shrink because I kept saying I hadn't stolen it. They drove me mad. They put me on drugs and when I was older they locked me up for three weeks. For my own good, they said. They made me think I was bad. Do you know what it's like to believe you're bad? Give me the monkey, I haven't got much time.'

I was casting about in confusion, trying to think where the key was, but she moved to the desk in her terrible, sudden, swooping way, taking the key from the drawer and swiftly unlocking the cabinet, where she seized the netsuke, scattering some of its companions on the floor.

Then, somehow, she was speaking in Greek, a deep voice with the hammering consonants of the island intonation, 'Your soul is like the netsuke. Small, hard and cold. It will sink like a stone in the seas of infinity.'

Then she had gone.

The storm rolled round and round and I sat on my couch, trembling, remembering; remembering the truth, this time, not the lie.

We had been sent out to the garden to play.

'I'll give you something if you let me see your private thing.' (It was my mother's euphemism.) 'What do you want?'

She smiled up at me in delight, 'I want the monkey.'

'You can have it, if you let me see.'

I knew she could not have the monkey, that what I was asking was too terrible for her to speak about and she would go home silent and empty-handed. But she had not. In her innocence, she had taken her reward.

In the early morning, Yanni rang me with concern. There had been a fire on the *Blue Star* and the storm had hindered the rescue attempts.

When the dawn filtered through my shutters, the monkey was lying amongst the others on the wet floor. Later, I asked the charlady to collect them together, saying that I had knocked into the open cabinet during the storm.

Clearly it was some kind of dream or nightmare in which I had had a somnambulist experience, but I never touched the monkey again.

A few days later my wife efficiently garnered all the details she could. Liz Caldwell was missing presumed drowned during the rescue attempts, along with two others.

In October Tom invited me to go with him to the annual monastery celebrations. He takes these things very seriously. I have even seen him crossing himself and kissing the icon, like the locals. I was embarrassed for him at the time, but it is the way of the island to accept each other's idiosyncrasies without direct comment.

I thought I would go to see what all the fuss was about. Tom enthusiastically led me round the museum, lecturing me on the artefacts which were quite adequately labelled already. We came to a large basket in which there appeared to be a collection of old plastic water bottles. I was about to make a comment about relics not being what they used to be, when he clutched my arm and pointed at a battered *AGRA* bottle.

'That's the one,' he said in a comically reverend whisper. 'That's the one thrown from the ferry in May, in the storm, when your poor cousin was drowned.'

I looked at it more closely. One of their superstitions is that, if they throw a bottle into the sea with a message for the Archangel, it will reach the monastery.

'*Immense Archangel save us,*' Tom intoned, finally telling me something which was not written on a label. '*Give peace to our souls.* That's what he wrote. The sailor. He was saved. Two hundred and fifty-seven were saved. A miracle.'

'For heaven's sake Tom,' I said. 'They were saved by the Hellenic Navy and three people died. Hardly a miracle.'

'And they are in peace,' said Tom crossing himself like a peasant.

There's nothing like the complacency of the believer, is there?

Outside I pressed through the crowds to sit on the harbour edge and watch the miscellany of craft which jostled together at anchor.

For some reason the awful monkey came into my mind.

There and then I made a resolution. I would sell the netsuke. I would give the money to my wife. She is a great one for good causes. Well, somebody has to be, I suppose.

The Shore of the Morning Sea

...Κι άς δώ κ' εγώ...
Θάλασσας του πρωίου...
...καί κίτρινη όχθη...
...Κι άς γελασθώ πώς βλέπω αυτά...

And allow me also to gaze at . . .
The yellow shore of the morning sea . . .
And allow me to fool myself that I see these things.
Morning Sea C. P. Cavafy

By the time she was eight, Angela knew that life was paradoxically both very dull and very frightening and two things made it better. One was to write and the other was to fall in love.

Perhaps the two strategies were born in the same year. It was that year in which Miss Grout gave them a bowdlerised account of the Battle of Hastings and asked them to write a story about the English army. School, like home, was devilled by rules of procedure and conduct which Angela unwittingly failed to observe. She was not talkative or naughty or lazy or stupid but there was always something which Miss Grout found to criticise. It could be the size of her margins or the fact that she had not underlined the title. At home it was the same.

She sat down at the dining room table to write the story after an uncomfortable supper loaded with her mother's exasperation that she had still not learned how to lay the table properly.

'Really Angela, fork on the left and knife on the right.'

It was not just the exasperation, it was the hurt in her mother's eyes, as if she were constantly rediscovering that her daughter was subnormal.

Angela wrote fifteen pages in her English homework book. She knew about terror and fearful anticipation and dread. She knew about long hours of waiting in fear for one of Miss Grout's tests. She knew about her mother's embarrassed anguish, if she failed to play Little Bobby Shafto perfectly when relatives visited. She knew about summoning up all her courage to face another day of ambush at home.

Miss Grout waved Angela's homework book in front of the class. Angela froze. Miss Grout said, 'Angela Kimberley?'

'Yes Miss,' she said with the correct intonation, polite respectful quiet submissive.

'This is the best story I have ever read from someone in this class. Who helped you with it, Angela?'

'No-one, Miss.'

'Hm,' said Miss Grout. 'Well, the best story is read out to the class, but just the first two pages, Angela, and then the last two, otherwise we will be here till lunch break.'

Later her mother asked her about the story. Miss Grout had been having a word at the school gate. Anything which prompted Miss Grout to have a word was not good news as far as her mother was concerned.

'Who helped you with that story, Angela?' mother asked, with one of her piercing stares which always made Angela feel that she had done something wrong.

'No-one.'

'Hm,' said Mother.

Nevertheless Angela had learned something. Writing the story she had been nowhere near 43 Frimley Avenue. 43 Frimley Avenue had ceased to exist.

She saved up her pocket money and, on one of her father's regular trips to Woolworths, she bought a notebook. He looked at her quizzically, 'Are you sure you want that?' he asked.

'Yes, yes,' she said, hugging it to her chest.

It was the same year that she fell in love with the milkman and his horse. The milkman was a bent old man with a peaked cap and an apron. His horse was a broad-backed cob mare called Daisy.

Angela was not allowed to put her light on before the alarm clock woke her father, but she was often awake at dawn. In summer she would sit reading on the wide windowsill behind the curtains. Thus she would watch Daisy and the milkman. Daisy would plod willingly onward while he nipped up each front garden to the doorstep with his clinking bottles in a little metal basket. Sometimes he would ask the horse to stop and when he spoke to her, he would give her a little pat or gently squeeze one of her ears. Daisy would turn her head and it was clear that her eyes behind the heavy leather blinkers were affectionate and trusting. After a while the milkman began to notice Angela's wide-eyed stare from the window and give her a little wave. She was too timid to wave back but she enjoyed this friendly acknowledgement. How she came to have the courage to go down to the road, she did not know, but a precedent was set and for many years these impetuous foolhardy imperatives would drive her thoughtlessly into action.

The upshot was a solemn and wonderful ride on Daisy all the way from No 15 to No 43. She perched on Daisy's table of a back, her feet sticking out on either side, clinging on to the harness and breathing in the acrid warm smell of Daisy's rough coat. The mare's firm swaying plod rippled up into Angela's slight body. It filled her with delight.

It had ended as everything seemed to, with her mother in a fury, dragging her onto the pavement in bellowing outrage. Mother berated the milkman in tones and words which made Angela feel ashamed, confused and bewildered. She was far too shocked to take note of the milkman's response, except that he did not seem terrified which surprised her. Until she was hustled into the house she thought that her mother was angry because she imagined Daisy might uncharacteristically bolt off down the road with her cart of milk bottles, throwing Angela to the ground. Apparently not. The issue was that Angela, in her nightie and dressing gown and slippers, had no knickers on. Like so much of the anger which she seemed to elicit, this was incomprehensible to her. She never wore knickers to bed and mother knew that.

After that she scrambled off the windowsill at the first sight of Daisy's nosebag rounding the bend in the road. Yet again, apparently, she had done something heinous and almost unspeakable.

Nevertheless, while it went on, being in love with the milkman and his horse had changed her life in No 43. There had been something lovely to look forward to every day. She had dreamed of riding Daisy and when it really happened, she hugged it to her. It had been an amazing secret. Daisy had looked at her with her gentle shielded eyes. The old milkman had said, 'Want to hop up?' and lifted her effortlessly over the harness and onto Daisy. They had been kind. They had wanted her to be happy.

The trouble with being a writer, she learned, was that when you had finished your story, you started to think that it was all make believe and no good anyway and who cared a spit? The stories poured through her onto the exercise books, making her happy, but afterwards weren't they rather silly, mawkish, a bit too much like Sherlock Holmes or Bulldog Drummond and not even a quarter as good?

Angela's mother was always going to evening classes and approached literature as if it were her job to pronounce judgement about the niceness or otherwise of the characters or setting. Mother thought Dorothea Casaubon was a frightfully dull and boring girl, rather ugly too, poor thing, who should have taken the advice to get out more and go to dances, which would have saved her from going off the rails so totally in *Middlemarch*. As if George Eliot were a nineteenth century agony aunt writing a cautionary *How Not To* . . . tale. Mother thought *Wuthering Heights* was a most unattractive place and it was just depressing having to read about it and it certainly did not give her any desire to see the moors. As if Emily Bronte were unsuccessfully writing for the Yorkshire Tourist Board.

Angela left No 43 and went to university, where she learned to convince people that she thought they were terribly clever and interesting, which was what they seemed to want. Some of the people she met were indeed clever and interesting, like her Literature Professor who absent-mindedly patted her on the head if he found her in the quiet little Middle English library which no-one used.

She revelled in her work, finding she could learn for herself, developing intuitive analytic skill, admiring the masters of Literary Criticism and their unashamedly biased but impressive knowledge.

She secretly smiled that none of her tutors objected to the required reading on the grounds that it was about nasty or boring people. Henry James wrote extensively about appalling shits and their stupid or naive prey but nobody seemed to think there was anything wrong in that. Terrifying Dr Kane, who bore down on the class like a thin waspish Valkyrie, never announced that they should not bother with Chaucer because some of his characters were not very pleasant.

Angela enrolled in creative writing classes and went to writers' groups. She either came away feeling that she should have been writing an altogether different story about completely different people in a totally different idiom, which the tutor would have preferred and could have written better, or she came away feeling sticky from the honeyed and unhelpful praise which everyone received from everyone: *That's so good, Angela, it made me cry.* Cry with pain? Laughter? Boredom? She wondered how Henry James would have responded to that. He sounded as if he were a complete stick, so probably with a sniff and an icy glare.

The writers' groups liked to warm to the stories. *Oh I do like the heroine. Reminded me of a friend I had at school.*

This confused Angela. Most of the people in Iris Murdoch's books, for instance, were so up their arses that

Angela hoped that in life she would be able to spot them at fifty paces and get out of their way, but that had not stopped her devouring every novel as it appeared.

When she finished a book which had entangled her, she had to sit still while a worm of thought wound its way through memory and meaning. She wanted to be able to make this happen.

The writing accumulated in files and folders. She learned that she was searching for a way of looking and saying, unfiltered by the committee of censors in her head. She was often despairing of this. She read the letters of the writers who, in spite of her envy, she admired. They were piercingly carelessly vocal. They had no qualms about spouting it all out. This was Angela's nemesis. She was scared to death of ever saying what she thought, because it always got her into trouble. She knew she was a coward and cowards never speak out.

After her degree, with circumstantial good fortune, she secured herself a job in publishing (she did temporary work cleaning and The Editor noticed her legs). She settled down to a nine to five slog through hundreds of nervously wrapped manuscripts, most containing overlong letters of introduction with superfluous and embarrassing biographical detail. Sometimes they were splattered with sealing wax. These were usually the memoirs of old colonels living in rural retirement.

The good stuff never came near Angela because it went direct to The Editor as a result of a cocktail party or a dinner where an agent had used some form of pressure, including, according to The Editor, sexual inducement, to get him to read it. Alternatively it was from someone already published by Swede and Garrett Limited and who was, therefore, a probable earner, given a shakedown over lunch and some strong editorial comment.

Angela had imagined that at five o'clock she would be free to scurry home to Tooting and sit at her old Corona portable, biting her nails and trying not to smoke too many cigarettes because her salary was pitiful. Apparently not. She was expected to go to book launches, agents' little get-togethers, dinners and parties for the firm's authors and any other excuse for a booze-up and a bitch, put-down or boast. She was absolutely hopeless at it. For hours she stood in weakly smiling silence by tables of sausage rolls with a glass of bitter white wine, wishing that she had enough money to chain smoke rather than having to ration herself to one every fifteen minutes. If she did open her mouth it was usually to put her foot in the shit quite comprehensively, viz, finding herself standing next to the firm's Real Spy Writer, with whose face she was not familiar, who asked her, the little turd, what she thought of the modern espionage novel. She told him that she thought the Bond books were popular because everyone liked the fantasy and no-one wanted to think about reality. She heard him asking The Editor who the hell she was.

Copy-editing *Desire in the Saddle,* the latest in a series of blockbusters which kept Swede and Garrett afloat, she raised the possibility that a horse kept hidden in a stable for three weeks and then galloped for forty miles to the clandestine wedding, would suffer serious lameness after ten minutes. The lady novelist wrote a blistering letter to The Editor, 'Whoever the hell she is, tell her to stick to the commas and the spelling.'

Angela learned that her mother's School of Literary Criticism had won. The Editor tried to help, 'It's about money, duckie. Find the big seller and then, if you want, you can bring out a lovely gem which three hundred people will read and enjoy. Otherwise it's the middle of the road stuff which everyone wants to read on the train. Something to pass the time, keep you hooked and not too bothered. Where's Dickens now with everyone watching *EastEnders*?'

After an appalling experience, when The Editor suddenly found himself tied up, perhaps literally, and Angela was asked to host a dinner at *Quaglino's* where the guest of honour was a very drunk author who asked her who the hell she was and spat out his food, she applied for a job teaching boys in a secondary modern. The holidays must now be her writing time.

The falling-in-love solution to life's grimness had, of course, not provided a permanent answer, but she could not forgo the delicious times of being and gaining the object of desire. She also found that she fell in love with teaching.

Then she met Sylvia, six foot two on her long brown feet, the daughter of a Trinidadian athlete and a nervous but beautiful blonde from Clapham. Sylvia moved in next door. With Sylvia, Angela went to gigs and festivals, learned how to cook pig's trotters, smoked dope, danced in a frenzy at a Brixton pub every Friday, sifted through material in markets to make bizarre clothes, tramped on marches and experienced police brutality, read books on all manner of strange phenomena which Sylvia fervently believed, and went to poetry readings because Sylvia was a poet. They told each other everything and, even when it was sad or excruciatingly embarrassing, ended up laughing.

It was the seventies, a decade which is credited with being perilously close to the end of civilisation in Britain. Angela hardly noticed the electricity cuts because she almost always used candles anyway. The marches were a good source of idiosyncratic acquaintances. The behaviour of the police came as no surprise to her, but she annoyed herself by saying 'Sorry' when a policeman poked her with his baton and told her to 'Fuck off out of it'.

With Sylvia, Angela went to Kapotheni. A trip to Greece was agreed, one wet Saturday, in a Notting Hill bedsit which was more like a cupboard, with Sylvia, a dusty man in a ragged sweater called Reg and an Indian woman with a sing-song accent, who was his yoga teacher. Sylvia said the man was a 'Duke or something'. The man said he had been to Kapotheni on a friend's yacht when he was at university. Sylvia thought he was really cool, Angela thought he was a drug-addled loser, but did not say so.

The journey was noisy and long. There was a plane from Heathrow to a milling shouting Athens airport where they pushed through crowds, in a panic, unable to interpret the departures board. There was a toy plane to Rhodes, where the airport consisted of what looked like a large bus-stop shelter next to the runway and a concrete building full of men in uniform with guns. They came out into blinding sun and nothing but empty road where they sat on the kerb and finally a car came up with some disembarking passengers and the driver kindly asked them if they would like a lift into town and where were they going? He drove at high speed down the rubbish-laden road which snaked along with the shoreline, passing derelict cottages and scrubland and one huge white palace of a hotel. The beach was deserted and rollers smashed endlessly along its length while they gasped in the hot breeze through the windows. At a quay the driver jumped out and talked to a man lounging on his bicycle. No ferry that day. There would be one the next day. Maybe. They could stay in the Old Town where his cousin worked in a hotel. The hotel was deep in the alleys of the Old Town and they were lost when they reached it. Outside Angela saw a big rat coming out of a wall and inside a cockroach on the floor of the hole which was the lavatory. She managed not to scream and laughed along with everyone and lay awake all night cursing herself for making the trip, trying to forget the rat's long shiny tail.

The next day the 'Duke or something' and Sylvia went out to try to find the quay and information. They came back and said a man had offered to take them because there would be no ferries for three days. The yoga teacher was very sick on the voyage, which was wet and bumpy. They huddled at the stern while her vomit washed from side to side of the deck. When they arrived four hours later, there was a lot of shouting and arm-waving from the quay. No-one seemed to want to help them dock. As they and their soaked luggage were unwillingly dragged out of the boat, they realised that the ferry was bulking up impatiently behind them blasting the port with angry hooting.

They staggered into a bar and, when they told the waiter how much they had paid for the trip, he put down his tray and bent double in laughter. He told a blonde woman who was fanning herself by the counter. She spat out her cigarette and slapped the counter making a noise like a death rattle. The pair of them took some time to recover. They came over and dragged chairs to the table, 'I'm Mustapha,' said the waiter shaking their hands. 'People, you have given us the gift of a bloody good laugh. This is Betty, my boss. We must look after you. You are babies in the trees. I will find Irini who has good rooms where you can stay.'

By this time Angela did not believe a word of anything anyone said, although she tried to look polite and grateful. 'Oh,' said Mustapha, noticing, 'cross my heart, lady. We are not all like that Rodos bastard. You will fall in love here. This is the most beautiful place in the world.'

Irini was found and she came with a man with a very small donkey. Angela watched in mute horror as he loaded the donkey with all their bags and said something unfriendly to it, which set it off nimbly up steep stone steps into the darkness above. Irini went off as fast as the donkey and they had no breath for anything but the effort to keep up through black twisting alleys of broken paving and sudden winding flights of uneven steps. 'Here,' said Irini, opening a door in a wall.

'Jesus,' said Reg. They stood in a paved courtyard with the night sky glittering over them and the scent of rosemary, thyme and oregano drifting in the warm air. The port seemed to be miles beneath them, glowing yellow round the dark flashing water. A tree hung with pomegranates bent toward them from a corner.

Irini showed them down steps to the two rooms below, the beds piled with sheets and pillows. In one corner a very old electric oven was attached to frayed cable which came out of the wall rather like the rat. The bathroom consisted of a hole in the floor below a menacing shower head, which looked like a cobra poising to strike.

'No water in day,' said Irini. 'Water in morning and night. No drink water, only bottles. Electric sometime. You no put paper in toilet. Put in box here. I come tomorrow. Goodnight.' There was no paper and there was no bottled water.

Angela fell in love. She fell in love with the heat and the journeying sun which cast deep shadows down white alleys. She fell in love with the colours of the houses and the mountains and the warm translucent sea. Ochre, cyan, azure, cobalt, sienna, pink, grey. While the others took enervating walks urged on by the yoga teacher, Angela lay on the little Port Beach and clambered across the boulders to tip into the water when she felt her skin burning. A permanently irritated man marched back and forth, ignoring sunbathers, dumping barrows of gravel onto the boulders in what seemed to be a fruitless attempt to disguise them.

Nobody on the island did anything until they felt like it. The bus set off when the driver had finished his domestic errands. The boats to the beaches waited for sufficient passengers or did not go at all if someone felt like fishing or there was a wedding or funeral to attend. The few battered taxis appeared and disappeared haphazardly. Angela, whose working life was segmented by rigid timetables, luxuriated in the insouciant chaos.

After three weeks the axe fell. 'Ange,' said Sylvia one evening in Betty's bar. 'Could you do me a favour? Reg and me are going to stay here. Could you crate up my stuff back home?'

Angela, who had immediately smiled delightedly and kissed them both, disconsolately joined the yoga teacher at the quayside.

'That woman will bollox his chakras,' said the yoga teacher in a startlingly new East London accent. 'Serve him right, the dozy bugger.'

Angela sat wrapped in her misery at Sylvia's betrayal, the colour and warmth draining from her heart.

'Kindly let me entertain you in my bed,' said Mustapha later at the quayside. 'That will cheer you up, baby.' But nothing did.

Angela came home and set to work in Sylvia's flat doggedly going through the list she had been given and packing boxes. Everything else she threw out with enraged force.

She rang the Head of History who had been staring at her at meetings and went for a drink with him and blubbed copiously about the infidelity of friends, while he waited, only slightly impatiently, to get to his item on the agenda. It was not a success. His knowledge of the Hundred Year War did not make up for his ignorance – or was it dislike? – of female genital anatomy. After several reruns, without improvement, she had to do the 'Not Your Fault' conversation. He was inexplicably annoyed.

Gradually Sylvia's rambling letters ceased to feel like poison darts injecting toxic envy and rage into her brain, but the empty weekends were every bit as bad as the years at home. The only thing which stopped Angela from taking a mixture of travel sick pills, paracetamol and whisky, an express route to blessed death, was the thought of the few seriously disrupted hopeless boys in her classes, with whom daily she negotiated a fragile truce in order to get them to sit still or write a few words. They, she knew, would be damaged by this evidence of her own despair.

Her resolutions to leave Sylvia and the earl to rot in their idyll, faded in the barrage of enthusiastic invitations. The next July Angela went out. The earl had bought a ruin, a house bombed by one or other of the warring nations who had serially 'liberated' the island. It had foundations, a few weed strewn walls and piles of roughhewn stones which had been walls. Everything had to be reconstructed exactly as before and the earl was in constant conversation with masons and plasterers and carpenters without any result. Sylvia and he had remained in Irini's eyrie at the top of the hill.

'Ha, my chicken,' said Mustapha. 'I knew you would be back. I am of course irresistible.'

Betty gave her a blast of nicotine and a bosomy hug.

Sylvia had whitewashed the eyrie and bought rugs for the walls and floor and painted a table and chairs and bought a new stove and a fridge in Rhodes. An easel and her paints and brushes sat under the pomegranate tree where she made large swirling images in the manner of a five year old asked to paint a seaside. Her poems, in purple ink, were strung about the rooms on ribbons.

At Betty's the earl concluded a conversation with a dust-grey mason ('*Avrio. Nai. Avrio.*' Tomorrow. Yes. Tomorrow) and told Angela that Sylvia was mad. Sylvia told Angela that the earl was an idiot. Mustapha said, 'Alas, all is not well in the house of love,' and Betty inhaled noisily and said cryptically, 'It's a small island.'

Angela took herself off to the Port Beach where the angry man, running with sweat, continued to pour gravel onto the boulders, covering everyone with clouds of dust. There was now a bar at the beach operating from a concrete pill box run by a speechless blonde girl who was possibly Yugoslavian. In the afternoon the man sat outside the bar growling at the few visitors in whichever language was appropriate, 'Nothing but trouble. I want electric for my kitchen. These idiots on the council say no. You want coffee. You can't have. You go and tell the mayor. You from London? I know London. Dirty place. Plenty of women. All women fuck in London.' He spoke to the husbands or boyfriends and ignored their women. Angela sat at the far end of the beach and skirted round him when she left, as if he were a snake on the path.

She sat on the sea wall and watched the island women doing their shopping and mending the nets. She took the old bus, noisy with conversation and plonking bouzouki music on the radio. She got off it wherever it stopped and wandered about the tiny alleys, where the houses squeezed together so she did not know where one ended and another began and there were glimpses of flowers and family meals through doors in walls. She learned to walk slowly and carry water. She found the other bay and the taverna where the bus turned round and after three visits was greeted as a friend by Yanni and Fotini. They called her Angeli with a hard 'g'. They were very old, their children were all in Australia they explained. Sometimes Yanni forgot what she had ordered by the time he reached the kitchen. They patted her back when they brought the food, like parents encouraging her to eat.

She did not avail herself of Mustapha's regular attentions, 'You have beautiful eyes, my fish. They become greener every day.' Brushing ash off the table, Betty remarked, 'Let's hope it's only her eyes.'

On the plane home Angela met an architect and fell in love, so she was not attentive to Sylvia's letters for some time.

At Christmas, when the architect's bad breath and habit of sniffing her dirty knickers extinguished her passion and she had to do the 'Not Your Fault' thing and endure his mystification, she read through the letters and found that Sylvia was in love with 'the sweetest, most darling man. Glorious in bed. Reg is being horrible about it'.

In February she answered her door and Reg leant against the doorpost, vomited a gallon of red sick onto the floor and fell into it. Fearing it was blood she rang for an ambulance. They informed her it was rum and blackcurrant, slapped him awake and left. For a wearisome week he lay on her sofa swearing about Sylvia. His house was still a ruin.

When Angela arrived on the island the next summer, Sylvia, bulgingly pregnant, hustled her into a buckled Mercedes and drove dangerously out to a series of shacks, some of which housed sheep. Entering a dark interior, Sylvia threw her arms round a man seated at a table, 'Ari,' she cried, 'meet Angela.' It was the man from the Port Beach. Angela smiled and put out her hand, 'Lovely to meet you,' she lied. They gave her a bed in a small room the walls of which were noisily occupied with busy small mammals and head-butted periodically by the sheep next door. She spent the night plotting how she could move out. In the morning a radiant Sylvia made her coffee and Ari delivered a monologue on the stupidity and corruption of the town council. Sylvia was pleased to inform her that the pregnancy had not diminished the sex and Angela was pleased that the animals, feral and farm, had made so much noise that she had not heard any of it.

Making the excuse that it was a long walk to the town and she had no transport, Angela arranged with Irini to rent an apartment. To her surprise, when she checked, the earl's ruin appeared to have acquired all its walls. A team of small donkeys pattered about delicately while two men unloaded bags of concrete.

On the Port Beach Ari took a proprietary stance and stalked noisily with his wheelbarrow between her and a barrister from Birmingham who wanted to find the monastery and also to know if there was a gay bar. There was even more trouble when she inadvisedly told Ari that she was in no danger from the barrister. Ari, muttering homophobic remarks, tipped a barrow of gravel at the side of the barrister's lounger and proceeded to scatter it broadside with an ancient spade.

Later, with the barrister, Angela went to the bar which Betty recommended. There she made some lifelong friends.

Years passed in which Angela filled her time with work and repetitious ascents into sexual ecstasy and descents into disillusionment. She became used to the grey bleak moment when she knew an affair was over and she was angry or bored. In the times of excitement and pleasure she played music. When the good times were over she wrote on the old Corona and, after some years, the keyboard of a big white box of a computer. Words streamed through her in the bleak night hours. She rose stiffly from her chair at two or three and wandered in her overgrown garden, smoking. It was crap, she always decided, when a story was finished, but it passed the time.

She did not want children and worried that she should. Her friends were all married, most of them with children. She heard too much about the guilt and anxiety this caused.

She lay on her sofa on a Sunday evening congratulating herself that the children she worked with were ring-fenced by the school timetable and at five the next day she would drive home to her quiet flat. She enjoyed finding ways to help them to learn and express themselves and felt something like love for a few of them, always the most badly behaved. But she was not to blame for their shortcomings. After the long years with her mother, Angela did not want to be blamed for anything.

Sylvia had come back to England with her son, Hermes, and threw herself into obsessive concern about his education and diet. The earl had gone out to Kapotheni. After six years the ruin became a house with wooden rafters and floors. There he lived, working in the summer on the pleasure boats pretending to be an old sea salt. He and Ali became friends while they angrily tried to work out why Sylvia had left them. Sylvia and Angela came out every summer bringing Hermes to visit his father, who dandled him proudly on his knee in every bar and perched him on his motorbike as soon as he could sit up.

The Port Beach slowly metamorphosed into a gravel beach with bar and taverna and a quay. Ari abandoned his outrage and established a gay beach on the other side of a rocky outcrop. There he built another bar, about which there were ten years of wrangling with the council. Ari said they should be very grateful to him for risking his arse every day and they might say it was 'Greek' but he was half Armenian. The bottom half.

At forty-five, Angela found herself to be a Head of Department and Head of Pastoral Care, that is to say the care of hopeless and disrupted children who were now to be called "young people", as if this somehow made everyone slightly less responsible for their unsupported lives. The school had become a co-ed comprehensive. She had not planned or schemed for this weight of responsibility. Her promotions were largely a result of the poor competition and the fact that, as a single woman, she could be relied upon to stay late in a crisis. She was settled in a respectable and, according to her married friends, enviable life. The old boxy computer and the Corona both sat on top of a wardrobe. At night, in term time, she closed her laptop and fell into her bed before midnight. Spreadsheets and protocols had crowded out even the memory of literary endeavours. One Saturday, Jimmy from the minicabs picked her up from the theatre and drove her home, 'How're you going?' he asked, the usual preamble to a full and frank discussion of their respective lives since they last met. She liked him for his punctuality, the kind way he always opened the door for her and the laughter and swearing that went on when he drove her about.

She paid him and got out and was walking toward her door, fiddling with the catch of her bag, when something hit her face and in a daze of incomprehension she staggered into the hedge and fell onto the path. She seemed to have gone blind. She could see nothing, although she knew her eyes were open. Everything was black. Terrified, she began to crawl toward her door. Someone touched her and she started to scream.

At the hospital she lay trembling in the white light, while a nurse wiped away the blood which had poured from a gaping split in her forehead. When they gave her a sedative, she was able to ask what had happened. 'You were mugged,' the nurse said. 'It happens more and more now.' Jimmy took up the narrative. He had clocked the cunt pissing off, decked him and give him a right which probably, fucking hope so, broke his jaw. The nurse raised her eyebrows but smiled. Jimmy was still gripping Angela's handbag incongruously in his undamaged left hand. Angela realised much later, with shame and embarrassment, that she had clung onto his bruised and bleeding right hand throughout the stitching.

Jimmy drove her home. On the path and doorstep viscous blood congealed on the tiles in splashes and pools, so that they took off their shoes when they went in. Jimmy made tea and they sat on the sofa, 'Don't look in the mirror,' Jimmy advised. 'You're gonna have a face like Lennox Lewis in the morning.' She wanted to clean the path but he would not let her and took a bucket of water out to sluice the tiles.

When he came back, he put out his hand, 'Come on darlin',' he said. 'You get to bed.' He waited while she climbed painfully into the bed in her blood soaked clothes, and pulled the covers over her, 'I'll be in there,' he said, nodding at the sitting room.

They had nothing in common but inexplicable need for each other. For a year they bounced in and out of each other's beds. None of it made sense to her. She hated and loved him without resolution. He held her in a bear hug, if he could get near her when she raged at him. If he could not, he left. Jimmy would not think about it and endured the pain like an animal in a trap. He led a formless life driving at night and picking up work in pubs by day, getting into fights and debt, moving regularly from one hovel to the next.

Nothing grounded her in the black hole into which she fell when they shot apart. She could not walk away in the comfort of justification. It was the only year that she did not go to Kapotheni. Later she could not remember whether it was because she was too happy or too miserable to make the journey.

It settled very slowly like a volcano which, after the apocalyptic eruption, will rumble and spit, unwilling to free anyone from anxiety. Exhausted, she eventually gave up trying to make him what she thought he could be and started to love him for what he was.

On Kapotheni, in the summer holidays, they lived in a tiny house on the waterfront of Little Bay. At night they sat outside their door bathed in the dark warmth of the sea and sky, playing cards for matchstick stakes or chess, at which he was much better than her.

Jimmy talked to everyone. He wandered around the port chatting to the fishermen. Her gay friends spent evenings showing him what they had bought, confiding their woes and reporting salacious gossip. People she had seen for years in the shops and bars suddenly became real. The man in the cigarette kiosk had been injured in an accident on a ferry. The old lady next door had lost two brothers in the fighting on the island during the war. One of the taxi drivers had lived in Clapham and hated the Germans. The beautiful Swede on the motorbike was having an affair with the harbourmaster. The man from Manchester in the *Dolphin* bar was a retired gangster.

They were invited to birthday parties and, once, a wedding. Everyone liked Jimmy.

In their twelfth year together Jimmy died of a heart attack in the last of his damp, peeling bedsits. It was an unattended death so there was an autopsy. His heart had been very damaged. At night Angela slept with his dressing gown wrapped around her. In the day she was pulled through one hour after the next by the schedule of work. In between she sat staring at the television. Nobody knew about Jimmy when he was alive or when he was dead, because Jimmy was not a possible escort to school events or dinner parties or theatre trips. Jimmy did not read poetry. Jimmy did not like looking at paintings. Jimmy did not enjoy concerts. At all of these activities, Jimmy was prone to falling asleep and snoring. They developed a knowledgeable appreciation of restaurants, because Jimmy did like to eat, and they went to the theatre or a film if it were something he fancied, but they always went alone.

Only Sylvia had met Jimmy. But Sylvia was always preoccupied with the full time job of nurturing Hermes's undoubted intelligence, finding the right tutors and then the right university, and making sure he did not drink or eat anything which might be contaminated by poisonous chemicals. Sylvia was conspicuous for her non-judgemental attitudes toward everyone but those who had the care of her son.

At school they knew that someone had died; Angela had to have time off for the funeral, but at fifty-seven everyone starts to attend funerals. It was not recognised as a "real" bereavement. No-one squeezed her arm occasionally or asked how she was getting on.

Five months later the young Head, normally bouncing eagerly with continuous performance management targets, solemnly sat back in his chair and said, 'Angela. I'm sure you know that this is the end of the road, professionally speaking. The family have decided not to press charges, which is one blessing. It *was* actual bodily harm, Angela, although we all accept completely that you had no intention of running him over or even of running over his foot. Of course, Carver is a troubled young man and we're lucky that the case of the disabled neighbour who was set on fire gave the police a bit of leverage, as it were. If only you had just driven off . . . the punch is very difficult to square, Angela, and it appears he did lose consciousness. You were due for retirement in three years. I think sick leave and early retirement. Perhaps some therapy would be useful?' The union representative and the Chair of Governors both nodded wisely.

He did not say anything about her sitting in her car all night on the playing field, frozen and numb with the knowledge that she had wanted to kill a child, until the Deputy Head came out and found her in the morning.

Everyone commiserated, 'It had to be Carver, the little thug'. 'The number of times I've wanted to punch *him*'. 'There but for . . .' But no-one had punched him, only Angela, leaping in a frenzy from her car, as Carver howled and hopped about in exaggerated agony.

She went to a therapist, who talked to her about destructive rage and her inability to grieve. It was all very interesting but she lived alone and dared not allow herself to weep, in case she never stopped. In July she went to Kapotheni.

The earl was waiting at Betty's bar, 'Christ, Angela,' he said, hugging her and crying. 'Don't know what to say. Christ. He was such a good bloke. The good die young, eh?'

She could not go back to the house on the waterfront. She could not go back to Little Bay. Irini found her a mousehole in the village at the top of the hill. It had one room and, up some steps a raised Greek bed, a sink and stove where the old bread oven had been, a tiny bathroom, a stone floor and a small garden. The front door opened onto a street which was too narrow and full of steps for anything but people and donkeys.

In the morning an old lady was always busy sluicing and sweeping. Their conversation amounted to greetings and smiles. On her first day Angela made a list and staggered back from the local shop, with frequent stops in the hot narrow streets, carrying four bags stuffed with provisions. She intended to retreat. Anywhere she went would be haunted by ghosts of laughter and happiness. In the evening she walked up the lane to a high place where, between pines, she could look down onto the glittering port. She stayed until the sunset. When she was walking back the old lady often appeared from a steep alley, smiling and nodding, carrying a large bag which Angela offered to take, but she laughed and refused, patting Angela's arm.

Every morning after she had sluiced and swept and hung washing on a line, the old woman came out of her house without her apron and set off somewhere, smiling at Angela.

After four mornings with the aid of sign language, it seemed clear that she was going to church. She cupped her hand to her ear and pointed. Angela suddenly heard a bell tinkling the nearby church's own ragged tune and understood. Church bells rang brokenly around the port every day for a multitude of reasons and Angela had learned, over the years, to edit them out of her hearing.

Two days later she went to the church and sat in the courtyard. She was worried that the woman might think she was stalking her, so she had waited until she had gone and would be safely inside. Churches, apart from the monastery chapel, had not been on Jimmy's itinerary and he had only visited the monastery because he liked the trip with Giorgio who took the tourists on his boat. The courtyard was cobbled in intricate patterns of round grey and white stones. Angela watched while the sun inched toward her white feet. Her feet which she used to twine round Jimmy's legs when they were cold in bed. Her toes which had carelessly felt his skin. As if she were in a trance she felt her arms rise up from her body, her hands reaching out into the air begging to touch him, her mouth opening in a wide noiseless wail of desolation. She began to cry and then to howl.

They called the doctor and he came to the churchyard. Three old ladies stroked her hair and patted her back. The priest sat beside her and prayed.

Tapping a syringe, the doctor said, 'This will help to calm you. Where are your friends?'

He rang Betty on his mobile. Gently they walked her back to the mousehole and brought her water. Irini arrived. Angela fell asleep.

In the evening the doctor came back. He said, 'You must drink water. You must sleep. You must eat. You must not be alone.' He gave her another injection and patted her arm.

Irini put a camp bed in the little room and Reg said he would stay, even though his house was only one lane up the hillside. This was a scandalous arrangement, but because they were English it did not matter.

The old lady came with cakes and a little icon of Archangel Michael, which she placed on the shelf above the sink.

Mustapha brought an embroidered shawl, which he shyly gave to Irini refusing her invitation to come in.

Reg sat outside the door smoking and drinking beer from the bar down the lane and when the bar closed he went to bed. For five days Angela slept and woke to eat the food which Betty and Irini brought. In the evening she lay in bed hearing Reg lighting his cigarettes and pouring his beer, until she slept again.

The doctor came every day, 'You could go to Rodos,' he said. 'I am not a psychiatrist. You could see a psychiatrist, but my judgement is that your heart is broken. Maybe there was a crack from long ago. This can happen, I think. You must be kept safe. Your friends will care for you. Maria and the priest pray for you.'

Slowly she became able to talk and think. Sylvia came over with Hermes on his annual visit to see Ari, who rushed him off to the house he had built in place of the shacks, which had exasperated the town council even further. Hermes, a corporate lawyer with all of his father's entrepreneurial talents, joyously drove Ari's hulking four wheel drive all over the island meeting his friends, eating as much pizza and hamburger as he could cram into his mouth and drinking with his father every evening. Sylvia came up to the village and sat with Angela, knitting. They went for walks and Angela clung to Sylvia's arm as they slowly laboured up the steep streets and sat on ruined walls staring across the clustering roofs, silent in the vastness of the perfect sky and the pearl grey mountains which towered up behind them and sank in monstrous prehistoric shapes into the glittering sea.

In September they journeyed back to London. In November they cleared her flat. In the garden they fed a small brazier with the shoals of reports and files and university notes which had gathered in tipping mounds on top of bookcases and in corners. There was also the writing. Box files full of yellowed pages. Folders with peeling indecipherable labels. Angela discovered the story of the Battle of Hastings in the grey homework book. Angela Kimberley Class 3, underlined. Sylvia demurred, 'This is all your stuff,' she said. 'Surely you don't . . . ?'

'It's served its purpose,' said Angela.

They watched while the wedges of paper curled and turned to ash. It was a quiet day and the smoke rose up to the leafless branches of the sycamores in an unearthly column like a votive offering.

'What are you burning?' Sylvia asked, as Angela placed another heavy armful into the smouldering container.

'Lies, I think,' she said. 'I want to stop having to make things up. I'm not sure I've ever been truthful. I was never allowed to be innocent, Sylvia, as a child. But I was with Jimmy. He taught me how to be innocent . . . to see him and to love him. I want to be able to see everything like that and write it down. Nothing is stranger or more horrible or more beautiful than what really happens.'

Sylvia looked at her doubtfully, 'Are you sure you're well enough, dear?'

Angela grinned and squeezed Sylvia's shoulders, 'You think I'm going up my own arse.'

Sylvia laughed, 'Well, that's a journey, I suppose. But are you sure you should go now?'

'I'll miss you badly, dear dear Syl,' said Angela, 'but we'll have the same sun above us. We'll look at the same moon at night. You'll be out in the summer.'

In December Angela packed a suitcase with a new laptop, two jerseys knitted by Sylvia for Ari and Reg, some clothes and a few books and went back to the mousehole in Kapotheni. In the grey light of a soft winter day, which was warm enough for the door to be open onto the street, she scraped her chair across the stone floor and sat down in front of the laptop.

In the Rooms of Heaven

...τα δώματα
χωρίς ν'αφίσω τ'ουρανού, υμείς αυτοί
την ψήφον μου θα χρησιμεύετε. Αστοί,
εις τον κατηγορούμενον επιθυμώ
πάντοτε να χαρίζηται.

. . . without my leaving the rooms of heaven,
you will exercise my vote. People,
I wish that compassion should always be offered
to the guilty.

Athena's Vote C. P. Cavafy

'The rose is very beautiful. You say do you do nothing to it. You are keeping secrets, Elli. Look at the blooms, look at the shine on the leaves.'

Irini put down her cup and walked across the courtyard to the flower. She squatted down to examine the plant.

'Nothing,' I said. 'I have done nothing but put it into a larger pot. Twice now. It grows like a weed.'

She tutted: 'Do not call it that.' She put her hand around a luxurious white flower, a faint bloom of peach on the edge of the petals. Her phone rang in her pocket and she stood up. 'Hello Mrs Parker . . .'

I was always surprised that she knew who was phoning, until she showed me that their names came up on the screen. Neither Angelo nor I have these mobiles. We have a computer which the children begged for, maybe twenty years ago. Since they have left, it has sat on the sideboard under a cloth. We have a phone in the house and one at the restaurant. Angelo refuses to have someone demanding his attention when he is not at work.

'. . . don't worry. Not at all. I will send Theo. I will give him a key. You get off to St Nick's, Mrs Parker. It will be the old wiring as usual. Not at all.'

Tap tap tap, she goes, 'Theo? Have you got time to go to *Villa Leone* this morning? Electrics are out again. Poor Mrs Parker cannot dry her hair! When? OK. No you must not tell her that, you rude man. Anyway she will not be there, she will be at the beach getting it wet again.'

Irini raised her eyebrows at me and we laughed.

After she left, I sat in the warm shade thinking about Mrs Parker and all the rich women I have watched, not only on my island but in Paris, when I was very young and worked in the atelier of Dior.

The old lady, who owned the *Sea Captain's House* on the waterfront and came for a month each year, needed some mending on an embroidered cloth and the dressmaker gave it to me. I was called to the house when the work was returned and the dressmaker, a malicious woman, would not tell me why. I was only seventeen and I was frightened of this old lady, who was so rich that even her name made us think of money. The old lady had soft skin on her face and hands and she carried herself like a queen. People had always turned toward her when she came into a room. She was the first rich woman I met. But she wanted to be kind and smiled and said that I was very talented and should work in a good house. I thought she meant *spiti*, a home, but what she meant was a couturier. She said I should go to New York and she would find me work, but my father was completely adamant. No, if it were true and I wanted to go, then I could go no further than Rome or Paris. If he needed to rescue me it would be possible for him to reach these cities, even if he had to stowaway on the ferries and walk.

It was a big adventure and we cried when I left. I was allowed to go home for a week at Easter and the October celebrations. Living in a place where no-one knows who you are, you must close your heart and hold your family within it. I would not have wanted this for my daughter, but when she was grown there were universities in Rodos or Samos or Athina to which she could go and return often and because I had gone all the way to Paris and met her father there, neither of us would have thought to object to the separation.

In the atelier, sometimes the clients would come in and we stood up respectfully and stopped work and were complimented, occasionally given presents, although Madame Harris did not like this. She thought we should not be interrupted. We were carefully chaperoned but flowers and notes were sent by men, although they were often homosexual and looking for a suitably adorning disguise. Some of the girls left because they said we were expected to live like nuns, but I was too young to think this way and glad of the care which was shown to me and I loved to learn. It delighted me to see the fine fabrics and the silks and jewels with which I was eventually allowed to work.

To see Angelo, one spring morning, walking toward me in a crowd, outside the Metro, was a big shock. For him too.

We stopped dead and stared and laughed and stared. He is ten years older than me and I had never spoken to him, but I knew who he was and which family he belonged to. We spoke formally and he walked me to the back entrance of the Dior house, where Madame peered suspiciously down into the alley from the windows in the roof.

Angelo was fun, like a boy. Madame, who made it clear she should meet him, eventually called him *mon petit fils,* despite the fact that he was much taller and only a bit younger than her. He has always been able to beguile women into this state of charmed security, because he likes them. He was even allowed to come up to the atelier, where he made the girls laugh and was openly amazed and appreciative of the profusion of beautiful fabric and colour. Madame thought he was very suitable, a man who could appreciate *tissu* and was not homosexual, a rare thing.

We went to see Johnny Halliday and danced in the aisles. We saw films with Doris Day and Brigitte Bardot, which made him drag my hand across his thigh and groan through clenched teeth, but we were both from the island. The consequences, then, of a mistake and pregnancy would have been savage. I knew he must go with women, how could I expect him not to, in Paris the City of Love? Madame was firm, 'He works at *L'Hirondelle,* it is three star, the women and the men who go there are used to buying what they want. You must accept this. It is better than the women of the street. Rich people have doctors and do not like disease. If he pressed you, you would not be able to resist because you love him, little one, and he is a man who gets what he wants. This is best.' I have wondered if Madame slept with him. She spoke with some certainty.

Once we heard Callas at the Opera. A customer had given tickets. We felt very proud of her, our Greek goddess with her dark toad of a protector. Angelo's uncle worked for Onassis as Captain of his private cruiser, a tall demanding man, bulging through his uniform, swaggering. Onassis was mean and paid badly but there were ways of making money as the cruiser glided from one country to another. This money was used on the island. In the seventies naked European women appeared on the beaches and the island boys and some of their fathers began to have a giant party, despite the disapproval of priests, wives and grandmothers. The island girls were closely guarded but doors were opening inch by inch. We returned into this feverish excitement to start a restaurant with money from the uncle. He was a prescient man and he knew the mayor. Together they planned. The uncle knew Monaco, Nice, Sardinia. There would be no theme parks, no tacky casino, no discos with vomiting children, no towering hotels. He knew what the rich liked. They would sail into their paradise island, a little primitive, a little rough, but a secret treasure, with good things for the connoisseur.

It brought wealth, but now I think we are becoming an island of the old. The old Americans and Europeans, who like the peace and quiet, and us, whose children leave to make lives in places where there are cinemas and chain stores. In a few years the island could be empty and our children's children will be coming over in the summer to work in the bars and boats. Like Onassis, maybe, we should have stayed with our own kind and not bought the American widow.

The restaurant sits at the top of a steep, perpendicular flight of steps, but there is a road from the town square which brings taxis up the back of the hill. I would be surprised if any of our clientele have ever walked up the steps, although some have had to be dissuaded from falling down them. It has the best view of the harbour and it is uniquely quiet. The *tzitzikas* is all you hear, unless the bouzouki players are with us.

The only blemish in our tranquil eyrie, is the helipad four hundred yards away, but even this has become an advantage. The ex-President always stops by for refreshment before he is driven to his villa and Galia, the supermodel, would sometimes bring her driver for ouzo and octopus when she arrived, although she preferred the waterfront bars. To the film stars in *Chanel*, the fat plain English Ladies in inappropriate debutante frippery, the second wives in *Féraud*, the Contessas and Princesses and the blonde peasant wives of Russian gangsters, Angelo is half friend, half retainer, who will provide their favourite table, their special cocktail, their particular dish with an invitation into the kitchen to discuss it with the chef. They ring him from New York and Brazil and Los Angeles to make sure that he will be waiting for them. He is very good at reassuring them that they are special. Like any small society, they include the lonely, the depressed and the hurt, but unlike other groups these women glitter within the silken thoughtlessness of wealth. Of course he makes love to them. He likes them. I think that has always been his code. He would not look at a woman he did not like, however many billions were scattered around the world in her family's accounts. His word for liking them (and thus being happy to sleep with them should they wish it) is 'lovely'. If he does not like them, in the privacy of our conversations in the house, they are 'crazy' or 'stupid'. I am not sure that he realises how informative his vocabulary has become. The only exception, so far, to this rule, was Galia, who was both 'lovely' and 'crazy'. But none of us on the island had ever really known who Galia went with. It might have been with everyone or no-one. She was always surrounded by fantastic tales, poor woman.

We returned and married. I was in my Dior wedding dress, so beautiful and delicately made, inside and out, that only I could see all its craft and luxurious detail. It was a tradition that Dior made the dress for any girl who left to marry and, in those days, if you married you were not permitted to stay. Our parents and grandparents and aunts and uncles and nephews and nieces and sisters and brothers settled in to wait impatiently for us to have children. Four arrived, safe and blessed. My quiet life of celibate dedication to extravagant beauty, became a noisy hurtle through days of laughter and weeping and preparations for other weddings and christenings. I lived within the circle of women in my family and our friends and in the early years fell asleep every night with one or more babies in the bed, who would be gently removed by Angelo when he returned. He always returned. I never woke alone. He never came to our bed with another woman's scent on his skin. He always showered.

He is what he is and two sons are like him. My third son fought him almost from his first breath. If they were in the house together, it was better they were not in the same room. My daughter went with him everywhere, wrapped in his love. The skirmishes and politics of our little kingdom occupied much of my time.

I emerged from this life at fifty-four years, plumper but not fat, still with my fine pale complexion that everyone admired. It was as if I came up from the depths of the sea and floated in an empty silent house, waiting for the grandchildren.

My parents were healthy and busy working in the newspaper shop and my grandparents were like old cats, limping about the alleys of the village, gossiping and bickering and sitting in the sun.

It was by chance that I went to work at the restaurant. Angelo hired English or French girls who had some experience in good restaurants and wanted an exotic summer in the sun. He had to pay for this, but his prices were high. People said, 'Angelo charges ten euro for every step you have to take to get up to his place and that's just for a glass of water.' He said, 'My customers would not understand anything else.' One of his girls broke her leg playing tricks while water skiing and she had to be taken to Rodos by another. He rang me to say that I should come in and help.

I stood in front of the mirror in my navy silk dress and held myself straight, like the old Rothschild lady, on my expensive heels. He likes me to have some good clothes and shoes.

I had not seen him at work although we hosted family celebrations, but on these occasions he was Angelo the son or grandson being cheeked and teased. It was exciting, to see my husband treated with friendly respect, consulted, obeyed, greeted with evident warmth by his customers. The nationalities were very different under the patina of good manners. The Italians went onto the balcony and rang friends to tell them where they were, while their wives sat behind large sunglasses, thin and observant. The Americans were usually Greek, so they roared and grumbled as we do. The French chattered in family groups, their adolescent children behaving like solemn grown-ups while they waited to escape to the bars. The Nordic men were heavier and quieter, self-contained, with wives who were beautiful and formidably capable. The Russians were grim and easily dissatisfied. The English seemed tired, on the whole. It must be exhausting making money in England. There were seldom Germans. Angelo's eldest brother was shot in the pine forests by the Germans. A German name elicited apologies, there were no tables.

I was delighted by this first evening. The chef stood back and motioned his boys to greet me when I went into the kitchen, just as I had greeted clients in the atelier. The Italians kissed my hand, the French paid me compliments on my accent, the Nordics told Angelo I was beautiful, the English made jokes, the Americans proudly used their best formal Greek. Only the Russians were surly beside their suspicious wives. There was a carnival air to the evening and *Crystal* flew out of the kitchen on the trays of the young man who attended to the wine and hoped to be sommelier at the Savoy in London or maybe the Imperial in Vienna. Our customers were familiar with these places. He quietly networked for introductions.

Everyone in the room knew of the others. Generally, these people are as close and knowledgeable about each other as we are in the village. Arguments, deals, propositions can be heard in the corners of restaurants and parties, as easily as they are in alleys and courtyards. They either came in on their gleaming silent boats or stayed at the *Napoli*, a hotel so discreet that it never advertises and is indistinguishable from its grand neighbour mansions, apart from a small brass plaque by the door. Angelo has to compete with the hotel chef and the expensive chefs who travel in the galleys and emerge at night to lean on the rails of the sleek cruisers, smoking outside the tinted glass. Angelo's allure, apart from his own chef who has published a book on the Greek American cuisine, is that he is authentic, a true islander. He is 'Angel', their good friend on the island.

As Stefano drove us back to the house that night, Angelo became romantic, which he knows is irresistible for me, '*Tu ne peux pas imaginer comme je t'aime,*' he said, kissing my fingers. Stefano growled at him to speak Greek because he must go home and tell his wife everything that was said in the back of his cab. 'Tell your wife I am saying my wife is beautiful,' said Angelo laughing. 'Pouf!' said Stefano, 'I will not. She will expect all that crap from me, if I do.' I sat next to Stefano in school and he was always a very rude boy, but a good heart.

For four or five years, I went to the restaurant on Friday and Saturday nights between June and September. I grew to like and care about some of our regular visitors. Old Maria, with the palace in Austria, told us about the excitement of finding a relic of Marie Antoinette in a locked attic room. Shy fat Peter, whose family were feudal lords in South America, wept on my shoulder while he told me of the flying accident in which his son was killed. Their lives were full of such tragedies. Thank God, we said to each other, our children could not get on anything faster than a donkey when they were growing up.

I will not pretend that I did not take particular notice of the 'lovely' women who came to the restaurant. You would never have known, from observing Angelo's behaviour, which of the women were 'lovely' and which 'stupid' or 'crazy'. His warm smile and gentle courtesy were extended to them all, but I had the information of his comments, when he was sitting on the edge of our bed puffing to put his socks on or throwing himself exhausted onto the couch at the end of a long hot evening.

I would say that on average there were usually three or four each season and some of them returned, so maybe two regulars and one or two new and beautiful faces each year. He did very well. I did not allow myself to speculate when and where he did very well. As long as he was in my arms in the morning, I was content. The women with their jewels are playthings in a game and his attentions are what you would expect from a man.

The Welsh woman had to explain to me that she was not English. Her husband was a Lord and they lived in a castle. She liked to swim from the Port Beach and I swim there too, in the morning, and our conversations became intimate. She hated the castle. They were very poor because of the castle and only came away because she had a brother who regularly sailed the Aegean in June. She did not like him or his wife. They were rich but they did not have a castle and held this against her. They had also lent her husband money so that her two children could be sent to a very expensive school where all the Lords go. It seemed that there had been a deal about the castle which involved turning it into a tourist attraction from which her brother could make more money and this meant that she and her husband had to manage staff and worry about making a profit. She was very funny about the castle and the rain coming through the roofs and the lavatories not working and the floorboards giving way and the drains blocking. She told me the cost of the light bulbs and it was more than I spent on the electricity in a year. But it was not funny, I thought, that her husband had gone away to sleep in one of the towers, with his four spaniels, after she had borne two sons. She slept alone, she said, in a fridge with curtains. This was a joke, I think.

It was clear that she had no money. I never saw her dressed beautifully like her sister in law. I could not understand why she had not been rescued from the castle, because she was entrancing. She was slim with breasts that were still high. She had a cloud of fine golden-red hair, which twirled round her face and down her back. When she was in her bikini, there was no trace of the two sons on her body. Her face was thin and worn in repose, but when she smiled, and she smiled often when we talked, her eyes were mischievous, as if she were always laughing at some absurdity. This is rare with rich people or poor people who live in castles. They tend to be serious about themselves. When Angelo said she was 'lovely', I agreed.

She, too, was an embroiderer. Tapestries and ancient coverlets were wearing away into cobwebs on the walls and four posters. She had learned by watching the expensive experts. When she showed me photographs of her work, I could see, even in these images, how fine it was.

I saw how her husband never looked at her or touched her. He drank steadily until, when they left, he was sleepwalking. I also watched Angelo, who did look at her, from his station by the door, with an impassive expression on his face and the powerful stillness of a stalking cat.

His women that season were a tall, turbaned American and an opulent, drawling Swede, but they had been netted in earlier years and the American had shown some faint rudeness toward me one evening and Angelo declared she was 'stupid', which meant that she would not again be receiving a neatly folded piece of paper slipped into her palm. I have never read one of these notes, but, knowing my husband, the details of the assignation would be announced without any entreaty. He is a pragmatist, not a seducer.

The Welsh woman was called Talaith. This is the same as our *Talitha*. It means 'maiden' and she was a maiden, despite the two sons. How the English do this, I do not know, but I have seen this before; women who ride horses or sail boats and give their children to other women to raise, or send them away, as if they cannot be mothers but must spend their lives as boys who put on dresses in the evening.

Pride, vanity, they were the instigators of my mistake.

I asked her if she would like to see the wedding dress. My relatives had been impressed but not professionally appreciative of its beauty. I had never been able to show it to a needlewoman, other than my excited fellows in the atelier.

In the great room I had brought out the wooden trunk, and, with her help, we drew the dress carefully from its linen cover and brushed the special tissue from its folds. Together we fitted it onto my tailoring dummy and laid out the train and placed the layered tulle veil above it. We were silent. We stood back. I confess, my first thought was that it seemed impossible I could have been so tiny in my waist.

'Oh!' she said, then, 'May I?' She wanted to examine the fabric, to understand the technique for the application of the little pearls, to marvel at the beautifully finished seams, so smooth and invisibly stitched.

My second mistake. I could not resist the need to see it moving in its fluid flawless cut, over a body, across a room, catching sunlight in its folds.

'Will you wear it?' I asked. 'You are the size I was as a girl, I am sure.'

She was reluctant, frightened that she might damage it. I urged her, reassured her that we would be careful.

'My daughter . . .' I said. 'When she was little of course, it was this dress alone that she would wear as a bride, but now . . . she is adult. She studies design in Milan. You understand, she has her own ideas of beauty although she sees the craft. But I may not see it worn again.'

She had no brassiere, she did not really need one and the bodice was cut and stiffened to hold the apples of youth. The slim lace sleeves perfectly fitted her honey-skinned arms. The dress gathered itself into place around her. The pearl buttons slipped effortlessly into their silk loops, tracing her spine. I drew out the train and placed the fountain of silk-edged tulle on her red hair.

Our great mirror, tarnished, venerable, which had reflected almost all of our family life, was filled with this image of glowing intricate perfection.

'Move,' I said. 'Walk. You will see how the dress gives itself to you.'

Hesitantly, she did as I asked, becoming more confident as she felt the beauty of the exquisite cut and drape.

I brought her back to the mirror and stood behind her, laughing, 'You see how beautiful you are?' I asked.

'It's the dress,' she said smiling and she looked up and saw him, before I did, in the mirror. Her startled blue eyes became sapphires and his, in answer, were the eyes I saw in our first nights together.

He had gone before we turned round.

'Is he angry?' she said. 'I should not have come into your home. I should not have worn your beautiful dress.'

'Of course not,' I shushed. 'He comes and goes. You know men. They have their own strange life.'

We packed the dress away and drank coffee and talked of our children and, when she left, I sat under the mirror twisting my fingers together. He had not been angry. I had seen his heart fly toward her. I sat and twisted my fingers and, later, when he came in to shower and dress for work, I said I felt unwell and would go to bed.

The next day the rose was in the courtyard.

'A present from the redhead,' he said. 'Are you feeling better?'

'A little,' I said. 'I think perhaps I will go to see Kiki for a week or so.'

'Ah,' he said, reaching for the newspaper, smiling. 'Our daughter needs some more clothes?'

I returned when I knew that the Welsh woman had left. I came over on the late ferry and Stefano brought me to the house. It was in the untidy messy state which any wife expects, particularly from a man who insists on a meticulously clean kitchen in his restaurant. The builders leave their own houses half finished. The plasterers live with boarded walls. Angelo had used every plate in the cupboard and they were all piled in the sink. I washed and dried mechanically.

Through the window, the rose glowed in the moonlight. I took my secateurs from the drawer and went out into the courtyard but I could not do what I thought I wanted to, to cut every petal from its stalks. I put the secateurs away. Why should I punish the flower? I should just as well cut off my fingers or rip up the dress. When beauty is found, is seen, we are all powerless in our hearts.

When Angelo came in I was not asleep and he did not come to our bed. I waited but he did not come. At three o'clock I got up and went through the house where I found him on the balcony in the dark.

'Are you alright?' I asked.

'Of course,' he said impatiently.

'Your daughter did need more clothes,' I said, wishing I was not making such silly conversation, but not wanting to leave him.

'Good, good,' he said quietly, but his eyes were like stones in the luminous night.

For five years the rose has grown luxuriantly in the courtyard. Angelo is always in my bed in the morning and the 'lovely' women come and go. He will turn to me when he wakes and sometimes he will kiss my fingers and speak in French to excite me.

I know the Welsh woman will not keep coming for ever, but he never speaks of her. This tells me too much.

I do not go to the restaurant regularly now. The grandchildren began to arrive, one in Athens, one in Sydney and two in Paris. I travel to them and they to us. The house becomes noisy and crowded with toys and cots. The table is not large enough for all of us at Easter. He annoys his daughters in law by waking the babies when he returns from the restaurant, lifting them out of their sleep and carrying them into the great room, playing with them as they stare at him in confusion or dismay, until they remember who he is, their *Papou*, and settle onto his chest.

In June and July I go to see the grandchildren. I say that I like to have them to myself for a few weeks, which is true. He comes with me in winter.

But really I go away because of his eyes. For a few weeks after she leaves, his eyes are the dull grey of stones from which the sea has retreated and, although he is motionless on the balcony at night, the house is restless.

Return

Επέστρεφε συχνά καί πέρνε με τήν νύχτα,
Όταν τά χείλη καί τό δέρμα ενθμούνται...

Return and return to possess me at night,
when lips and skin remember . . .
Return C. P. Cavafy

Everything had been planned. She had booked first class on an expensive airline with reverential transportation in wheelchair and buggy. Walking more than twenty yards was difficult now. At Rhodes, Niko himself came to meet her and manage the bags. With unsentimental Greek plainness he said, 'Is very bad now. Yes?' It was a relief to be with someone who was able to see her death.

She had had to reduce the morphine levels to restore some sharpness to her wandering mind. A gruelling night followed.

Niko took her to the ferry, the small catamaran where the passenger seats were on the same deck as the luggage hold and the ramp. She would not have been able to manage the stairs on the larger boat. The perpetually exasperated crew, normally aggressively indifferent to struggling tourists with unmanageable baggage, came down to grab the suitcase under Niko's belligerent commands and one put her hand in his arm and walked her carefully to her seat. She gave herself another shot from the implanted syringe under her T-shirt. The boat was bumpy and uncomfortable if the sea was choppy. She crossed her fingers that she would be sufficiently aware of their arrival.

While the busy little ferry ploughed round the barren grey mountainside, she could not go out to wait with the other tourists, to watch the town appear, climbing up the hills from the harbour, decked out for summer in fresh blue and yellow and ochre. The commuting Greeks dozed and read their newspapers, oblivious to the excitement.

The crewman remembered her and led her down the ramp with her suitcase, where Sevasti, ducking under the arm of an officious policewoman, walked her to Theo and the four wheel drive.

Her legs were woolly and wayward, 'I'm sorry,' she said, 'this will take some time.' She had no strength to propel herself up into the seat. 'Theo,' Sevasti ordered quietly. He lifted her, telling her to bend her head, placing her on the seat gently, as if her bones might break.

'It's so beautiful,' she said as they drove up the winding road to the village leaving the horseshoe harbour to appear and reappear through the trees, each time slightly different, smaller, wider, like a kaleidoscope. 'It is always so beautiful.'

Theo took the suitcase, Sevasti took her arm. It would be the worst part of the journey. There was no other way of getting up the steps. 'Let's try three,' she said and lifted her leg. It felt like a prosthetic limb, attached but unconnected to her brain. After three steps she leaned against the wall and Sevasti shouted for Dimi who would be in the restaurant puzzling over his orders. Dimi peered suspiciously from his doorway, as if Sevasti might be a tax inspector, then bounded down the steps. Between them they hauled her up.

At the top of the steps, she asked them to stop. The cobbles felt like sponge and her ears were hissing. Lefteri was in front of her talking, but his voice was far away. 'Wait,' she said. 'Wait.' She stared at her feet, forcing herself to feel the stone beneath them. Her consciousness rallied.

'*Kali mera*, Lefteri,' she said.

'*Kali mera*,' he said. 'I say to Sevasti who is this sea urchin?'

She put her hand up to the spiky white hair which had sprouted out of her scalp. Sevasti clucked and frowned at Lefteri.

'No. No,' she said to Sevasti, smiling, 'it's good. In England everyone pretends they see nothing.'

'You are very tired,' he said. 'I bring you something?'

'Orange juice,' she said. 'Dear Lefteri, thank you.'

Theo and Sevasti walked her slowly to the house. She lay on a sofa. Sevasti insisted that she would unpack her case, Theo unbolted the shutters, Lefteri arrived with orange juice. She slept.

Sevasti had left supplies in the kitchen. Water, bananas, sugar, juice and milk. She had brought porridge oats from England. Porridge and mashed bananas sometimes stayed down, if she only ate a little.

She had had to leave. She could no longer countenance the doctors and the nurses with their need to be optimistic and upbeat. She had been told there was nothing more to be done, but at their last meeting Dr Hamid happily waved her results saying 'These are much better than could be expected' as if he wanted her to congratulate him. She had schooled herself to stop saying bitter things, which embarrassed or irritated them. She had had the lecture on how much worse it got for some people.

With her children it was difficult. They wanted to look after her, but their lives were bursting with the logistics of their families and jobs. Her own parents had dwindled down the years, until it ended in stroke for one and viral infection for another. She had been able to visit and shop and do hospital runs. It was a slow halting process, with periods of remission in between. Death slunk up to their hospital beds, with nobody really thinking about it until it arrived.

Her children had had no experience of her as a failing or disabled person. They had complained for years that the only way to talk to her was by email. Visits were organised weeks ahead because of her schedule. Emergency baby-sitting was left to the more traditional and accommodating in-laws. When the treatment made her so ill that she had to tell them, she spent hours at her dressing table carefully applying makeup so as to appear as healthy as she could, before their visits. They wanted good news. They researched on the internet and spoke to friends in the medical profession and looked up all the drugs and told her of others. It was exhausting. They told her she was being defeatist, pessimistic. They sent her success stories of people who had lived for years. They wanted her to be brave. A mother is an icon, not a person. A lonely place to be. With her husband, she had grown through the pain of seeing that she was the mother of his children, not a woman, but she never lost the anger, which became cold and hard until she divorced him.

Only Mina, her old friend, still a practicing GP two days a week 'to keep her hand in', looked at the letters and the results and said, 'Fuck. Oh Fuck.'

Thank God. Thank God and all the Archangels and all the angels. Thank them all for brave Mina.

So the holiday was a last little trip, 'No,' the children said, 'Mother, don't say last. You must stay positive. Your mind could actually make you ill, you know.' If she had bitten her lip on these occasions, she would have had no mouth left.

She was to go to the doctor at the clinic near the harbour with the letter from Mina. 'It's only fair,' said Mina. 'He should know what he's up against and it will save you from any unnecessary emergency treatment. I'll give him the rundown on the medication. Well, most of it.'

Going down the steps to a taxi might be easier. She had been dismayed that the steps had almost defeated her, but, in a few days, she would get to the doctor.

She took the medication, another small pump and a toke of cannabis, which she had smuggled out. Cannabis gave her a tiny appetite, which made her try to eat. She slept for another six hours.

When she woke it was the pink dusk of the island. The mountains were glowing in the sunset from Turkey. Carefully, she walked to the balcony, holding on to lintels and chairs to keep her upright. Her balance was precarious with the drugs and the weakness of her emaciated limbs.

'Is romantic,' he had said, 'you sit on balcony. I watch.'

Sometimes, if she had looked down, he was standing against the wall in the shadows. She was always surprised by his unashamed acknowledgement of his yearning for her. She waited for it to fade into ownership and complacency, but it never did. When he had the luxury of her bed, there were long whispering nights, at other times they came together instantly as opportunity arose. But there were hours, days, in which simply the delicious contiguity of their bodies, in the same street, the same shop or bar or boat, bound them nearer and nearer together. They tried to explain it to themselves and each other, but it was a knot which could not be undone, an unfathomable mystery. With love came pain. In the winter she kept it all alive in her heart.

She had never been able to go to his grave during the three years after he died. She had continued her visits, unable to stay away from the places where they had talked and laughed. Maybe she could have wandered, like an inquisitive tourist, around the cemetery, but she would have wanted to sit beside him and leave him something and this was impossible. It was always gently understood between them that their families were the bedrock on which they conducted their lives.

Before the divorce, he was just a face seen on a boat and around the bars when she was on holiday. Later, when she came out alone, it was just a seduction like any other. She was never one to forego an adventure. Their shadow selves had fallen in love slowly and reluctantly, but the passion was contained away from the duties, responsibilities and love in their outer lives.

She must leave no evidence of her existence, at his grave, to cause perturbation, after the years of discretion.

There would not be a grave for ever and this was almost a comfort. In time, his body would be exhumed and the family would take his bones to put them in a place of their own choosing. They were not rich and so would not be able to afford a permanent plot. If she could have chosen she would have taken a distal phalanx. Relatives kept these relics sometimes. When he held her hand, he stroked her knuckles with his thumb.

She was glad that he would never see her as she now was, because he would have suffered and she could die without leaving him behind. It was probable, she believed, that the cancer started when she read the news, on an island blog, that his boat went down in a freak storm, that he was lost while out tuna fishing in the February seas. It was his winter fun and it brought a little money. No life jacket. Old sailors believe the sea will take you when she wants.

For a year she was under water, with him, clinging to his body. But the sea did not want her. Her life marched on in the upper world of work and birthdays and gardening and Christmas. When you are not old, your heart is bruised, sprained, damaged, but there are healing years. When you are old, she discovered, your heart breaks. The cancer lay like a black spore in her soul, waiting to flourish in her untouched flesh

She eased herself into a chair. The pain was at its biting worst. When it was like this, everything hurt. Her toes, her eyes, her breasts, even her poor strange hair.

She gave herself two pumps. She was over her limit.

He came to her as he always had done, with quiet certainty and, as they always did, they smiled at each other in silent delight. Thank God, it's over, she thought, this waiting is over. They sat hand in hand for a while, until her fingers felt the small packet of powder, which Mina had not mentioned in her letter to the doctor.

He leant toward her and they kissed like children softly on the lips, '*Kali nikta*,' he said. 'Good night.'

The Horses of Achilles

...άρχισαν τ' άλογα νά κλαίνε του Αχιλλέως
...γιά του θανάτου αυτό τό έργον που θωρούσε.

. . . the horses of Achilles began to weep . . .
. . . on seeing this deadly achievement.
The Horses of Achilles C. P. Cavafy

Michali was the youngest of four brothers. After their mother died, the house became dirty and cold, filled with their father's grievance and self-pity. Michali taught himself to clean and cook and one by one his three brothers went off to the ships. Unusually, for the island, there were no female relatives to step into their mother's shoes.

Two of the brothers returned, when they were about to be married, to make sure their father's suit was clean and take him away to the wedding. Each had been given marital advice in the littered, weed-infested courtyard.

Michali first heard the diatribe when Young Andreas, his eldest brother, returned. Their father perched on an old wooden chair which creaked under his unsteady weight, 'Now,' he bellowed, bending perilously toward Andreas, 'now you put your seed only in your wife's belly. It is for children now. Yes?' He waved his hand imperiously, 'With the other women go where you want, but not the belly. See? This is why your mother had four sons. How would I get a son, putting my cock in your mother's mouth? It is necessary to have respect. Eh?'

Michali sat on the doorstep beside the bucket of water he had hauled from the standpipe, sad at the thought of his mother. He remembered the day of the funeral, when he stood hopelessly by the old stove staring at the joint of lamb, which the butcher had given him for the funeral meal. Little Maria, who lived nearby, had brought rosemary from her courtyard and cut onions and said nothing about his tears.

The next brother, Taki, always recklessly outspoken, growled at the homily and said, 'Fuck off, old man. And leave off with the bad words about mother, God rest her.' This caused a fight and Old Andreas went to the wedding with a clean suit and a black eye.

Marko, the third brother, had settled in England. He did not come home to collect the old man.

Soon after, Young Andreas found work for Michali on the ships. Maria and Michali sat together on the old bench speaking of marriage. They wanted peace and security.

Maria's father was not happy about their friendship. Old Andreas was a wastrel, he said. This Michali would be the same.

Maria's mother went to their priest, who had watched Michali grow. The boy was as thin as a feral cat, but his smile was loving. He had a honeyed treble voice and when it broke, a deep brown bass emerged. The priest patted him, when they met, even when he was grown, knowing that the mother's death had left a hole in Michali's heart.

The priest talked to Maria's father, who relented enough to agree that they would see, in two years, if Michali were able to be a respectable affianced.

Small but strong as a donkey, Michali found his place in the bunkrooms. He was the little brother. The men laughed at his neat ways and took him to the whores. He used the women exactly as his father advised. He was waiting for Maria.

On one foul voyage the deck master pursued him with gifts and threats. The men were amused, having seen this before, and laid bets on how long he would be able to resist. The deck master broke three of Michali's ribs. Michali knotted T-shirts around his chest and tried to wash his bleeding bowel each day. The men laughed at his limp. By Cape Town there was an infection and he had a fever. They left him at a mission hospital, where he shrank in terror and disgust from the pink-palmed black nuns.

Eventually, the marriage was grudgingly agreed.

On the eve of his wedding, Michali went out with his brothers, who had all come home to celebrate. Bounding up the thousand steps, they pushed and shoved him as they always had on the way to school.

'Get ready to be told how to fuck,' laughed Taki, grabbing Michali round the neck and trying to trip him up.

Marko leapt up five steps and raised his arms at the panorama of the glowing port, 'He's the lucky baby,' he said. 'He'll have this for ever.'

'And he'll have the old bastard,' shouted Andreas, plodding up the steps ahead of them in the dark heat.

The problem of the old bastard was solved by the decision that Maria should stay in her parents' house.

Michali returned to the ships and was away for eight months. Sitting on deck, as the tanker throbbed slowly across the brooding Bay of Biscay, he remembered the solemn proceedings in the narrow bed, separated by a curtain from the snoring parents of his silent wife. Each morning he had been relieved to see that Maria smiled at him, when she returned with the bread, but when she woke she did not look at him and dressed modestly with her back turned. The beauty of her glowing skin aroused him, but she never looked back.

On their last night he asked her, 'Do you love me?'

'Of course,' she said, her eyelashes lowering over her gleaming eyes.

In Rotterdam he found the woman he used and threw himself into violent relief, while she shouted and pulled his hair and gasped and moaned.

'What is matter?' she asked, as she sat smoking in bed while he dressed. 'You come but you no like?'

He smiled at her and said nothing.

When he returned to the island, Maria was almost ready to give birth, pale and swollen, surrounded by the women.

When the baby came, Michali stared at the crumpled face of his son, before an aunt whisked the child away. He was dark with sadness that he would not be able to show his son to his mother. He would not see her sitting in the shade, fanning the child on her lap. In Alexo's bar they toasted him and slapped his back. Michali went to the cemetery and sat by the grave, remembering the funeral lamb.

He returned after another year and, at the sight of him, the child whimpered and buried his face in his mother's skirt. The crowded house was jubilant with a wedding and there was discussion about accommodation. He found a house. It was dusty and damp from neglect and it faced West, but it seemed sound and he set to work with whitewash. Pieces of serviceable furniture arrived, roped precariously onto the donkeys or carried by staggering cousins.

On Michali's last day, he ate his first meal in his new home. The child clung to his mother, upset by the unfamiliar rooms, crying. She was still suckling him. The nights were pierced by his demanding wails. Her dreamy preoccupation with the baby stirred up a black temper in Michali, which sent him off in silence to the bar. On his last night, he held her jaw to make her look at him as he came into her. In the morning she placed the bread on the table and tentatively stroked his cheek. He put his arms around her waist, burying his face in her stomach.

Years passed and there were two more children. He became a deck master and, although he could laugh and tease, there was a violent edge to him which meant that he was generally obeyed. His dark voice rose through the bunkrooms. Anyone who turned out to be lazy or stupid felt the glowering menace of his contempt. He found work on a ferry line and was able to come home more frequently, but the children sat wide-eyed at the table, looking at their mother whenever Michali spoke to them.

He was not pleased to discover that Maria was cooking for the Englishman who lived nearby. He was paying well for the extra plate which was brought up to him, but Michali clenched his teeth at the sight of the man's smile when they passed in the streets. Michali chose his own friends.

The accident, which brought him permanently ashore, happened in a force ten rounding Kos. He was checking the vehicles in the lower deck, when the ship caught a crashing broadside and rolled heavily, dislodging an overloaded truck. The tipping truck knocked him across the swilling floor. He lay in hospital in Athina, while the doctors debated if he would walk again, but he returned to the island two months later on crutches.

He had offers of work but he could not bring himself to smile and flirt with the tourists. His father wept in the bars, soliciting sympathy and a drink for his misfortune at having a crippled son. After angry months of black looks from his father in law, God stepped in. The old chandler fell off his stepladder and decided to retire. Michali made a bid for the shop. It was a dark cave, crammed from floor to ceiling with rope, sails, chain, engine parts, tools. Between towering shelves, ran two small passageways, hazardous with falling merchandise. The chandler had been partially buried by a cascade of mildewed waterproofs, when he fell.

Michali recruited his children and they cleared the shop. In the afternoons he trudged painfully up the thousand steps for the siesta, while the children leapt like goats around him. They made him smile and sometimes his daughter stood above him on the steps and reached out her small plump arms to kiss him as he laboured up. He held her, breathing in the sweet fragrance of innocence, filled with her beauty.

The shop did well. The yachtsmen passed his name around because of his English and efficiency.

In Alexo's bar after work, he laughed with the others, idly watching the trails of visitors lumbering round the port. In the winter they gathered there, the shutters closed against the wind and rain.

After the third baby, the doctor had told Michali in the bar that there should be no more. Maria had suffered complications during the pregnancies. Michali listened to this in silence. When he went home, he surprised Maria by kissing her tenderly before they slept. It was his farewell to her body. When they were very old they were to care for each other silently, until God decided who should be first. Maria felt herself to be fortunate. She had a good man and, when the children grew up, she enjoyed a gentle affair with a bachelor lorry driver, who bewildered his mother with his unwillingness to marry.

While Michali was collecting Maria's daily commissions, he had noticed the breasts of the ironmonger's wife, and one evening on a chance meeting in a lonely alley, he slid his hand up to her cunt and an unspoken agreement was made, which satisfied them both.

Maria attended scrupulously to the children's needs, overseeing their homework, planning their futures, taking them to music lessons. Michali was secretly transfixed by the fluent sound of his son's violin, but he said nothing to the child and grunted at the news of examination successes. None of them ever knew that the boy had inherited his father's perfect pitch.

By dint of his good-natured acceptance of Michali's surliness, Reg, the Englishman, slowly became a friend. He brought a violin from England for Young Michali, which was rapturously received by Maria and ignored by Michali.

Michali hated gifts, which he found humiliating and incomprehensible. He was amazed by the open delight of his children on their name days, when they shouted with pleasure and squeezed him in rushes of gratitude for the presents their mother bought and wrapped.

Reg's younger sister began to come each year with her husband on a chartered yacht. The husband was a loud fat man, spluttering and swearing at the wheel as they manoeuvred into a berth.

One year he appeared in the chandlery yelling furiously on his phone. The sister grinned apologetically at Michali. A mast stay had snapped. She suggested her husband should go for a drink before his blood pressure exploded. Michali went to the yacht with the woman to assess the damage. Afterwards, she gave him water and they sat in the tiny deck well, 'My husband loses his sense of humour when things go wrong,' she said.

'My wife would say the same of me,' he replied smiling.

Her name was Rosemary. When he returned the next day, he gave her a sprig from the bush in his courtyard. She said she would smuggle it home for her garden.

It became a regular thing each year that she would have an ouzo with Michali, when she arrived. They shared a gallows humour, a compensation often bestowed on unloved children, but the details of their early trials were very different and undiscussed. She had suffered boarding school at eight and a glacial mother. He had survived a drunken father and a ruined home. They exchanged stories of their wayward children, followed eventually by weddings and constantly photographed grandchildren. Her children flew away to Switzerland and Brazil, his to Rodos and Athina. They agreed it was sad to lose them. She swore often, words which he only liked to hear from a woman's mouth during sex and not at all from his wife, but she just grinned at his joking disapproval. He learned that she was an artist. She made pictures for children's books. She grew orchids. She liked to find the hidden icons on the island. She had a huge ginger cat.

He would see her wandering around the port in the evening, her hand on her husband's arm, listening to the man complaining. Reg called him the 'fucking city-boy bastard' and contrived to avoid him. Every winter she emailed Michali a photo of the rosemary bush.

One winter day Reg thrust his phone at Michali in Alexo's bar: *Percy dead. Heart attack yesterday. Let you know arrangements. Love Rosemary.*

'I am sorry,' said Michali.

'I'm not,' said Reg.

She did not come that summer. In November, as usual, Michali went with his wife to visit the grandchildren, who no longer clambered onto him, stroking his face and smiling, but melted away politely, their eyes fixed on their phones. He saw how old he was to them and felt that he must seem like his decrepit father.

The next July she came.

In the chandlery she raised her glass and then lowered it onto the table, weeping silently, scrabbling in her pockets for a tissue, which she did not have. He gave her a dishcloth, tearing it from its cellophane.

'Sorry,' she said, blowing her nose. 'Even here it feels so quiet without him ranting on about something.' The sun was slanting through the doorway and the light caught the tears in her eyes.

'Your eyes are blue,' he said, suddenly fascinated by the purple turquoise colour. 'Like the English flowers. Under the trees. I see them in your forest by the Southampton Water. There are many.'

'Bluebells?' she said.

'Is that. Your eyes are like the bluebells. Very beautiful.'

'Oh, fuck,' she said, smiling behind the dishcloth, 'how romantic.'

'Blue eyes. Blue mouth,' he said, sighing.

'Sorry,' she said.

When he passed in the afternoon, she was sitting in her deck well, 'Come and have a drink tonight,' she said. 'Won't blub. Promise.'

He knew what she wanted and it was understandable and she was a nice woman, everyone thought so. But in the evening, when he took her hand and nodded toward the dark cabin, she drew back and shook her head and laughed, stroking his cheek as if he were a child.

He got away as fast as he could, hiding his anger.

He stayed away from her and smiled politely, if he saw her with Reg.

She came to say goodbye and kissed him on the cheek before he could step away, which made him brusque with the customers who came in afterwards. He did not want kisses. He got them from his family.

The next year he put the glasses of ouzo triumphantly on the table. She had come back and why else would the woman come back?

'You like me?' he asked, with only the suggestion of a question.

'Michali,' she said, laughing, 'of course I like you. I especially like your voice.'

'My voice?' he said.

'It's like treacle,' she said. 'I like the sound of it, when you're having an argument or a joke in Alexo's.'

'The rosemary has grown?' he asked, failing to find any way of responding to her strange pleasure.

'It does very well,' she said.

'Tonight, I come to the boat,' he said, firmly.

She smiled at him, 'No,' she said.

'Why not?'

'Michali, all I want is some bloody peace now.'

'It will be nice,' he protested, grinning.

'No it won't,' she said, laughing, 'it will be fucking uncomfortable.'

'It will be fucking. Yes?'

What can you do? he thought, as she left the shop waving. She drinks with me every year, even when she has a husband, and now she says No.

When she came to say goodbye, the shop was full of a

loud American crew and he annoyed himself by waving to her, as she stood in the doorway blowing him a kiss.

'Rosemary is mad,' said Reg in the winter. 'She's bought a bloody boat and she's living on the Thames.'

There were no emails.

She raised her glass of ouzo four months later and before he said a word, she said, 'Reg is going to Rhodes for three days.'

'You want?' he said, relieved that there would be no more of this game.

She nodded.

He never kissed, but she wanted to kiss and, as it was the first time, he made a silent concession. Then he did what he wanted, but she smiled and even laughed throughout it all, as if it were a joke. He needed to hear her telling him he was big, he was good, like the prostitutes and the women in the porn films and the ironmonger's wife, but she would not even use the bad words, which was infuriating. She rolled and twisted above and beneath him, her eyes sparkling in the dark. Grimly he tried even harder to break into her, but all she did was struggle free and sit next to him, sweat rolling between her drooping breasts, gasping, 'Pax.'

Her stomach was pouched and creased like silk, where the babies had stretched her skin. Maria had never lost the bulge of her stomach and now it was like a small barrel. He had never seen the ironmonger's wife's stomach. On the whole he did not waste time noticing such things.

'Tell me,' she said, stroking his chest, 'what is the thing you most desire in the world?'

He frowned and tried to pull her toward him.

'Tell me.'

He tutted impatiently, 'A new back,' he said, smiling in case she thought that he needed sympathy.

'No, no. A thing.'

He shrugged, 'Nothing.'

'Percy wanted things. The day he died he was getting a new car. He could not understand that people can have lives which are more important to them than money.'

Why does she speak of that *mounopano*? he thought, pulling her firmly toward him.

She did small tender things with the loving touch of a child. She did things the whores did and things the whores would not do. Unlike the ironmonger's wife, she seemed to have her own ideas. Slowly he sank into an abyss of her devouring wishes. He could not master his need for her in the command of her opened body. His mind filled with her desire.

He came inside her, lying on her belly between her legs, like a husband. Fading helplessly on her breasts, submerged in a wave of pleasure and shame, he fought his way up toward the steady gloom of the room, the litter of potions on a table, his clothes scattered on the floor, the woman softened and still.

Could she be? Despite being the sister of an English lord, growing up in the pillared house which Reg had once shown him, a house twice as large as the town council building, was she a whore? A whore witch? Even his favourite prostitute in Rotterdam had not overcome him with her tricks. He had never committed this desecration, this blasphemy, as terrible as pissing on the icon of Archangel Michalis, to whom his mother had prayed.

She put out her hand to touch him, but he moved away to get dressed, 'That was so lovely,' she said. 'You are beautiful. Like the bluebells.'

'A man is not a flower,' he said, grimacing at her and pulling on his T-shirt.

'Sometimes he is,' she said.

He left amiably, but as quickly as he could. Outside he ducked into a tiny alley the width of a man, littered and broken underfoot. He leant back flat against the wall, breathless and anxious as he used to be in childhood, when his father was out looking for someone to beat. He padded through the streets to the old bench, shaking his head, trying to come back into his old self, his real self. Above him the patterned stars sat in their arching canopy. Below him the town lights were mirrored in the dark plain of the sea.

The thing about finishing sex properly was that it had to be where you wanted and when you wanted, anything else was just little boys playing with themselves. Control was everything. He said this angrily to himself, as if he might be talking to his son. With a grunt he stood up and walked home.

He woke suddenly in the night, out of a dream of the heaving gloom of the transport deck from the top of the iron stairway, gripping the rail while the ship heeled and bucked, staring into the hold, knowing something was loose, hearing the crash of metal within the constant roar of the storm. He crossed himself, thanking God that the other dream, of the deck master, had not pounced on him.

He stayed away from her and he busied himself at the back of the shop, losing custom sometimes. Reg came back and went off sailing with her. Michali waited for her to be completely gone, as if she were the sullen winter clouds. He worried that she might talk to her brother. She might be so shameless. But, when they returned, Reg chatted with him in the bar and, when she came in, she gave Michali her smile and a wave, as he made some excuse and left.

He knew when she was leaving for England and he thought about shutting the shop that day, so that she would not find him. Instead, when she came in with the beautiful smile in her eyes, he stood and reached for her hand and said, 'I am sorry,' and she smiled so kindly, he said it again, 'I am very sorry.'

'Michali,' she said, 'It's only love. See you next year.'

It was a strange time. The winds came too early and annoyed the tourists. In November rain slashed the paving stones day after day and the mountains spewed a torrent, which raced down the steep streets carrying away dry-docked boats at the port and an old lady who had ventured out to shop. The tuna fishing was ruined for weeks, which made him bored and irritable.

In Alexo's bar they watched the football and the porn behind closed shutters.

To his annoyance, the films made him think of her and it subdued him. The memory, sharp with searing contempt for his frailty, shuddered through him. He hated her. On the big screen, the perfect globes of tits and arses did not stir him. He saw her pendulous uneven breasts and felt her pleasure overwhelming him again and wished her dead in her coffin boat on the grey Thames.

The first time this happened he had stamped home angrily and in the morning in the shop there was an email from her. Was this her magic, this infuriating coincidence? She sent a photo of the rosemary bush in a huge earthenware pot on her deck. In the background glistening racks of apartment buildings rose like liners above the dusty dark water. Angrily he closed down the machine. Let her sink with her rosemary down into the mud where she belonged.

He went in search of the ironmonger's wife and made an assignation, so that she could take her knickers off in preparation. He did not like to be hindered by fumbling and pulling. At the back of the shop, after his preferred preliminaries, he came in her mouth, which was a relief. He had wondered if the witch might have made this impossible. The ironmonger's wife put on her knickers and left, taking a packet of kitchen sponges. It was her custom to award herself a small gift on these occasions.

Later, he sat before the bright screen staring at the email, biting his nails. He had humiliated himself with this English woman. Why had he apologised to her? What had he to apologise for? She had wavered and teased him for years.

It would pass. He remembered his son, snarling at his mother at the evening meal, running out of the room, banging doors and when Michali threw up his hands and bellowed, she explained the boy had fallen for Giorgio's girl who was going away. He went after his son and sat him down in Alexo's and told him the girl had just entranced him, to take no notice, he would learn there were women everywhere.

I am not a child, he thought. Is this the childishness of old age?

But he was right with his fatherly advice, the days passed, the porn films regained their ephemeral power and the ironmonger's wife satisfactorily embodied them.

The woman did not return until the brazen heat of August and by that time both of them were orphans. His father had died, after weeks of unheeded complaint. Her mother had faded beneath a pastel coverlet until nothing was left. Reg went home for the funeral and brought Rosemary back. She was pale and dry-skinned.

Solemnly he poured the ouzo and they touched glasses. She drank it in two gulps.

'That's good,' she said. 'It's so fucking good to be here.'

He poured her more.

'Take fucking water,' he said smiling and giving her a bottle, 'or you'll be fucking drunk.'

She laughed, 'Jesus, Michali, you've made me laugh. Bless you.' Nothing had dimmed the dancing light in her eyes, the glow of mischief and playfulness and love. It was like the love in his mother's eyes, he thought, deep and wholly benign.

He said, 'I love you.'

'And I love you,' she said, smiling. 'I don't fuck men I don't love.'

They smiled and smiled at each other, with his bare foot on hers under the table.

'Here,' she said, after a while, taking a package from her bag. 'I brought you something.'

He hated opening presents and having to be grateful. He took it from her and went to the back of the shop, leaving it on a shelf. When she left, he opened it. It was a personal locator beacon, very small and very expensive. She knew he went fishing in the treacherous winter sea. What did she think of him that she would spend three hundred euros in this way, as if he were a gigolo like the waiters in Rodos?

He watched her in Alexo's bar. He saw her waving at people, shaking hands. How many men? he thought, his mind clouding over.

Reg annoyingly seemed to have no plans to go away and she would not let Michali come to her, as quiet as a cat, in her small bedroom, while Reg snored on his *moussandra*. In the evenings, Michali could only sit frowning with his noisy friends and watch her.

He sat in the shop biting his nails, consumed with plans and strategies to get her under control. Then Reg was forced to return to the lawyers in England.

She had wine, but he would not drink. She did what he wanted, while he tried hard to keep his mind on the porn films and the ironmonger's wife. He took his hand away and shook his head, when she asked him to do the things which he knew would please her and threaten to drown him in her desire.

While he dressed, she sat in the crumpled sheets, looking so forlorn that he sat next to her and stroked her cheek. 'What's the matter?' she asked. 'What's wrong?'

'Nothing,' he said. 'We're good friends. Yes? Next time . . .'

'Not if it's like this,' she interrupted. 'Not like this.'

He stood up and looked down at her, doing up his belt, 'You are English,' he said quietly. 'You want men like dogs who do what you want and take your presents.'

The silence in the little room followed him into the street. He had meant to give her back the silver beacon. He placed it under one of the many loose pavings, where it would be smashed by the rumbling trucks, and he walked home drenched in moonlight.

He saw her in the bar with Reg a week later and a few times after that. Reg said she had conjunctivitis from the sun. She always wore her large black sunglasses.

In October, Reg told him that she had gone to live with one of her children in Brazil. Now, thought Michali, swallowing down the last of his beer, she will have many black men. He patted Reg on the shoulder and left the bar to walk round to the fishing boats by the gas station. The fishermen were tenderising octopus by slamming the creatures onto the flagstones. He picked up a grey tangle and joined the men, smashing the soft mottled tendrils repeatedly onto the stone.

He swore at her rhythmically under his breath, hammering the octopus until his arm ached and the men were laughing at the unusable shreds of flesh which remained.

The Flowers of the Masque

η Αρετές...με πίκρα ακούνε...
...και βλέπουν...
τα φώτα, τα διαμαντικά, και τ'άνθη του χορού.

The virtuous . . . listen in malice
. . . staring . . .
at the radiance, the jewels, the flowers of the masque.
In the House of the Soul C. P. Cavafy

When I look at the old photo albums I am sure we were happy, but Megan had not been easy to live with for a long time.

Take, for instance, the question of lights. I am all for lights when it gets dark, but not for turning the house into a Christmas tree as soon as dusk creeps up the garden. I turned them off. She turned them on.

She took to parking her car nose up to the back gate, which made the front look untidy. Every time she did it, I told her to park it next to mine. Apart from anything else, I could hardly get through the back gate. She told me to lose some weight. Her excuse was that the broken arm she sustained over a year before, tripping over the boot scraper, still meant that she could only carry one carrier bag of groceries at a time and she needed to be near the back door.

The broken arm was the source of a great deal of aggravation, necessitating disruption to all my routines, with hospital visits and shopping trips. I told her to take taxis, but she objected on the grounds that I was doing 'nothing'. It was only because I was going up to fetch her from the supermarket that I ran into the back of the stupid woman who decided to brake without reason on Lakey Hill.

Thank God, Megan spent most of her time in the expensive shed in the garden, where she painted all her little pictures. I noticed that the broken arm did not stop her doing that.

In the last years, she took to going out without warning. It was hard not to see this as deliberate provocation. Several times I arrived back to find that she was not in. She knew I never carried a key. The first time I had to break the kitchen window, stand on a milk crate and squeeze through the window, with resultant cuts and bruises. All she said was that there was a key in the potting shed. The second time I ransacked the potting shed with no success, only for her to say, when she sailed home, that she had meant the tool shed. It is the lack of remorse which grates.

Well, everyone is always saying that marriage is hard work and I suppose that is what they mean. She had stopped listening to me. If I tried to tell her my schedule, she told me to write it on the diary in the scullery, in case I needed a late dinner, and when she started, which sometimes she did, in a rush of revelation about some exhibition or a film she had seen, it would be because there was golf on the television, which seemed to be a signal for her to come in yabbering.

She could bore for Britain about the island, too. I told her it was an obsession and not everyone is interested in an expensive little tourist trap, but on she went at every opportunity, eulogising the views and the weather and the 'lovely people'. It was quite embarrassing.

Even though I had been retired for several years and did not need any rest and relaxation, she became quite difficult about holidays. I would have been happy staying at home, archiving my postcard collection which is a major task. I make quite a tidy sum on ebay. Then there is the gardener to manage. He is inclined to do things on his own initiative, unless I am vigilant. I play a bit of golf, alone because people don't take the game seriously enough. I have also been helping out at the library, although this may have to stop. The Dewey system is superb, but most of the volunteers appear to have trouble with the alphabet and all my time seems to be taken up correcting their mistakes.

For these dratted holidays, I had to pack a few clothes around my juicer and my steamer and my water purifier, which, as she pointed out, did leave very little room in my suitcase, but the meals in the restaurants are soaked in oil and teeming with germs and unhealthy ingredients. She did the buying from the local shops and I took good care of the preparation. My stomach is only used to unprocessed, organic, fibrous food. I would feel quite ill, watching her pouring olive oil onto her feta. Cheese has not passed my lips for several decades.

My blood pressure had been giving cause for concern, but, frankly, I think that was down to her. If she had only compromised slightly, we might have had less friction.

We arrived for the last holiday in appalling heat. I had made a comprehensive list of the comestibles we needed, so that she could do a shop when we arrived, but she was determined first to go down to the bar and renew her acquaintance with other holiday makers with whom she kept up an email correspondence during the winter. She knew all their names and told me inconsequential details about their lives from time to time. I had no idea which of them she was talking about. I waited for her at the apartment for at least two hours until my patience ran out.

I could not see her at any of the tables, where cheery strangers greeted me enthusiastically. I did not ask if they knew where she was. Not knowing where your wife is demonstrates a certain lack of control on your part and, clearly, a lack of concern on hers. Fortunately someone mentioned that she was at the butcher's and that she had left two crammed shopping bags from Tavrakis's shop under a table, while she completed her errands.

Beer gives me wind and wine gives me indigestion. The orange juice at that bar is produced from a machine which does not look as if it ever sees soapy water. Soft drinks are simply poison. I ordered a bottle of water, which I opened but did not drink. I have heard about the warehouses, where the rats run around the crates urinating freely as they go. Even unscrewing the top of these bottles is probably hazardous.

One of the women was asking me about some award or other which my wife won a few months before. I couldn't remember what it was, the Women's Institute prize for pictures of trees perhaps, she is always painting trees. She appeared, at last, with annoying lack of concern, and another carrier bag.

'How's Sotiri?' asked the woman.

'He's good,' she said. Her capacity to appear to be friends with the shopkeepers always amazed me. 'Little Yanni has joined the Navy, it doesn't seem possible, does it? I remember him running around after the big boys playing football in the square.'

I was anxious to return to the apartment to purify some water and make sure I consumed my three litres, so, shortly after, I prised her away and we trudged back with the shopping.

It is a large apartment with two bedrooms. When the children left home, which took far longer than either of us expected, she commandeered a bedroom and spent weeks removing Blu-tack and painting the walls and buying completely unnecessary new furniture, carpet and curtains. When she had finished and I glanced in, it appeared to be a mixture of Turkish bordello and rustic Greek. She is a great fan of Lucien Freud, so the reproductions on the wall were nauseating. How she could wake up each morning to meat masquerading as people, I do not know. We had had no discussion about her moving out of our room and we never did. She seemed to feel less and less need to ask me about anything.

A few years before she told me rather curtly that she was 'seeing a therapist'. I think I had been anxious to know if she would be in on a particular morning to receive a delivery, and that was her reply. My reaction was relief, this seemed to annoy her, but women do get awkward and moody after the change, it's well known. How she was paying for it is a mystery. We had a joint account which was supplied with money for her to use for the housekeeping, but, when I checked the statement, I could not see any anomalous amounts. If she was getting her therapy from the NHS, she must have been a very expensive nut to crack, because she went for years.

I was irritated by the lack of consultation about the bedroom, but frankly I was more comfortable without her. She moved about a lot in bed and got up in the night, sometimes going to her shed to paint, and there was a whole lot of bother when she went through the change, with her complaining about sweating, which I found rather coarse. Also, she snores. She says I do, but I never hear it.

Thus we had a holiday apartment with two bedrooms, so that we could continue our arrangements as normal and she could enjoy, as she inexplicably did, the stifling heat of the night, and I could use the air con.

Locking up is a regular part of my routine which did not stop on the island. The door into the courtyard had to be barred and, as our rooms had separate entrances, I ensured that I locked my own from the inside and did my best to remind her to do the same. Her room was part of the main apartment with the kitchen and I was thus able to check whether she had heeded my words, when I got up in the morning to make my St John's wort tea. Very often I found the door unlocked, but she maintained that getting up to let me in was an unwarranted annoyance, considering that the main door was barred and there was a seven foot wall around the courtyard.

When I got up the first morning, I immediately noticed that the iron bar was hanging from the front door rather than securely fixed into its bracket. She had left her door unlocked and when I went into her room to rouse her, the bed was empty. I was extremely annoyed at the carelessness of all this, so that she found me in the courtyard with a very strong camomile infusion to reduce the stress. She was wearing a billowing beach garment and had bought bread. Fresh bread is completely outside the competence of my stomach.

None of this made me feel well disposed toward her, so I was grumpy about the invitation to the children's folk-dancing. Nevertheless in the evening I agreed to go down to the red chair bar, which is on the harbour road and offers a constant panorama of boats. While she had wine and I had water from my thermos, she began to talk to a plump redhead, who was sitting at the next table smoking. It was one of the real drawbacks of that place that no-one seemed to understand the extreme dangers of this activity. Let them kill themselves how they wish, but don't include me. I did a bit of polite smoke-waving and throat-clearing and, thankfully, the woman took the hint and put the cigarette out.

An old man came limping past and my wife shot up and waved. He was introduced as Sotiri and gravely shook my hand. Apparently Sotiri's granddaughter was dancing in the show and off they went for a few hours of stultifying boredom, watching small children stumbling about or freezing in fright and, no doubt, bawling when they got it wrong.

The woman had refused an invitation to go with them and it turned out that she had made the same estimate of the evening's potential as entertainment. We had a little chuckle at this. We discussed our grandchildren. Being a woman, she knew a great deal more about hers than I do about mine, but I do remember their ages and their names and one of them seems to be shaping up quite well in Maths, which is promising.

Her name was Celia and she was a frequent visitor with two other friends. To our surprise, we discovered that we lived in the same county. She had a shop which sold bric-a-brac and vintage clothes. I supposed she meant secondhand junk. She was very interested in my postcards and, as not many people are, I had an unusually enjoyable evening telling her all about them. I thought she was very attractive, rounded and feminine, with delicate hands. By the time my wife appeared it was far later than my normal time for retiring, but we walked Celia back to her apartment and managed to catch the last bus up the hill.

I felt quite elated. It's a long time since a pretty woman took any notice of me. My job as a risk engineer did not provide me with many opportunities to meet women, until equality started to bring the young female graduates amongst us and, by then, I was stuck behind a desk with the tiring and repetitive task of arguing with the Board about the costs of health and safety.

My wife had yet another island event to attend, three days later. This time it was a lecture on birds, with slides and a local English translator, organised by the Women's League. There was no question of my going and she suggested I have a drink with Celia, who seemed to spend her time either at the bar in the evening or having a variety of massages and beauty treatments, all of which were very successful, from what I could see. This would have been delightful but for the extraordinary behaviour of the waiter at the bar, who seemed to have taken a particular dislike to me and sat at the back, positively glaring straight at my face. I tried buying Celia her wine, so that my parsimonious thermos did not cause any offence, and I tried braving the obdurate scowl with a smile, but neither had any effect. It may have been this inexplicable hostility which contributed to my fright later that night.

We had spent a very pleasant evening. Celia had developed an idea that she could sell my postcards and I was pleased to discover a business-like brain under her jolly, strawberry blonde curls. My wife could not add four and six.

It was early morning when I woke, with a start, and heard a completely inexplicable, loud noise in the room. I sat up in alarm, but I could see no-one. The noise was human, I was sure, but it was not words. It was a mixture of a groan and a menacing growl. I put on the light and made sure that I was alone, then I opened the window and looked out. There was no movement in the small alley that ran below the window. The sound still rang in my ears and it occurred to me that it may have come from the other rooms in the apartment.

Typically, this one time, my wife had remembered to lock the door. I knocked urgently, because being in the courtyard, which was open to the sky, made me feel unprotected and anxious. Eventually I heard her impatiently fiddling with the lock.

'Did you hear that noise?' I asked.

'No,' she said. The door to her bedroom was shut, so I supposed that she might not have heard the noise, which definitely came from the front.

'Someone was . . . I don't know, shouting or groaning. It woke me up. I thought someone was in the room.'

I went through the sitting-room to the balcony. She followed me. We stood on the balcony, 'Oh look,' she said, pointing down to a rectangular patch of rubble where there had once been a house, 'look down there. The goats have come in to forage.' Immediately the imperative call of an alpha goat rang through the alley and he appeared, herding a few more bewildered animals toward the weed strewn ruin.

'Good God,' I said. 'I could have sworn it was human.'

'Well, it wasn't,' she retorted and stumped back to her room.

She had been wearing a lacy slip. Presumably she wore these things because of the night heat. It was the kind of thing I was beginning to imagine Celia wearing.

In England before breakfast, my wife was invariably wrapped in a bedraggled furry dressing gown, covered with paint splatters. She looked extremely unappetising, but she is frigid, of course. I realised that some years into the marriage.

Celia and I met most evenings for a few companionable hours, watching the passers-by and laughing at the red-faced tantrums of the yachtsmen trying to moor up in the harbour, which is almost as impossible for parking as my local Waitrose. Sometimes we wandered gently round to the elite moorings near the ferry quay. Here monstrous, white vessels, two or three storeys high, afforded us the occasional glimpse of cream leather interiors adorned with carefully lit works of art. It was always a disappointment to see the people who came from these boats. There was nothing glamorous about them. Most of them looked old and tired. Celia said she had once seen a famous model hurling champagne bottles from the helicopter landing-deck of a glossy black Russian cruiser.

On our perambulations, Celia would take my arm and tell me sad stories about her life. She did not seem to have been very lucky with men. Walking with her, I felt as if I were about nineteen and all the sick anxiety of being nineteen came with it. I wanted simultaneously never to see her again and to spend every hour close to her body.

Meanwhile my wife was deluding herself that she was part of the community, going to concerts and film shows and art exhibitions.

'I seem to be monopolising you,' said Celia, one evening as we walked back to her place, 'are you sure your wife doesn't mind?'

'She's busy mixing with the locals,' I said.

'Yes,' said Celia, 'Sotiri is very fond of her, isn't he? I suppose, because he's a widower he has some licence. It's rather unusually open, as it were.'

'That's my wife all over. Anything unusual. I'm afraid she's a rather silly woman. She's off at the monastery tonight, which doesn't sound like fun.'

'Oh I think it will be,' Celia said, stopping outside her house, 'it's a kind of boat blessing thing and there's quite a party. The girls have gone.'

'Why didn't you go?' I asked.

Her reply was to seize my hand, pull me through her doorway and push me backwards onto her bed, where something happened which had never happened to me before. I won't go into the details.

In the deserted hours of the night, when I finally reached the top of the thousand steps and pushed open the courtyard door, there was no sound from the apartment or light in the fanlight. I undressed and went to bed, where I spent a very happy half hour creating an ineradicable synaptic pathway, in my brain, to every event which had occurred on Celia's bed.

I woke into an agonising mixture of adolescent excitement and plain terror. Performance anxiety in retrospect was part of this disturbance, but also dread of what might be expected next. I was unable to tell whether it would be more awful if something else were expected, or if it were not.

As I sat in the courtyard with my camomile, a motorbike roared deafeningly up the alley and stopped. My wife opened the door, waving over her shoulder to the motorbike, which set off again in a blast of smoke and noise.

She was dressed in one of her wildly-coloured gauzy things. Her clothes reminded me of Gloria Swanson in *Sunset Boulevard*, bordering on tawdry and thoroughly unbecoming on a skinny old woman.

'I trust you have not been out all night?' I said.

'Do you?' she said.

There is a point at which patience fails. I decided immediately that this would be the last time I brought her out, to cavort about the island behaving like a fool.

I had absolutely no idea whether I was supposed to take Celia's behaviour seriously or dismiss it as part of her normal holiday repertoire. She was a stunningly attractive woman and there would probably be no shortage of transitory partners.

My wife had not emerged from the bedroom all day and I had become thoroughly exasperated with my cage-pacing mind, which prowled around every eventuality in a monotonous circle. In the end I decided to go to the red chair bar and find out once and for all if I had got a first or a third, as it were. Frankly I had been so astonished by what went on, that I only partially believed it had happened, despite committing it to memory in every detail.

Celia was not at the bar, but I was earlier than usual. The furious waiter glared at me and made a contemptuous movement of his hand, as if to say, don't expect me to waste my time coming over. However a few minutes later I was alarmed to see him winding his way between the tables toward me. He sat down in the opposite chair.

'Why you no drink?' he said. 'Why you come to bar and no drink?'

The bloody nerve of the man. 'I am waiting for the lady,' I said.

He lit a cigarette. 'I'd prefer it if you did not smoke near me,' I said.

'You fuck off,' he said.

I was definitely not going to go, so I stared out at the harbour and he glared.

'What you do with your wife?' he said.

I was not sure how to interpret this question due to the unsophisticated syntax, but I was not going to become embroiled in any conversation with the brute.

'I think you do nothing,' he said, 'which is why Sotiri has good time. Very good time.'

It was, of course, obvious what he was implying and I suppose a certain sort of man would have immediately stood up and hit him, regardless of the utter nonsense he was talking, but I gave up hitting people in nursery school. The idea that anyone would be interested in my stringy wife with her ludicrous clothes was so ridiculous that I could only answer with a snort. Also, she had demonstrated to me quite conclusively years ago that she was not interested in sex. An elderly butcher with a club foot and a devotion to his grandchildren, would have appealed to her mawkish sentimentality but nothing else.

Nevertheless I was extremely relieved that Celia arrived at this point.

'Hello, dear,' she said to me. My heart rose.

'Nasso, can I have a spritzer please.'

He stood up, 'Of course,' he said, then in an urgent whisper, 'but what you do, Celia? What you do?'

'Nothing, Nasso,' she said firmly, sitting down. 'I'm not doing anything. And Nasso, stop staring, it's rude.'

'Is the look,' he said. 'Is looking.'

'I know what it is,' she said. 'But it won't work on him, will it?'

'You think?' he said. 'Looking is very strong thing. You know, yes?'

'My spritzer, please?' she said sounding cross.

'What's he talking about?' I asked, as he snaked away.

'They have this weird thing about staring. The evil eye, I suppose,' she said. 'This is a spooky old place, despite the Sky TV and the kids with iPads. How's your wife? The girls are still in bed, groaning.'

'Fine. Fine,' I said. I took the plunge, 'Celia. Celia, was it alright, last night?'

'It was lovely, darling,' she said, patting my hand.

'Are we going to . . . ?'

'Oh, I expect so.'

I felt gratitude. Simple gratitude. It was the first time someone had wanted to give me pleasure. My wife and I had been far too young to know anything about sexual pleasure. Believe me, the Sixties only happened in London, not Shrewsbury where we both grew up. When we married, it was amazing enough to be able to get contraception and actually do it;

then the children came along and what with them and my wife's rather long list of what she didn't want to do in bed, which amounted to everything but the most basic first position and be-as-quick-as-you-can-because-I-have-to-be-up-early, it all came to an end.

On the final night (my wife had gone to a firework party in honour of a baptism) Celia persuaded me, quite easily, to have a small glass of champagne. By the time I reached the apartment, indigestion was raging in my throat and chest. Although we had exchanged phone numbers and Celia swore she would meet me in England, I was miserably unsure of her and the pain underlined my fear that I might never again have what I had unknowingly denied myself for so many years.

My wife returned silently and went to her room. When I knocked on her door, she was not inclined to be sympathetic about the indigestion, saying, 'The medicine is in the kitchen.' And that was the last thing I remember. A wave of agony seemed to travel through the room and hit me like a truck. I went down. And out.

Sickness and frailty took over our lives. I spent a week in Rhodes being stabilised. A viciously uncomfortable plane flight on a trolley brought me to England and open heart surgery, which left me weak and raw and stiff with pain.

At home, every previously unheeded daily task required patience and time. Making my way to the lavatory left me breathless and aching. Getting out of a chair seemed to require the strength of ten men. I became a slumped, open-mouthed, drowsy invalid, staring for hours at the television. All thoughts of Celia had vanished like the swallows in autumn.

Then, one November morning, I woke up to the sound of voices at the door and she was coming into the room in a long red coat. I was furious with my wife for not warning me of this visit and I sent her a look which should have withered her on the spot. Half my porridge oats were probably in my lap and I had not summoned the energy for a shave.

'Oh don't get up,' Celia was saying, 'you poor thing. I've brought you some DVDs. You must be bored stiff. I wondered if you wanted us to start looking at the postcards? Megan said she thought you wouldn't mind.'

My wife melted out of the room, muttering about tea, with a facetious smile on her face.

Celia stayed for a sensitive half hour and left me tired but happy. We had agreed to work slowly on the collection. I hauled myself up the stairs and ran a bath. Although they kept telling me I could have one, I had been too frightened of stepping into its shiny high-sided depths and of being unable to lever myself out. Dressing slowly in my room, I glanced at Celia's films. They were definitely not family viewing. Some of them had caused audience revolt at film festivals. 'These will get you going,' Celia had said with her naughty smile.

'Nice of Celia to come over, wasn't it?' my wife said at dinner. 'She's been very worried about you. Perhaps you will perk yourself up a bit, now? I need to talk to you about some plans for next year. I want to spend more time on the island. To paint. Maybe three months.'

'I couldn't,' I protested. 'I couldn't go there. The heat. Look at me. I couldn't possibly manage the steps.'

'The doctors told you. It will take time, but there's no reason that you won't be perfectly alright. Anyway I don't expect you to come. I'd rather you didn't. I could get in some help if you're worried.'

'Help' conjured up images of being bossed around and force-fed. I grimaced at her.

'Perhaps Celia would pop in and make sure you aren't starving? She's going to be around anyway, isn't she, doing something with the collection?'

'What do you mean, you'd rather I didn't?' I said, waking up belatedly to this gratuitous rudeness. 'I've got no intention of either of us going back to that over-priced, over-heated bit of rock.'

'Oh Clive,' she said, 'do stop it. I can go where I like. Anyway, let's be careful of your blood pressure. Celia seems terribly fond of you, I'm sure you'd be well looked after. She's a very nice woman, if a bit simple.'

'Simple? That's rich coming from you. She can do her VAT returns. You can't even work out the twenty-four-hour clock. What do you mean, you can go where you like?' She seemed to be bent on provocation.

'I mean, I can go where I like,' she said, in a gritty tone, 'and I mean that Celia does not seem to have learned much from experience. Are there three, or is it four, appalling men in her past?'

'No idea,' I said. 'It's extremely bad luck if there are.'

'Bad luck or bad judgement,' she said, determined to twist the knife. I realised that Megan was probably jealous of Celia. 'Well, never mind, you can show her what it's like to be looked after properly, can't you?'

'Yes,' I said, surprised at what amounted to an accolade coming from the mouth of my wife, 'yes, I can.'

Three months. . . I thought.

'Just one thing,' Megan said. 'Remember the saying, What makes a woman good in bed? A man who's good in bed.'

She was pouring tomato sauce onto a wedge of glistening lasagne. Not for the first time, I silently begged God to explain why I had had the heart attack not her. I did not know whether to be more disgusted by the lasagne or the remark.

But, three months. . .

I put a forkful of mashed carrot into my mouth and found that it was the sweetest, most ambrosial carrot I had ever tasted.

A bit like Celia.

Silence

Σκιά καὶ νὺξ ἔιν'η Σιγή, ο Λόγος, η ημέρα.

Silence is the shade and the dark, the Word is daylight.
The Word and Silence C. P. Cavafy

Reg woke on his *moussandra* and stared across to his long windows which framed the dawn gloom of grey Turkish mountains beyond grey sea and sky. He never closed the shutters, unless there was a storm or the island's notorious wind was rattling the panes. His house floated above the panorama of the port and the sea, its windows like eyes always open to the view.

He was curled under two duvets and an old blanket but the damp chill of the winter night rested on his face.

Groaning with the effort, he leapt raggedly from the bed in a convulsive jerk, jumped down the three steps and ran to the two battered electric fires on each side of the room, switching them on rapidly before stumbling back up to his bed to wait for the air to be more hospitable. He was a tall ungainly man, his body still wiry and strong, deeply tanned on his arms, legs and face by the fierce summer sun. He had grown a glossy ponytail and a beard in his twenties but now his hair was thin and iron grey. He lay flat in his bed and waited, his face lined into a frown, the result of years of squinting into the sun.

He must have dozed because little Kyriaki was knocking on his door with the bread. Dragging the blanket around his waist, he padded out to the narrow courtyard, where the double doors were bolted in the old Greek way with a solid bar from wall to latch. He lifted it and let it clang against the wall.

'*Yeia sou Kyriaki. Euharisto. Kala?*'

'*Kala, Kyrie Rheggi*,' she said solemnly, holding out the carrier bag.

He took it and slowly withdrew the biscuit, which was her fee. Giggling at this reliable game, she snatched it with her small brown hand and scampered off with her family's bread.

Reg latched the door and turned, hugging the warm bread to his chest. The sounds of voices in the lane came over the courtyard wall. Kyriaki and a man. Not her father, whose voice boomed like a foghorn. He listened. There was something timid, hesitant about the child's voice. He turned back and opened the door, peering out. There was a breath of a second and Paul came toward him on the cobbles, carrying one of his kittens. Kyriaki skipped away round the corner, swinging her bag.

'Hi Reg,' said Paul. 'I see we're wearing Dior today.'

Reg gripped his blanket.

'Entertaining Kyriaki?' said Paul. 'She's a little gem, isn't she?'

'She was bringing the bread,' Reg said, immediately annoyed with himself for caring to explain.

'Told her about my kittens,' said Paul. 'Bootiful ickle babies.'

'Yes,' said Reg, shutting the door brusquely.

He stood for a moment staring at the unkempt rose and oleander bushes in the round raised bed, which he had made one winter with discarded paving and stones from ruins. His bare feet were cold on the cobbles and he went inside, troubled by more than his feet. A bizarre memory of the school swimming pool, cloaked in the usual miasma of shuddering revulsion which accompanied any thoughts of his schooldays, caused him to hurry to his CD player and switch it on.

Reg was an outlier. He preferred this word to "outsider", which suggested loneliness and banishment. When he came to the island with his great love, Sylvia, he had blossomed in the sun and stretched his arms out to the world, inviting all the bounty he could imagine. Contented marriage. Children. The house, which was then a ruin, would be firm and sturdy, decorated with Sylvia's murals and warm with her exotic curries, but before the first stones were collected together to rebuild the walls, Sylvia had been kidnapped by Ari, a pirate of a man. She had gone to live with him in his shacks on the headland, like a D. H. Lawrence heroine, which was probably why she did it. Reg went home in anguish, but there was no home and never had been. He returned to find Sylvia pregnant. At twenty-eight, Sylvia was a black matriarch, wearing her hair in a huge halo, clothing her towering body in billowing African colours. Reg wove pleasurable, vengeful daydreams of a West Indian sixth Earl, for Reg was the fifth and he knew that this would be the ultimate family horror if he could find a way of legitimising the child. He hoped to be the father and to have a son, but with her determined honesty she explained that she had no idea who the child belonged to, and when he was born, his black eyes and thatch of dark hair were those of the pirate. Reg took the ferry, was drunk in Rhodes for months, then precipitately bought a plane ticket to England and trailed around acquaintances' bedsitters and flats, sunk in misery and cannabis.

Sylvia sailed off to England with the child, installed herself in a Brixton house and hauled Reg off a sofa to live with her and sober up. His house on the island was being built, she declared, he must go back and manage the work. Her curries, the little boy's innocent affection and Sylvia's hawk-like ability instantly to confiscate any illegal substances, brought him back slowly to an accommodation with his life. He returned to the island, where Ari the pirate sought him out for evenings of pleasurable commiseration, mutual sympathy and misogynistic psychology. Reg watched his house become a home and he stayed.

Reg made toast and sat on his balcony to eat it. Beneath him Maria patiently swept her alley and waved at him. Two plasterers, white with powder, came round the corner and looked up to call *Yeia sou*. He heard Angela's door opening, under the balcony. Angela came out from her doorway until she could look up and see him.

'OK?'

'OK,' he said. 'Cold one, eh?'

'Nonsense. Wimp,' she said. 'Come to dinner tonight, will you? Helen's coming.'

'And Rufus?'

She tutted, 'Typical English, more interested in a dog than a woman. Will you play the Bach again? We'll come up to you for coffee.'

He grimaced, 'Tom plays much better than me,' he protested, 'and Young Michali used to trump us both.'

'Tom's busy with the ladies. The folk-dancing. Anyway I like the way you play. It's nice even if you get it wrong.'

In the evening, they ate in Angela's tiny kitchen-cum-sitting-room, warmed by the stove and liberal moussaka. The flagstones were covered in rugs and the shutters were closed. Helen had brought a box of wine. Rufus was stretched out in luxury at the doorstep like a medieval hound, except that he lay on rough wool and not rushes. Angela, who had never stopped being a closet hippy, lit the room with candles in old bottles.

Helen was a new resident. She had bought a house near the headland which was fitted out with a kitchen and bathroom worthy of any up to the minute English suburban semi. The Greeks knew what the English liked. Angela had first met her in the shop by the customhouse. Helen was almost in tears because she could not find ginger. Nobody ever knew why she wanted ginger, but it was found.

It was discovered that Helen had brought all her books with her, of which she had many on expensively carpentered shelves. Angela and Reg were delighted. Both of them were frugal. Angela because she had to be and Reg because he was. Someone else's books cost nothing.

Helen did not object to cannabis, which Reg was smoking, although she herself refrained, and she was broad minded about bad language, having spent her working life as a forensic psychologist. Helen was pragmatic, ironic and extravert, all of which had saved her from the dangers of her job: cynicism, drink, depression or chronic rage. She had been married, but her husband had died suddenly while they were on holiday on the island. Helen never mentioned it, but Angela and Reg had heard about it.

Reg handed a spliff to Angela, 'I've got to do something about this,' he said, pointing at the spliff. 'I don't like that weasel Paul but I've been getting it from him. I need another dealer.'

'Well, ask around,' said Angela.

'What the mouth doesn't speak of, the heart doesn't know,' said Reg. 'I don't want to upset anyone.'

'Is that an old Greek proverb?' said Helen.

'No I've just made it up, but it might as well be,' he said. 'Like: To keep the masses quiet all you need is bread and circuses. They're all ancient cynics, really.'

'Michali? You can ask him,' Angela suggested.

'Michali can be a very touchy little bear and he has no vices, apart from the ironmonger's wife.'

Angela slapped the table in delight, 'Delphini and Michali?'

'Maria told me,' Reg grinned, 'it's one of the island secrets. Been going on for years. Everyone knows and nobody speaks. Maria wasn't bothered. She said, Men are pigs Rheggi, but he is quiet pig, so *ti pota*. As far as Maria is concerned, I am an honorary woman, so not a pig. Crazy English with no wife. They don't understand it, if you're not gay.'

'Giorgio?'

'Not sure. You know what they're like. They have the charm of merchants, but you don't want to upset them. Thing is . . .' he leant forward, '. . . I don't like Paul, that slimy little bastard. Something happened this morning. He was talking to little Kyriaki. She's such a trusting little thing.

He kind of insinuated that I was . . . that I had some kind of thing about her. I think I'll have to tell her to stop bringing the bread, but she'll be upset and she hasn't done anything and the family will think it's odd and want to know why and . . .' He sat back throwing his hands up.

'Do I know Paul?' asked Helen.

'The one with the kittens,' said Angela. 'Professor of Theology, or was. Oxbridge. I thought he was gay at first, but he doesn't mix with Grant or Jim and that lot.'

'He was married,' protested Reg. 'Until she pissed off.'

'To Dawn,' said Angela, as if this was an explanation.

'Dawn?' said Helen.

'Dawn would not have noticed if he ate children for breakfast. She was passionate about cats. Cats were her mission. The older, the mankier and the more infected the better.'

'So you think he's a paedophile?' said Helen, 'This Paul.'

'I didn't say that,' said Reg, in surprisingly vehement tones.

Both women stared at him.

'But it's perfectly obvious that *is* what you're saying,' said Angela. 'He *is* slimy and he hangs about on the beach with his horrid kittens talking to the tourists' kids. I've seen him.'

Reg put his hands to his head and began rubbing his hair in agitated circles.

'Well, something will have to be done,' said Helen.

'Helen,' said Reg breathlessly, 'you're not a psychologist now. You're not a bloody whatever. You've got no power here.' He scraped his chair back and began to cough. Angela patted him on the back.

'I had precious little in UK,' said Helen, sighing. 'Are you alright?'

'We . . . can't . . . do . . . anything,' Reg gasped, between coughs. 'I can't get my breath . . . Forget it. Just . . . leave it, for fuck's sake. Jesus . . . I can't get my breath.' His chest was heaving.

'Is something stuck?' Angela asked, banging his back as hard as she could.

'It's a panic attack,' said Helen, getting out of her chair. 'Have you got a paper bag?'

'A paper bag,' echoed Angela, in bewilderment. 'What makes you think I've got one of those?'

'He needs to breathe into something,' Helen knelt down in front of Reg and took his hands, 'Reg, look at me. Now slow down, put your hands round your mouth and nose, breathe in, now breathe out. Do it. Just do it. It's alright, you're not dying.'

After a few minutes, Reg sat back. Helen returned to her seat. There was an uneasy silence.

'Sorry,' said Reg, standing up. 'I think I'll go. Thanks and all that.'

Before they could say anything he was at the door, tripping over Rufus who yelped and jumped up.

'Oh,' said Angela.

'Poor Reg,' said Helen.

'I'd better go and see if he is alright,' said Angela. 'Reg is a sociable old cove. He doesn't storm off.'

'He had a panic attack,' said Helen. 'He'll be alright.'

'Why? How? What about? Reg has been chilling since nineteen sixty-nine.'

Reg curled in his bed, shaking with what he told himself was cold. He heard Angela calling him from the courtyard, but he buried his head under his pillow. Angela came in and sat on his bed, putting her hand on his blanketed back.

'Reg?'

'Go away. Please. I'm alright.'

'Fuck off, Reg.'

He sat up and took hold of her hand, 'What's that woman saying?'

'Nothing. What are you frightened of?'

'Her.'

'Why?'

'What does she think she's going to do?'

'Nothing. She can't do anything. Paul's horrid, we know that. But she can't do anything.'

'I won't say anything, Angela. I'm not going to say anything.'

'What is there to say, old love?'

'Nothing. Nothing. Leave me alone, Angela. Please.'

All his childhood had been cold. He had been born in an English country house. The winter ice patterned the inside of the windows. He had been sent away to school where, every night, he shivered under one harsh blanket. At University the old buildings had streamed with chilling draughts and gathered the damp into their stone walls. To his relief he was sent down for setting fire to the wastepaper basket and his room, with an un-stubbed spliff.

The first time he felt warm was in the Notting Hill house, partitioned with hardboard into small rooms, chaotic with a shifting tenancy of students, West Indian families, ancient residents and drug addicts. His tiny cupboard of a bedsit on the first floor, with its elaborate fireplace sadly blocked up, a remnant of a far grander room, could be heated into a cocoon with one electric bar.

His father died when he was twenty-one. He had lain in his bed in the cupboard, imagining the consternated discussions which would be buzzing in Staffordshire and Kensington. His mother and his older sister, Primrose, summoned, asked and finally pleaded that he meet with solicitors and tax consultants. Only his little sister, Rosemary, still at school and bunking off to find him, could make him agree to the meetings. Beneath the agitated faces of his family and their exasperated lawyers, he obediently signed documents and yawned and watched the room and the people swim lazily around him. He was then supposed to do many other tedious things, but he did none of them.

His mother, who had always ridden life as if she were schooling a powerful hunter, kept the reins. The money they could not safeguard eventually arrived in his account in a benevolent avalanche, causing his bank manager to come out from the counter and gingerly shake his hand, with an appalled and envious grimace. There was a property in Devon, which he later sold to buy and rebuild the Kapotheni house. He gave the rest of the money to a school friend, a boy with alopecia and glasses, with whom he had spent silent hours cowering in shrubberies to avoid cross country. It was a good choice. Even now, many years on, the little mound of gold had not appreciably diminished. From his gleaming office, the boy with glasses regularly sent him incomprehensible annual statements and lengthy analyses of the financial situation, which Reg carefully filed and forgot. Every year he was asked if his circumstances had changed and every year he said no. He earned about two thousand euros working on Giorgio's boat in the summer.

When his mother died, crumbling into a scatter of twigs under an eiderdown, he had been forced to meet Primrose in the City of London, where she quivered and bellowed about the house and the taxes and he signed more papers and fled to Stanstead and the first available plane home.

Helen watched Paul. She was sitting on a bench eating a 'small bread' filled with tomato and feta. The harbour had reverted to its winter persona. Fishing boats and little craft clustered together and the deep horseshoe of grey sea reminded her of the old sepia photographs of the sponge divers outside their black shacks, staring sternly at the camera in moustached splendour. When the harbour was filled with the ocean-going private yachts and the towering cruise ships, it seemed nothing more than an extension of the land, but in winter it reasserted its dominance over the town.

Paul was fussing with a kitten as he sat in Alexo's bar. She noticed that Alexo swerved slightly sideways, away from Paul, if he had to walk past. Paul's musing remarks, either to the kitten or to Alexo, were not acknowledged. Feral cats had almost overrun the island years ago and there were locals who detested them.

Helen had talked with many paedophiles and she knew that there were no identifying marks. Also she was aware that the men she had met had been convicted of their crimes and were in varying states of denial, rage or hysterical remorse. Her understanding of their invisibility in the world had been deepened when a trusted friend from student days, who picnicked and played with her children, confided that he was a member of a paedophile group and wanted to assure her of the beauty of sexual experience with the innocent. He saw the expression on her face and left the café where they sat. She had remained there for an hour, reviewing every moment when he had been near her children, feeling sick at the thought of the photographs of them all together, the children sprawling around him. To her relief she could not think of a time when he had been left alone with them. The guilt at her unwitting neglect led her to keep it secret from her husband. When Bill asked after Jeremy, she muttered about a sabbatical. She told a police colleague what she knew, but there were no grounds to pursue it.

She wondered whether this was why she was now stalking this man. Paul picked his nose, examined it and wiped it on the kitten. She flinched in disgust and Rufus settled himself protectively against her legs. We are a failed species, she thought, the majority of us are unable to provide our young with the delicate and sensitive care they need to grow into a force for good in the world. We will finally obliterate ourselves with our perverse addictions to revenge and power.

Sevasti sat down beside her and stroked Rufus, '*Yeia sou.* You are looking thoughtful.'

'Dark thoughts,' said Helen smiling. 'How are you?'

'Good,' said Sevasti. 'You think of your man?'

'Not really,' said Helen. 'But I'll never forget how kind you were when he died. It was such a shock.'

'Yes,' said Sevasti.

'Sevasti, there is a man here . . . he tries to make friends with the children. You understand? An Englishman.'

'I know who you mean. Is not nice man,' Sevasti said, glancing at the bar and sighing. 'We do not like but we could not survive if we turned away the people we do not like. And it is not only English. Is in every country I think. But here is an island, small, everyone know everyone, see everything. And, for us, you know, to hurt a child is the worst thing.'

Helen thought of the grandfathers parading their tiny grandchildren in buggies during the warm evenings, while their daughters worked in the shops and bars. Old Mr Tavrakis was to be seen every night with his granddaughter in his arms patiently walking up and down the alley outside their house, kissing her little hands and singing to her.

'But if there was a child . . . if we knew he was interested in a particular child . . . ?'

'Then you must protect,' said Sevasti. 'You must growl, like Rufus, yes.'

'Reg is avoiding me, isn't he?' asked Helen when she bumped into Angela in Mr Tavrakis's crammed shop, where it was impossible not to bump into anyone who happened to be there as well.

'Well,' said Angela. 'I don't think it's just you. He seems to have holed up. Maria's worried. She went to put some of her *kleftiko* in his fridge and she couldn't get in. You know what Maria's like. As long as she's feeding Michali and him, she's happy.'

'You see, I think I know what might help,' said Helen. 'I think there's something Reg could do.'

Reg had not left his house for two days. When Kyriaki arrived he took the bread quickly, covertly. He could not meet her smiling eyes and pushed the biscuit into her hand, as if it were a bribe. Unable to tolerate food in his mouth, he sat in his overheated room and stared sightlessly at his laptop screen playing gangster movies. He knew some of them so well that he could recite chunks of dialogue and often did, to amuse himself or vent minor irritations, but now he was silent while the air grew muggy and stifling.

He could not find words to explain to himself what was happening. His mind felt both blank and agitated and he was very frightened that this was insanity. Dread seemed to be lurking in all his thoughts. He blamed the ganga and he blamed the whisky and he blamed himself.

Angela doggedly knocked until the door was abruptly opened. She followed his silent back into the house. He slumped down into a chair and stared at his nails.

'Christ, Reg, it's stifling in here,' she said. 'Open a window.'

'No, I'm cold.'

'Are you ill?' she asked, moving toward him to feel his forehead.

He shrank away angrily, 'Stop it.'

On the screen a man in a bar was systematically blinding another man, using a biro, with repeated efficient blows, while his colleagues stood around looking faintly irritated, as they might if he were making an unnecessary fuss in a restaurant. She looked away.

'What on earth do you see in this stuff?' she asked

'The dark side,' he said.

'Turn it off, I want to talk to you.'

She had thought he might refuse and was relieved when he stilled the little screen.

'Listen Reg. Just hear me out.'

It was not an easy conversation. He huffed and bounded

out of his chair and paced and told her to Shut Up and, later, to Fuck Off. Even more alarmingly, he then sat down and wept and she found the whisky and gave him a medicinal draught. Finally she left him, with a promise to meet her at Alexo's in the evening. As she carefully stepped down the steep alley to her front door, she found she was trembling with the tension of the meeting, but he had eventually agreed to do what she asked and wiped his eyes and blew his nose, on what looked like some old underpants.

Reg was waiting in his courtyard for Kyriaki's little knock. She was clearly surprised when the door was wrenched open so promptly.

'Here,' he said, giving her the biscuit. He stepped out into the lane, leaving his bread on the doorstep. 'I shall walk to your house,' he said in his accurate, but dolefully English, Greek.

She giggled and skipped by his side as they walked up the lane to the line of pine trees, which were sighing heavily in the morning breeze. As they turned to climb a narrow flight of steps, Paul appeared at the top, the kitten perching unhappily on his shoulder. Reg felt the child edge close to his side and he opened his hand without looking at her. She placed her small fingers into his palm and he closed his own around them.

'What a charming picture,' said Paul, standing above them in his long black raincoat, sounding like Dracula trying to be nice. 'I had no idea you were such friends. Hand in hand, my lor', are you to be married Kyriaki?'

'I am walking her home,' said Reg. 'I shall walk her home every morning.'

'Well, fancy,' said Paul. 'That will be . . . stimulating for you.'

By then they were abreast of him and within sight of Kyriaki's house. With a squeeze of Reg's hand, she skipped away with her bag of bread and disappeared into her home.

'And,' said Reg, poking Paul hard in his chest, 'and you can fuck off out of it and if I ever see you near her or any kid, I'll knock you down every one of the thousand steps. Have you got it?'

'Well,' said Paul breathlessly, staggering against the wall, 'dear me, we are in a naughty temper this morning.'

'Actually, you piece of shit,' Reg hissed, grabbing and twisting Paul's right ear, 'I might just cut your balls off.'

'Ow! Stop it,' Paul squeaked. The kitten dug her claws into his shoulder to keep her balance as he tried to duck away.

Reg turned and leapt down the steps. Behind him there was an ear-splitting wail from the kitten, but he did not stop.

Back in his house, he tore off a hunk of bread and lathered it with butter and wandered about his room, biting and chewing, letting the butter run down his chin. He felt wild and exultant and beautifully happy, as if all the good in the world had suddenly deposited itself in his mind in a glowing heap, warming his soul.

'Fucking bastard,' he said to himself out loud, 'fucking fucking cunting bastard. And I will, too. Just let me see him. Just once. I'll fucking knock his lights out.'

He went onto his balcony and gazed out at the layered houses of the little town which had offered him a home and friendship. He felt a love and gratitude so intensely peaceful that his legs would not hold him and he slid down onto the floor, leaning against the wall, thinking how lucky, how wonderfully lucky he was, to be alive. The sun had decided that it would remind everyone of its power and was pretending it was May. The stones of his house were warm. He was warm. He had been in hiding, all these years, from the horrors in the clammy dark of the swimming pool, but now he knew he was safe for the first time. Little Kyriaki was safe. He would make sure.

'How did it go?' Helen asked, as she walked with Angela along the rocky path to *Agios Nikolaos* beach.

Angela clambered round a boulder, 'Alright, I think. He's in a very good mood. I got a big hug this morning. What on earth was the matter with him, Helen? You know about this kind of thing. I've always thought he was totally laid back. He was brilliant with me, when I cracked up a few years ago. Why should he be so bloody scared of tackling that little shit?'

'Because a bit of him was still a small terrified child,' said Helen, 'with no-one to protect him.'

'Oh,' said Angela, 'poor Reg. I'll give him another hug tonight.' She slipped on some shale, 'Bugger this path, one day I'll break my ankle.'

They unlatched the gate into the sandy courtyard and found the key to the heavy door into the white chapel on the beach. Rufus sat down patiently in the weak sunlight. Inside Helen found the broom and did a bit of sweeping, while Angela lit the two candles she had brought and contemplated the cracked brown icon.

'Look after us, please,' she said. 'One for me and one for Reg. I'm sorry I didn't bring one for you, Helen.'

'I expect St Nicholas doesn't need candles to take notice of us,' said Helen, 'and he has a very soft spot for children.'

The Glowing Night

. . .έπηγα μές στήν φωτισμένη νύχτα.
Κ'ήπια από δυνατά κρασιά, καθώς
που πίνουν οί άνδρειοι της ήδονης.

I went into the glowing night,
And drank of dark wines, such as
the daring in their body's passion drink.
I Went C. P. Cavafy

Helen and Angela heard the screaming as they were about to plunge their spoons into a chocolate and cream sponge which they had not been able to resist when passing the patisserie. Rufus, the deerhound, raised himself to his feet in alarm. In the street they found Mrs Samagdios leant against a wall, her mop abandoned at her feet, a tea towel clutched in one forlornly waving hand, the other hand on her heart. Her screams had subsided into moans.

'Is kaput,' she gasped. 'Danish is kaput.'

Angela put a consoling arm around the woman's shaking shoulders. Helen and Rufus, with forensic interest, peered into the opened doorway at the sprawled body. There was a fusty sharp smell of faeces and a circling cloud of flies. A black quivering stream of ants had settled round a congealed dribble of blood which had issued from somewhere in the blonde motionless head. Helen rang the police station.

Dimitri sat without thought in the air conditioned cold of the Danish embassy. His journey had been infuriatingly difficult to arrange. The flight from Toronto had been long and sleepless; the changeover at Heathrow confusing and crowded; the taxis at Athens apparently on strike. Sweat was trickling down his body under his ironically unsuitable sweatshirt. He had not thought about clothes for the heat, he had forgotten his sunglasses. Everything was wrong. He was travelling toward the death of his best friend, a woman whom he had known for twenty years. They had been bound together by their academic and literary interests, their increasingly intimate correspondence and their meetings at conferences on this or that continent, in which they talked as intently and passionately as they might, in another life, have made love.

The door opened and a neat young official returned with forms for Dimitri to sign. When he had signed, and was apparently accepted as the person who belonged to his passport, he was given a spatter of facts. The police declared it an accidental death. Haemorrhage caused by the skull hitting a marble internal step. A trip or slip, maybe, no-one would ever know. Sometimes only a slight blow could cause this catastrophic outcome. The post mortem had been conducted in Rhodes. The body, unofficially identified as Sasha Holm, sixty-nine year old single female Danish national, now reposed in Rhodes and needed a formal identification, collection and transport to wherever was wished. The effects were still on the island, in safe keeping in the office of the letting agency. This was their number. They would arrange shipment of the effects, if he wished, or he could collect. The young man would arrange the identification process in Rhodes. Someone would meet Dimitri at the airport to accompany him to the mortuary. Did he have a flight?

He gave the details, 'Then I will go to the island,' he said.

'I am sorry for your loss,' said the official, with the first intimation of humanity in his quizzical expression: who was this old woman to you?

'She was my sister soul, my anima, the mother of my work. Irreplaceable,' said Dimitri, not caring that the question was not audibly asked. The answer produced concealed embarrassment. The smooth-skinned young man cleared his throat and tapped the form on the desk absent-mindedly, as if politely ignoring a fart. Dimitri found himself thinking that if the diplomatic safety of Denmark was in the hands of such emotional cretins, it was likely that they would soon find Russia on their doorsteps.

Irini and Helen and Rufus sat with Dimitri in *T'Asteio*. The locals were respectfully subdued at their table, refraining from loud tetchy commentaries on the events of the day which usually occupied them at this hour. Everyone knew that the young man was a friend of the Danish woman. He had visited her in past years.

He had wanted to see the room where she was found. Irini begged Helen to accompany them. Irini found it very difficult to switch off her happy holiday manager persona and become a kind of undertaker. Helen, on the other hand, had been used to dealing with people who were in the throes of absorbing bad news. Dimitri had stood silently in the little *salone*, until Helen touched his arm and intimated it was time to leave.

'I am sorry,' said Dimitri, shifting in his chair and moving his glass of beer on the table, 'I cannot seem to find any words.'

'You must be exhausted,' said Helen. 'You've been travelling for four days. We'll eat in tonight.' It had been decided that Helen would offer her spare bedroom. Nobody liked the idea of him being alone in a hotel or a holiday apartment.

'I hope it is good we have delivered the suitcases to Helen's house?' said Irini. 'I don't know, maybe you do not want to take everything home?'

'I will go through it all,' he said, 'but she needs nothing now,' and for the first time he felt the tears gather in his eyes.

'Helen?'

'Yes.'

'Could you come here?'

Dimitri was sitting with Sasha's laptop open on a small table, with Rufus companionably at his feet, 'I was looking for her contacts, to start letting people know. I found this.' He clicked on a file marked *Dimitri*. 'Sit down,' he said, getting off the chair.

Helen sat down and read.

The Island

Tuesday 5th

11.45 am

I am writing to you, Dimitri. Whether it will ever be sent and whether you will wish to read it, is not clear. But you are the only person who might, at least, receive it. Some of it you will know very well, you have been a generous confidant over the years, as I hope have I, but now I am going to try to write without sparing myself any of the stark details which I have ignored, glossed over and edited in the constant story-telling of my life. I will pretend that you are here and I am speaking to you . . .

'I should not be reading this,' said Helen, turning away from the screen.

'She's dead,' said Dimitri curtly. 'Please, Helen. Read. I need a cigarette. Read.'

Dimitri went out onto the balcony. Helen obediently settled into the chair and read.

. . . For the past four nights, sleep has been achieved, fitfully, through alcohol, cannabis and diazepam. Maybe what I write and the effort of writing it will, at least, be a more benign soporific. For me, I mean. It may even be for you, in its tedium.

You know how it has been with me these past months. In March, which now feels like the calm before an endless storm, my only discomfort was the mild ache of separation, assuaged by the winter phone calls, in which his dark solid voice steadied me.

Then they found the cancer and swiftly, giving me no time for thought and fear, they cut it out. The surgeon smiled plumply and said how well I had done, meaning how well he himself had done I suppose.

For two weeks into May I was dissociated, withdrawn, struggling to manage my students (who, in turn, were struggling with end of year papers) without infecting them too heavily with the burden of my dismay. It sounds a slight, trivial word but it seems the best one to describe how it felt, as if I were a child. Profound dismay. Bottomless dismay. I could not fully understand why I felt this fall into a different world, a different person.

The phone calls from the island had diminished when the holiday season started. He had relatives arriving. The yard was busy with people suddenly deciding that work had to be done, despite the long months of winter having come and gone with little or nothing to do. He could no longer ring me and be sure of an uninterrupted conversation.

There had been missed calls, while I was miserably being processed through the hospital's managing machine, but this had happened anyway. My schedule is not regular. I did not tell him of the corruption in my flesh. When a call was made which I could take, I sat staring at the trilling creature on the table. This time I let it ring, as if I were a stranger staring at someone else's calling phone. I was a stranger to myself. After five silent minutes I touched his number. When he answered, I could not speak. When I finally spoke, my words were dead, uninformative, confused. When I pressed End, I knew that something had been damaged.

A week later, another phone call. This time the old delight was almost resurrected. I was able to give a version of the truth: cancer, but dealt with, no sign of any more, I was alright. I almost believed it, too, but, but cancer is not like that. Cancer brings with it permanent disease. He sounded anxious. I said it was all fine, all good now. The first lie I told him.

I was due to leave in two weeks and there was silence from the phone.

There was something new in this silence. It was as if a great fissure had opened up from which a dark stream was pouring. I had tried to close it, to pretend that it did not now exist, but he had not spoken to the same woman in those last two phone calls. I had been mutilated and it felt more powerful than the nine years of our . . . what should I call it? Association? It was the beginning of the end. I was to know myself as truly old, dogged by scans and hospital visits, watched for more blight which would have to be cut out, until my body became nothing but a battlefield on which death would win.

It had changed everything. I was no longer the woman who had slowly opened again, after we met in the little bar (you know it well) where I often went with a book to read in the evening, when people have showered and dressed and come out like butterflies emerging from the chrysalis of the hot sweating day. I like the noisy constant movement and the colour of the fairy-light streets at the port, where the sea lies, like a huge docile animal resting on its paws in summer idleness.

We spoke occasionally if we happened to be sitting next to each other. I have always felt comfortable with men who use their hands to work. It comes from the hours with my father watching him making and mending things at home. Sewing our shoes on a heavy iron last, if they came apart. Sweating and grimacing over the obdurate clay soil to grow vegetables. Mending window frames, chair legs, wardrobe doors. Once he made a great snake of a rope ladder with rope as thick as my arm, so that we could climb up into our horse chestnut tree. I still have it, slowly rotting to dust. I watched him, later, with his sturdy, stout-bellied cruiser; rubbing down, varnishing, oiling, scraping, his strong forearms burnt brick brown by the sun, the hairs golden.

Sailors are careful with the vagaries of wind, current, tide and respectful of the elements. They must make a pact with powerful wild things, through their bodies.

I felt at ease with Damiano, with his sawdusty hair and battered hands. It was possibly in the second or third year of my innocent safety that he proposed a visit to my rented house, one street back from the busy sea front. Maybe these echoes of my father and even the small similarities to Bjorn, the sudden smile which transformed a grim rain-beaten face, the shrewd and kindly assessment of the eyes, had lulled me into undue familiarity. I was ashamed to think that my sexuality, which I thought was mingled with Bjorn in his ashes, was alive and seeping out of my pores, like a scent. You know, Dimitri, that I was stunned and grieving at that time. My persona, not chosen but imposed upon me, was that of the sexless widow.

I did not tell you of this, did I, Dimitri? It felt like a betrayal of Bjorn. You know, and I will always bless you for it, how losing Bjorn smashed my life into bits. It had been the first time I allowed grief to overwhelm me. But 'allowed' is not right; there was no choice.

I told myself that it was the sad silent emptiness of my life in our country which drew me back to the island and its constantly shifting beauty, humming with music and laughter. Visitors came. They were protection from the importunate anachronistic flirtation which Damiano pressed upon me, watching me with meaningful steadiness, if we found ourselves occasionally in the same place, a shop or a taverna; seizing my hand and kissing it, if we met in a quiet street; muttering what I thought were ridiculous comments which no sane woman would take seriously, if we passed each other, but which reminded me of Bjorn and those moments when he whispered words I could believe. My skin. My eyes.

I did not stay away from him, Dimitri. Like a shepherd clothing a new born lamb in the fleece of a stillborn to deceive the mother into suckling another's baby, I clothed him in Bjorn's shadow. It was ravishing to feel wanted again.

That foolhardy mantra triumphed: the only deathbed regret is for things you have not done.

Although the couplings could never be frequent or assured, I was very surprised to find that he remembered them, as if they were individually beautiful beads on a necklace. I have the habit of remembering, because all experience is fuel for the engine of my work. Every meeting had its own mood and pace, like different pieces of music by the same composer. Years later, they were often the starting point of our phone conversations. For him it was usually the first time, when what he had thought would be a quietly routine encounter, although he never said this, turned into a thunderclap of pleasure. (This is my word, of course, to try to capture the breathlessness and stammering excitement of the way he spoke about it.) The other times, in their more leisured and adventurous ways, were always available to us, recreated between us: 'You remember when . . .?' For me, it was when I took off my kaftan on one of our last mornings, and let him take me in his arms, naked in the daylight. This was the only pleasure I had ever refused him. Remember how old I am. It may be the bravest thing I have ever done. As I pulled the silk over my head, he drew his breath through his teeth. This small sound of delight and gratitude lingered in my skin, like a caress.

Dimitri, this was real. It is also a construct of my mind. Can we ever know the difference? Must we know?

I have never been beautiful but, with Damiano, I began to be happy again. First gently, unexpectedly, then wildly happy. This was what shone in my eyes and the way I moved. It flamed out like a beacon, so that there began to be other men on the island who stared and smiled and started conversations and offered me lifts up the hills and shade on their verandas and held out their hands to guide me onto their boats to look at the fish. It was as if I were swimming in a sea of sexual desire.

You saw this, one year when I came back. I lied to you, Dimitri. I knew I was lying when I said that nothing had happened, but I dared not admit the crude facts. I apologise. You would have understood. This is why I am writing to you, now.

And so to now. To the terrible Now. No visits. No phone calls. No message codes. Three and a half days of silence and an empty street and an empty bar and only the noise of him in the workshop which I can hear on my terrace. He has always come to me in the first few days, so that we can join together properly, but not this time.

I do not know where you are, Dimitri, on this day. I think you are going on holiday soon. I have thought of ringing you, emailing, begging you to come here. This must show you how desperate I have been feeling. What do I want? I want your tall calm body beside me, not sexually, but as a kind of loving son, as you could be and you so often gently behave. A son who can be told these secrets and who will not be embarrassed and discomfited by the knowledge of my absurd frailty, my final unslakeable thirst. I want your humour and your sensitivity and I want you to make me feel that there will be something else, somewhere to travel toward. Because Now, there is nothing.

When I arrived he had come to me as he does, magically appearing as soon as I had finished all the unpacking and had changed out of my travelling clothes. He had started to find me like this, as soon as I arrived, some years ago, and, if there were only seconds of possible time, he would hold my face and stare into it, cupping his hand between my thighs, as if re-establishing his ownership. I don't think he could ever believe that I had no other sexual partners, until, maybe, this last winter.

I flew toward him.

We hugged and drew away to look at each other. Smiling. Those greeting smiles were like the smiles of children when they see someone whose love they trust. I was struck by how young and well he looked. He is almost my age but we are worn out much earlier than they, with our complicated lives of luxury. His skin was very smooth and tanned. I buried my face in his neck. We drew apart again and I saw in his eyes a cloud of . . . what was it? Something disconsolate, saddened? It was fleeting and I could almost dismiss it, but it took an unusual disconcerting minute for him to get an erection and we were both aware of it. We were awkward and unbalanced together. It felt that this was all being done because we had expected it to happen and could not think of a way of not doing it, without admitting to something too complicated, too difficult to know. These first encounters were always very quick because they were dictated by my arrival and not by opportune times. They were about possession, not pleasure.

There had been something wrong about this coupling which crushed my heart.

I knew, and I had known, that it would end. Had it ended now?

And, of course, also I do not know, cannot know, do not want to know, hope, pray that I am wrong, that I am misinterpreting, projecting my own distaste and disgust with my ravaged body, or maybe fiercely not wanting to know, what I always knew, that at some point he would simply see what I am, an old and exhausted woman, worn out by loss and work and life.

Since then, eighty-seven and a half wakeful hours of hell, more than three days in which memories have been masochistically flayed, opening wounds in my mind. Or was it *all* the product of a wound in my mind? The place where reason cannot reach?

It is now 3.30 in the afternoon. I have been writing and staring across the sea and aching with loneliness for three and three-quarter hours, on the roof terrace under my umbrella, where I can look up and see a rectangle of dazzling blue between the sharp white walls of the houses and, further out, the broad dark water.

Since that meeting, every moment in the day when he would normally come to me has come and gone in silence. The morning on his way to work when sometimes the street is empty and he can slip through the door. The evening, before returning home. Once he came in the dead of night. Three times, when anything else was impossible, we made love in the rubbish-laden back of the yard, filled with crates and timber and broken machinery. This was desperately reckless.

Danger was our constant companion. His English, the *lingua franca*, is very limited. I am equally poor in his language. We developed a complicated series of codes and signals. It reminded me of the spy stories. We were spies, communicating secrets, making assignations. If his motorbike was placed next to the oleander, it was safe for me to go in. If my green towel was hanging over the roof terrace railing, it was safe for him to come. If there were a knotted rope on the little table outside the workshop, he would see me late in the evening at the bar. Every day, if he had not abruptly disappeared, there would at least be some 'chance' meeting at the baker's perhaps, or at the top of the steps to my house, where I would look up and see him leaning against the wall in the shadow and, if there were no-one, we could touch. We only once used the phones. They were too dangerous with the possibility that someone would lean over his shoulder – *Who's that?* When the winter phone calls were decided, there was another code of signals.

No visit. No phone call.

I go through every possible permutation of the meaning of this severance. Have we been found out in some definite, proved way? But this is untenable. He has often apologised for the difficulties we sometimes had in finding ways to meet, told me of unexpected family developments or important work, which meant he could not come. So there have been days of silence before, but then I had the life jacket of physical confidence; now the cancer has left me in a dark sea without the strength to stay afloat alone. The cancer has shattered the illusion of my invulnerability, even though the fat man, surrounded by his meerkat students, told me in his self-congratulatory way that it was all clear, all gone. It has killed something joyful and innocent and hopeful, which, despite so many years, was still alive in me.

I sit with Angela or Helen or Reg or Tom, trying to listen to what they are saying and to laugh in the right places.

His absence at the bar, in the street, every time he is not there, is like a paper cut, invisibly splitting open my skin, bloodless and painful.

The yard is on the way to the closest beach. I cannot feel any need coming from him, when I walk past like a ghost and hear the sawing and hammering rattling out of the cavernous workshop.

I try to keep busy. I work on the saga book, surprised that I can do this, but still mildly anaesthetised by old expectations and hope.

I need to stay safely for periods of time within my writing mind, the private place where words on paper are all that matter; even in writing this searing eulogy I have to keep searching for words and expression, which makes my brain feel alive and of value.

By some synchronistic chance, I brought out the English edition of Lawrence Durrell's *Alexandria Quartet*. His preoccupation, mania, obsession is the careful, linguistically pyrotechnical delineation and dissection of the layers of pain connected to the experience of the pathological uncertainty and endless questioning of those who find themselves helplessly bound to another. His meticulous compassion for the idiocy of the human heart consoles me in a bleak way.

Durrell loved Cavafy. When I was young, studying in America, I discovered Cavafy, the old Alexandrian who wrote with such tenderness and gratitude of his secret homosexual couplings. Repeatedly he conjures up his memories of the beauty of experiences of furtive hasty fleeting erotic encounters, knowing with candour how obscene they were thought to be. Showing us, with his quiet unshrinking acceptance of his pleasure and love, how obscene the disapproving contempt was.

Back to the demented old woman that I now am: mad fantasies and urges pounce on me.

I want to beg him to tell me that he is not coming back, so that I will stop hoping. Nothing would stop me hoping, however cruelly he spoke; but he would not be cruel. He would be polite and possibly even say *Sorry*. Over the years he has learned to say *Sorry* when I made him see that he had hurt me by one of his unexplained retreats and this is a courteous place. The politeness would send me mad with pain. Besides, we do not have enough common language for this conversation, and it is impossible in any.

I tell myself: you do not need to ask, when there is silence. Silence is the answer to the question.

I imagine threatening to make a terrible scene, slapping him, taking up one of his chisels. He is not a violent man. He would simply walk away. He has done nothing but ask and take what he was given.

I have often wondered where he really lives in his mind. He and Bjorn are, were, the same. Their minds are, were, not clothed with words. Even if we had language, I do not think I would know more of him.

The sky is roaring with heat. I live in a silk shirt. But the beautiful clothes which expressed all my wild happiness hang in the wardrobe as if brought by some other woman. I shiver, and the shaking is a kind of physical disbelief. How can the whole world have become so changed?

The night is a bad time. The hours from ten to one are filled with my longing. Every creak and rattle of the house is the sound of his footstep. I still leave the key under the paving stone. I cannot bear to bolt the door. One night I slid the bolt, feeling that it might give me some peace to know that, even if he tried, he would not be able to come in and I might sleep, but then I was unable to sleep, listening for the sound of the latch and the door straining against the bolt, so that I could leap out of bed and run to open it.

Could deathbed regrets be any more painful than this?

I am not a good crier. Tears do not come easily. I cannot bawl into my pillow. In the deep heat of the night I sit on the roof, when the whole town is sleeping, and stare without sight at the dim black sea. This is my grief.

It is seven o'clock on this hot evening. I am making a tomato salad with the enormous Greek tomatoes, which are the only ones which still taste like tomatoes and not to be had in our country. I have bought lamb and made a kind of stew with beans. I could have eaten like this last night, but a friend was going to Katerina's and I suddenly wanted someone to make me a proper meal. I ate far more than I needed. Katerina told me about her damaged shoulder which is making it hard for her to manage the trays and how they are now demanding even more tax on all the drinks in the bars. Her husband has not had work for two years. She looks tired. A tiresome garrulous Norwegian woman, with a totally silent husband, talked non-stop in a guttural self-satisfied tone about some extraordinarily inconsequential details of her wealthy life. Katerina smilingly listened with her island courtesy.

I am a woman who has made her life alone, because, although my heart and body were shackled to Bjorn, our lives were separate and he was rarely able to have anything like a holiday. I left him and came alone to rest and refresh myself. When he died, my holidays continued like everything else, except that there was the dull physical ache, in my stomach, of his absence from the world.

I became an icon for Damiano, painted with the red of strength, independence, self-sufficiency. The gold leaf, the gleam of sex, was slowly applied. I was not to slide into dusty atrophy, after Bjorn's death and the years of silent mourning.

I became what Damiano wanted; a wild happy hedonistic bird of paradise, alighting gently into his life, for him to enjoy without any need for either of us to be weighed down by reality, reproaches, regrets, or fears. He falls in love with this fantasy. He can reveal any dangerous wish, expose his need, beg and plead for this or that favour like a pilgrim, give licence to the tenderness which lies in the shadow of the island's traditional life and in their songs. All of this in halting words translated into the language of hands and eyes and bodies.I am his private dream of flesh and blood. I am his secret woman and he has me in his hand. And then, this last winter he proposes a new game of telephone make-believe: that through the winter, we extend the fantasy that our mundane, conscientious, task-filled lives are simply the periphery of this golden worship. I thought at least the sound of our voices would link us, if not the words.

Dimitri, all I can say is that this is how it felt and, if I were swindled, what did he take from me without giving of himself?

For the long months apart, the telephone held us together, and then . . . and then on the phone he hears fear, distress, depression, even a trace of anger, and worse, fatigue and dismissal. All of these things were in that incoherent phone call after the surgery. We try to patch it up, but a bird of paradise with patches is not the same.

And what did he see when we met? Did he see the struggle in me to be what I had been and what I could not be any more? Reality had broken through. I was powerless to prevent him from feeling that something had changed. He felt me unresponsive and heavy, like a badly trimmed boat. Damiano and Bjorn and my father and their boats. These men do not use words. Just before Papi sank into his morphined death, he kissed my face in an agony of passion, but he never told me he loved me.

10.25 pm

The house is panting in the heat. The streets of the town are muffled by the suffocating weight of the dark air, as I am, by the weight of my loneliness.

Wednesday 6th
10.00 am

Today is slightly less burningly hot but the wind blows everything back and forth. The old shutters bang about tirelessly.

Did he see that I am nearer death than I know? A friend went to a healer who used crystals. She met the woman once and did not go back. She said that in the room she had a certainty that this woman was going to die very soon. The healer, who had appeared to be perfectly well, died within three months, of lung cancer. She had never smoked and was a devout Baha'i.

I wonder if he felt this chill, which perhaps he could not interpret, except to want, like my friend, to leave and not come back.

He has also had his threats. He had a small stroke four summers ago. We are both being besieged by death, which is padding around us, snarling.

There have always been these times of sudden withdrawal. I know how he can chill with his displeasure; the hard edge which he turned to me if he could not get his way, if there was some obstacle to our meeting. I have seen him screw a child's ear, making silent tears flow, if the boys have been playing in the dust near a freshly painted boat. The stray cats are hurled out by their scruffs. The schizophrenic man and the Down's woman are angrily growled at to leave the workshop, if they linger.

On the other hand, the children confidently go in to him, a little too confidently to my risk-averse eyes, with small items for him to mend. I also very much like his delicate references to his family, always respectful and filled with a proprietorial affection. I parenthesise the times of passion, when things are said to express the heat of the moment.

If he were denied a meeting he would click his tongue, walk rapidly away. This might lead to a day or two of brooding silence, sometimes more; but this time there has been nothing to spark his disappointed anger, only the fumbling meeting in which we somehow missed each other's grasp.

The writing yesterday was exhausting, but it has helped. Or am I, even now, still reconstructing this nightmare into a story, a fairy tale, a myth?

Thursday 7th
11.00 am
I woke up to the rose-grey dawn and walked to the beach to wait for the sun to top the mountain ridge, a sparkler turning into a ball of fire, instantly blazing over the harbour, taking the air out of our lungs. The water is warm and I lie on my back, giving myself to the undulations of the tideless sea. It is early so the beach is deserted, patiently waiting to be filled with people. Drowned in all the noise of my chattering brain, until today I have foregone this habitual tryst with the crystal island water, the sea, which was my father's mistress, which called me to buy my stone house on the headland above our own dark slanting ocean.

I went to the WiFi bar at three o'clock where I catch up on the emails, with a double espresso, my small fee for connection to the world.

On my ambling way home, Tom was at the bar, so I joined him for a glass of beer to see suddenly, with a shock, that Damiano was sitting at a table in his dark glasses. Why do I never recognise him in his sunglasses, as if his eyes are all that I see and know when I look at his face? He would whisper to look, look at him, touching my chin with his fingers, making me stare into his eyes, while he fucked with the single-minded determination of a marathon runner. I am angry. I am so angry that he sat there as if nothing has happened.

We finished our drinks and Tom and I walked together up the side of the town square. Damiano came up and walked between us, his hand firm, unseen, on the small of my back. This used to be a signal. What is it now? A joke? A habit of flirtation?

I was more drunk than I should be on two glasses of beer. I remember a phone conversation, after which he rang me again to say, 'I love you'.

'Sleep well, darling,' we would say.

'Take care. I love you.'

If love has died between us, like a child, I will not refuse to remember it.

Trudging up the thousand steps, I hardly saw the constant snapshots of beauty, a narrow view of the port glittering with sun and boats between the walls of two houses, the yellow and blue mansions rising grandly in their balconied splendour behind the giant sighing pine trees where incongruous lines of washing blow in domestic banality, the glimpses of dark, leafy courtyards, radiantly pink with flowers. In the village I sat alone in the taverna which juts out from the hillside and drank prosecco, ate yoghurt and honey with strawberries. The boy waiter was helpful and sweet, but he stared from his doorway at the old woman who drank alone and contemplated the olive groves, over which the shadows inched, as the sun sank below the mountain ridge.

I was thinking, as if picking at a scab, of the times Damiano had come to me and watched me sleep and left me undisturbed. He would carefully describe the things untidily lying about the room, as if it were important to prove that he had been there. I had no idea if it were true, although it seemed to be. I found it annoying, a waste of our precious time.

I had a good friend a few years ago. A very beautiful woman. She was sixty-five when I first met her. We used to go to the theatre together and she was always catching someone's eye. 'The twinkle,' she called it. 'I do love a twinkle,' she would say. She told me one day that she had been tweezing a white hair out of her chin for five years and suddenly one morning she saw it and could not be bothered. Shortly after she succumbed to Alzheimer's and in six months was a nappy-swaddled derelict.

I walked back down the uneven steps. I was too drunk to do it without weaving slightly. I stumbled against the wall of Katerina's taverna whilst negotiating a greeting with her husband.

I was going to return to the bar and get a drink at eleven when it is usually busy and sociable at this time of year. I lay down to rest for an hour or two.

I woke at one. The rooms were all lit. The *salone* was untidy with my clothes and shoes and towels. There was a plate of quartered orange on the floor, covered in ants. The tap in the bathroom was running softly and it took me some time to identify the sound and turn it off. The shutters had been bolted against the sun and the rooms were stifling without the soft sea breeze.

I turned off all the lights and crawled back onto my bed.

This morning I see myself with my hair sticking up and the deeply etched wrinkles and eye makeup smeared down my cheeks. I am reminded of *Death in Venice*, with poor Dirk Bogarde, dying on the beach in his dribbling mascara.

What is this narcissistic sludge which I am writing? Is it doing anything? Perhaps it is keeping me sane? I notice that I am starting to find small sparks of humour. Humour and mental illness are incompatible. 'Cosmic humour', Kohut called it. One of my heroes of psychoanalysis. An American. He believed that we need it for sanity. The art of seeing the deep absurdity of our demanding hearts.

8.45 pm

Donald from the English book shop and I packed up to go our separate ways, sometime in the late afternoon.

We had been joined by various ex-pats and their visitors, during the two hours in which we sat chatting. I eschewed the beer which had such a disastrous effect yesterday mixed with the prosecco. I found my watch and my glasses on the bathroom floor by the toilet, a cup of coffee was in the shower tray, my bra was entangled in my feet when I woke and it appears that I may have singed the tablecloth. I'm afraid it made me smile, which is not a responsible attitude to inebriation.

The conversation on these occasions is usually concerned with the minutiae of events on the island. The issue of whether the dance club should have decided to charge an entrance fee for the children's show that night took up at least twenty minutes. I feel that I am in a genteel old world of small but mighty concerns.

As I walked back to the house he came up the steps from the sea front, carrying a coiled length of metal stay, his reason to be away from the workshop. He spoke quickly. He had come the night before, there was no key, he had banged on the door without result. He said smiling, miming, that he had been knocking for a long time. I said I was asleep. These conversations in the street are fraught with the pressure of discovery. I was shocked, too shocked to show anything of my rage and regret.

Why did he leave me alone for so long to wander in the labyrinth of my disordered mind? That graceful happy woman may be lost for ever. I have met a hopeless shadow of myself which has enshrouded me and my anger encases my body like armour. I cannot imagine myself able to lay my hands gently on his skin. I want to punch and scratch and bite. I want to leave scars.

Friday 8th
11.30 am

I did not know whether he would come again. I wanted him to come and I wanted to kill him in equal measure. It was very hot in the house. He cannot understand why I do not use the air con and is grumpy if it is off. I put it on. I worked on my eyes with my brushes and colours, trying to recapture the gleam of happiness.

When he came in he put something soft carefully into my hand. It was a pink rose. 'Sazzi,' he said, his way of saying Sasha. The perfume was powerful, stronger than that of any flower in my garden at home, filling the room with fresh sweetness impossible to capture in a bottle.

We climbed into the bed and pulled the sheet over us like an old married couple.

I was nervous and tense and did what always pleased him, which made him groan and suck in his breath, which pleases me. Then he did the things I like, in his methodical stern way, manipulating my body this way and that. I like best the expression on his face, which is of deep seriousness at these times. His eyes compel me to see him as he contemplates each way we are joined, as if it were an image that he is burning into his mind.

He pulled me onto him and held me still, stroking me. I began to cry out, louder and louder as he started to move, unable to control my voice as if I had become his sounding board. Even at the time I thought, anyone hearing this sound would know what it expresses. The sound of the body singing its pleasure, triumphantly independent, at last, of the mind.

Normally he is very concerned about any noise we might make, because the windows are open and voices are heard everywhere from the interiors of the houses. It surprised me very much that he did not put his hand over my mouth warningly, as he has done sometimes. The family next door are away, however, and there are only tourists like me on the other side.

The effort of holding back had disappointed his penis into sulky retreat. He took the smooth silky thick curve of flesh in his hand with urgent brutal action, rebuking and exciting me. When he was ready I took him into my mouth.

With him, it was a *directed* process, always toward pleasure. His pleasure, my pleasure. I was cherished lover, hesitant virgin, rampantly demanding mistress, adored plaything, cuddled child and whore. Through the years, as we became confident with each other, it sometimes became impossible to distinguish who was losing whose mind.

We ended in our usual way. He puts on his clothes, while I sit by him and stroke and kiss him. We go to the door, where I wait while he gently opens it and listens to see if the street is empty before he slips out.

I did not sleep.

Again, this meeting was out of joint. I had not been able to let him join me and he had felt it. I had been alone in my pleasure and, thus, still lonely. His was functional and did not resonate within me. Even his absence of concern about the noise feels like a small dismissal, I cannot explain why. Something has gone.

You see, do you, Dimitri, how, with overweening arrogance, I decide on the reality of what is happening between Damiano and I? Where is my unknowing? Where is the zen? I fashion a tragedy from each small event. My mind is bent on destruction and there is nothing more powerful than the perversity of a despairing disappointed heart.

Sunday (I think) 10th
2.55 am

No sleep, despite my remedies.

Yesterday I got up and found the sun shouting through my windows. A fresh heat. I thought I would walk to the sandy beach. I saw him as I passed, he was outside on his phone, speaking affectionately and animatedly, his back straight and one leg bent behind the other in a relaxed youthful attitude. By the evening his body is stiffened and his face is etched around the jowls. The long hot day takes its toll.

At the packed beach, Lefteri was raking the shingle. I had not seen him before today. He shook my hand and what do I think of the cactus garden which he has made? I tell him it is beautiful and how fit he looks.

In the evening I half ate a tomato salad and went to the bar. I sat with my iPod listening to something which had been part of the musical accompaniment to the affair. There is so much music which I cannot bear to hear. I asked for a small metaxa and received what seemed to be half a litre. Metaxa was an adventure for me. I never drink metaxa. I seriously wondered how long it would take me to sip away this enormous drink and whether I would be able to handle dignified payment and the walk home.

He was not there.

I tried to look with proper attention at the houses climbing up the steep slopes surrounding the harbour, each one painted separately in its own allotted colours, each slightly askew from its neighbours, so distinct and sharp in the last rays of the sun that they look like cardboard cut-outs from a child's book, the ochre of the tiled roofs, the yellow and blue of the walls, the green of the shutters, the white and blue painted steps, the mosaic pattern of the flagstones on the street, the icon red of the archways, the small bunches of drying flowers hung upside down at doors, the murmur of voices at tables, laughter, the clatter of dishes and trays, the faint scent of herbs always in the air from the hillsides and the herb shop close by, the smell of the ovens, where the lamb and chicken and beef are drawing in the spices and the wine in the slow heat. I wanted to imprint it all in my mind, to create a place where I could go and know I had been, with a solidity of experience as deep and concentrated as that of this moment. I wanted to feel that it was etched so far down that, even in the dark clouds of Alzheimer's, I might be able to reach it, this memory steeped, like the lamb, in strong deep pleasure. I want these images and sounds and scents tattooed on my brain.

When I leave this island I shall be sailing into a hell of emptiness.

The mountains have faded from pink to grey in the setting sun. This fading is like my own. It is, for some minutes, a huge glowing rosy display, dwarfing the houses, mocking the little yellow lights of the town, but it subsides as quickly into blank grey darkening rock.

I was thinking that although I constantly assured myself that this would 'obviously' end, I had no more idea of the torturing reality than a child's or a suicide's idea of death. Like an adolescent I had simply flirted with the abstract formulation of the end, in terrifying dangerous ignorance.

But then, it is more than the end of us. It is the end of me.

Dimitri, do you remember how broken down and husked I was, after Bjorn died? How there was almost pleasure in feeling that no-one would ever lay their hand on me again? As if this final mourning would continue for ever, as it should. He had given me so much, unstintingly, never asking for anything more than the domestic irregular evenings of food and wine and beautifully familiar, utterly satisfying love. I know, I'm skirting over the blackness of his addiction and the horror of his final descent into uncomprehending death and my anguished guilt that I had not given myself to him in a publicly recognised way and set up home and poured the booze down the sink. But afterwards there was that peace, that what I could give him was my infinite fidelity.

This reawakening was a betrayal of Bjorn but he would have understood in his straightforward, animal way. Bjorn saw through every one of my personae: lecturer, writer, respectable house-owning feminist. He saw through them all to my skin. He smelt the need in my skin.

I am quite aware of the psychological explanations as to why I have remained so powerfully the servant of my body. Why touch is more necessary than food or drink. We are supposed to 'grow out of this'. But some of us do not have it in the first place and the lack of it haunts us. I have gone through my life bewitched and enslaved by my body's need to be stroked and wondered at and kissed and pleasured. My mother was a cold woman, a nurse. I was handled like an infectious patient.

I still keep coming back to this death, like a dog to a pile of unfamiliar shit. Why? Why?

Perhaps Damiano needed most of all to convince himself repeatedly that he could have me, however and whenever he wanted. It had nothing to do with me at all; everything to do with his need to feel this power.

The rubbish strewn backyard of the workshop, where we made love three times, is an interesting metaphor. The mess of love in the discarded debris of life. It is strange, this disgusting backyard, when, inside, the tools are neatly hung on the wall in oiled rows, the machinery carefully covered against the dust and the floor swept each night. Perhaps, despite all the tenderness and the sophistication and ingenuity of his love-making, despite his assiduous attention to my pleasure, his sex lies in a filthy backyard of his mind.

Oh Cavafy, how you would understand! Although, as with most gay men, the thought of female passion would produce a shiver of disgust. None of us have open minds.

Sometimes I remember, with longing, how Bjorn, too, rejoiced in the sight of me, would often walk behind me to watch my body moving. When we had losses and miseries together, Bjorn took me to his bed and fucked me through the passion of sadness into calm. He swaddled me up and held me, when I was exhausted and weeping and unwashed from the two days at my brother's deathbed. But Bjorn had no wife or family, I was all of that to him. He had the space for me.

Dimitri, I put the key in my bag and closed my bedroom door, so that I could not hear anything in the street. Now I will take three more diazepam to slam my mind shut.

There was a way of being without this man, before it began. There must be now.

Monday 11th
8.05 am

There is not a soul to whom I could reveal all this without seeing contempt, pity, in their faces.

You know how pragmatic we are about sex, as a nation. Of course, they say, have some holiday fun with this bit of rough; but they do not remotely agree that there could be anything authentic in this relationship. In fact it is not a relationship at all, is it? Where is the commonality? The equality of intellect or education?

I am so over-educated that the pool of available men with whom to have a 'relationship' is as small as a mosquito's arse and, besides, I have not met an intellectual man who can fuck. They can have sex, but they cannot fuck. They think too much and cannot get out of the habit.

I feel weak, this morning. I feel unable to walk to the beach and experience the few seconds in which I may see him, I may not. I cannot bear the silence of today's emptiness between us.

9.45 am

I walked to the little shop near the beach to buy cigarettes. I walked with the uprightness of a model, the balance true and the hips forward and the back straight, because I know that he might see me from the dark noisy workshop.

This is my defiance. He will not see me broken. I wonder if even you, Dimitri, if you saw me laughing with others, an attractive, happy, worldly, self-confident woman, even you might be deceived into thinking that I am alright, more than alright.

Only once have I pleaded with Damiano, one day before I was leaving, when he was behaving like an angry disappointed disapproving father or brother, stalking past me in the street, glaring with folded arms from the workshop doorway. I rang him from the beach begging him to explain his coldness. He laughed and said it was just a joke, a tease about my talking to some tourist from Holland in the bar the night before; he loved me, stop, stop, he loved me.

My sadness is not his doing, it is mine.

We have all experienced this, have we not? Suddenly a light goes out and the moth of our attraction flutters away into the dark never to return.

If we think carefully we can see that the light had begun to flicker, the current weakened by small moments of distaste, ugliness, misalignment, or there is the power cut of something which cannot be forgiven.

The darkened other is left distraught, bewildered, maddened.

I have done it. I have done this to four people and you know that one of them was Bjorn. Four years before he died, the light had guttered and died, drowned by alcohol. He staggered about the port, roaring pornographic accusations of treachery at men we had known. His Skipper would not take him when the fleet went out. Punctually, somehow, a birthday card would arrive each year, *I love you, B*, although the only times we met, at funerals and seasonal celebrations, were stiff with my appalled misery.

He sold things, borrowed, retreated into the cottage, where the dispossessed scavengers, scenting remains, took possession of his father's gold watch and his rings and sat in his cheerless parlour, drinking vodka, until he died, alone one night.

Tuesday 12th
9.48 am

I can hear the big ferry gently rumbling in the harbour, having picked up its load of passengers and freight.

Yesterday the company at the bar had become quite raucous in the increasing wind. The talk turned to those island *habitués* who were felt to be strange, to be avoided, annoying. The stories were increasingly candid, leading inevitably to the out-of-the-side-of-the-mouth revelations about which tourists were going round giving and receiving fellatio this year.

When everyone had left, I read my Durrell, trying not to care that Damiano was not there. I went to the restaurant where I always have veal. The manager, a handsome man but shy, who has known me for years but rarely makes a show of it, put his hand warmly over mine when we shook hands at this first meeting. I blessed him silently for this small comforting gesture.

The wind howled about the house all night, making everything bang alarmingly but bringing the temperature down slightly.

I wish that we could have one proper conversation, but the one who is being left always wants the conversation.

The conversation has no starting point because there is only one person who wants to talk and, in this case, we have always been unable to talk in that way.

The familiar places and faces, the warmth and welcoming hugs and kisses from locals, the light and the mutating beauty of the sea and the mountains, are all counterpointed with this discordant descant of my disbelief that I am being set aside.

Two Swedish women asked me to join them for dinner last night. After the meal they decided to go to a bar at the second bay, quite a walk, and I was tired of being funny and entertaining and of hearing the locals contemptuously reduced to caricatures. I left them wandering along the port road, beside the packed rows of obscenely expensive boats, arm in arm, laughing, the sea beyond the boats rippling calmly like cobalt silk.

He passed me hurriedly in the street and gave me a muttered, routine greeting.

How do you do that to someone who for so long you have trusted to hold your secret, to behave carefully, to turn her mouth and body to yours, to answer when you called?

You do it because the light has gone out. I tell myself, there is no malice in it, no hatred, no deception. He did not want to hurt me or deceive me. His body was generous to mine and honest. When the light went out, the resonance had gone and, without it, there is nothing.

Last night I looked almost as good as I used to look, in the forgiving twilight of the street. I might as well have been a corpse.

You might say that I met my match. At heart this man was my counterpart, capable of letting himself be swept into a frenzy of imaginative passion, with one foot firmly on the hard floor of the workshop, just as I used to have one foot planted on a solid floor of books.

C. G. Jung was against the 'nothing but . . .' attitude. You have read him, Dimitri. I tell all my students to read him. Unlike some, you did as you were told. Jung felt this attitude reduced the mind. The human heart cannot be reduced to psychopathology. The Freudians say Jung is 'nothing but' a fantasist, which has its high irony.

No-one is 'nothing but' a mindless automaton of selfish neuroses. Everyone is 'both . . . and'; both Don Juan, feckless callous seducer, and yearning lover; both rapacious devouring nymphomaniac and tender sister.

Maybe he wanted to feel that he had been given a place in my life and my complicit secrecy indicated to him that he was unimportant or that I was ashamed of him.

Did he fear that he was just a part of my holiday entertainment, like the round the island trips, to be giggled about in the dim corners of the bar? Why should I assume, with contemptuous female sadism, that his endearments and gentle kindnesses (he mended a broken shutter, put a wheel back on a suitcase, brought me salts and water when I was sick one time), were only the ways of seduction? 'Nothing but . . .' you see. 'Nothing but . . .' We reduce everything in order not to see the complexity.

Maybe he, too, is exhausted by constant uncertainty. He has watched me obsessively for signs of boredom, weariness, retreat. He phones throughout the winter, trying to keep my sexual interest alive, to be reassured of it. Maybe he, too, yearns to be safely held.

Has he ever been sure which woman he is with? The lover or the amused dilettante picking up funny stories of sexual high jinks to relay at home or, with bursts of contemptuous laughter, to my acquaintances at the bar.

Emotions, like words, thoughts, are not his medium. He could only feel the intensity of my actions, my body.

'Show me,' he would say. 'Is good for you?'

'It is love,' I would say, 'it is always good with you.'

See the ambivalence of those prepositions, *for*, *with*, Dimitri. What do they reflect of how we were? There is no such thing as one truth in this dangerous pursuit.

He comes to the house, the lights are on, the door locked and no answer. Am I sitting inside deliberately making him vulnerable? Am I lying with someone else, laughing? If it were me I would have these fantasies, why not he?

Is this the final sad simple truth? The light went out because he is exhausted by our entanglement, as I too felt sometimes.

Dimitri, what do you think? For whatever reason, Damiano and I are now apart.

I have tried to imagine what you would say. I can see your gentle shrug. *These things come to an end. Love is an independent force, like the weather, outside our control. It does not rain only on the bad.* Despite the years between us, you can be so much older than I.

Wednesday 13th
7.30 am

I will have to read this all through carefully, because words are what you know, Dimitri, and I would not want you to be pained by sloppy clichés or shallow-minded banality.

I woke from a long tortuous dream in which I and my baby were waiting to be ejected from the house of the father, who insisted we leave. Could not be plainer. Or should I subject myself to analysis with some dour doctor in the city?

I sweat so badly at night that the colour from my kaftan has leached onto the sheets. Often I leave my sodden bed, to sit blindly on the terrace.

It is being packaged up, this pain, into a small parcel which can be put in a cupboard, like the photographs of Bjorn's beautiful cock which I cannot throw away, although now all of him is sunk in the black depths of the Baltic.

Our fantasies were interwoven. Damiano and I shared these aspects of each other: the idealistic, the romantic, the profoundly and determinedly sexual. We reflected each other's needs and the sides of ourselves which we could not see; my unquenchable phallic desires, which I so firmly placed in him and saw, for so long, as his; the grace and tenderness of his spirit, which he saw as mine and gave me in the rose.

Perhaps, every sexual act contains a seed of hope for growth and, for us, there was never anywhere to grow.

Is this compassionate understanding of us both, the fruit that will grow out of the flower? Can it sustain me in the wilderness of old age?

I still want to kill him.

3.00 pm

Sitting in the sandy beach taverna, eating Paulina's homemade dolmades, I wondered if it would be possible for me to return to the old love affair; the one with the island which started twenty-seven years ago. A *coup de foudre*, in which the mountains and the sea and the little town rising up the hill, finally made me understand the power of the mother world and its constant kaleidoscopic shifting colours and scents and sounds, moving, changing, revolving silently into itself, while we run in files like the ants up and down its surface, trying to keep ourselves alive until we die.

'Sazzi, why you laugh?' he would say crossly, in bed. Why did I laugh? Because so much of it felt like divine play to me. I was laughing because we were so incongruously lucky to have found so much pleasure together.

I remember the funny times and my heart smiles. The time he left his wrist brace behind (his left arm was weakened by the stroke) and had to return in a panic, which dissolved into our amusement at our ageing selves.

The time when we got our signals muddled and he came in, to surprise a visiting couple at breakfast. Out of their sight by the door, we held on to each other shaking with childlike suppressed snorting. 'So sorry. So sorry,' he whispered, as tears of laughter ran down our faces.

The many times when we caught each other's eye and delight passed between us, making us smile.

On the phone it was his laugh which warmed my spirit for another week of winter ice and snow. The sound of his laugh and the image of his smile filled me with glowing love.

And I want to kill him.

Sunday 17th
10.05 am

He came up behind me in the street. As he silently passed he put his hand softly on my back, rubbing it gently in the gesture which they use to show care, concern, pleasure. It used to mean that he would come to me, now it feels like a farewell.

I have found the music which I can bear to hear. Callas, with her incandescent voice, which the imbeciles criticised for being too passionate.

Thursday 21st
7.10 am

Oh Dimitri, I am so exhausted with this folly.

Last night I woke to see his tall shape standing at the foot of the bed. He was made of darker air than the dim tortured shadows of my room. How he got in, I don't know. I held out my arms; a child needing comfort after a nightmare. He lay with me like a trusted animal, passively allowing me to stroke and hold him, while I trembled and wept my first tears about my death.

'Why, Sazzi?' he asked, the sound of the words deep with sadness and bewilderment, 'why you not let me come to you?'

I stepped into the sea and swam toward him.

One night I will drown in this sea.

Helen sat back stiffly in her chair. Dimitri had been standing fidgeting impatiently behind her for the previous ten minutes.

'Yes?' he said.

'I had no idea of this,' said Helen.

'Who is this man?'

'Damiano? Just a local in the boatyard. It's all here.'

'I must speak with him.'

'No, you must *not*,' said Helen, twisting round in alarm.

'You do not think this man should be questioned?'

'Why? What on earth would be the point?'

'She was . . . losing her mind. She says that she might make a scene. She wants to kill him. Perhaps she breaks the rules. She threatens to make it all public, known. So, he hits her and she falls. I am Greek remember. My father came from a small island like this. Fled from the Colonels to Denmark. You do not break the rules on these islands without paying a price.'

'He had turned up. A happy ending,' Helen protested, pointing at the screen. 'I agree with you, she was lonely, drinking, smoking weed, making herself paranoid, taking all that bloody diazepam, making herself angry. Diazepam does that, you know. She was traumatised by the cancer, but she is aware how unstable she is. She says he is not violent.'

'Tchah!' Dimitri spat out, slapping the side of his head in frustration. 'You threaten a Greek, he will be violent. My father was Greek,' he repeated, 'I know about this shit.'

'Calm down,' said Helen. 'You're a Professor of Medieval Languages, not a peasant. She was an intelligent independent woman in a relationship she chose. What could you say to this man?'

'I would tell him that I hold him to account. I would tell him that I shall always curse him while I live, for taking possession of her beautiful spirit. Read it. Did he really come that night, Helen? Read it. The door is locked. She was living in her nightmare dreams all those days and nights. Perhaps a hallucination? Her mind was breaking up. Why didn't she ring me, email? I would have come and taken her away. We could have gone home to her house. She could have recovered herself. My God, what a waste. All for what? This island fuckwit?'

'It wasn't his fault,' said Helen. 'Even she says that, Dimitri. She was in shock when she came out. We could all see she was not herself. She had lost her spark. Cancer does that. We're not all brave souls who can walk through the Valley of the Shadow with a smile on our face. Sometimes I'd look at her and see the defeat. Don't blame anyone for this.'

Dimitri sat down heavily at Helen's feet and began to sob. Helen stayed quietly with him while grief filled the room. Rufus rested his head solemnly on his paws, watching in sympathy.

'My best friend,' Dimitri said. 'My beautiful friend. Why could she not see how precious and needed she was? By me. By her students. She was loved by so many people. She drives herself mad for this filthy *malaka*. For fuck sake.' Dimitri threw his hands in the air in impotent rage.

'She seems to have thought you would understand,' Helen said.

'I would have given her a slap and taken her home.'

Helen raised her eyebrows, 'How very Greek.'

'Metaphorically,' he amended. He thumped his fist on the floor, 'She should have told me. There are rules. This kind of love is just a game with words as counters. The Greeks will say anything to get what they want. They are traders.'

'She was so confused,' said Helen. 'She slumped further and further into a depression about it being over, while he seemed to be coming to her when he could. Also, frankly, the poor man couldn't do anything right. Her mind was disordered. It's given me a headache.'

'I am sorry to be brutal, Helen, but she was his whore, not his icon. He would not expect her to be faithful any more than a cat. She was pursued, stalked, staked out and possessed, then she must be available. If he lost interest, he would expect her to turn to someone else. She should have tossed her head and gone shopping, had a party, invited friends out to stay. This primitive cunt could not possibly have understood what she gave him, how she loved him. My father was the same. He left behind a string of women wailing at his grave. It's a game.'

'It was a long game. If it was just a conquest it would have ended years ago,' said Helen, reaching out to his bowed head, stroking his thick dark hair as if he were a child. 'It was a game she was happy to play.'

'But I needed her,' he said. 'I needed her. How could she waste herself in this way?'

'We don't know what happened,' Helen said. 'The truth is usually banal. She was drinking and taking drugs and she tripped and fell.'

'When I saw her,' he said, 'lying there in a white shroud, I could not touch her. People kiss their loved ones, touch their dead hands. I could not. I could only stand by her, asking *Why?* I have been with the dead. My father. My mother. They had gone. Their bodies left behind. But she had not gone, Helen.'

'She's left you with her anguish,' said Helen, stroking Rufus who had edged close to her, disturbed by Dimitri's anger. 'You'll help her to leave by forgiving her.'

Dimitri stood up brusquely and went out onto the balcony, 'So brilliant, so lovely and so fucking stupid,' he said, lighting another cigarette. 'People come to these islands and think they can make friends as if they were buying souvenirs, but these are medieval communities. In winter they shut their shops and retreat into their claustrophobic houses and their narrow alleys and their unquestioned loyalties. They have souls of rock. She would have had no deeper meaning to this man than a migrating bird.'

He stared at Helen's expensive view of the beautiful harbour, which laid itself out like an opulently jewelled, dazzling whore, bewitching, charming and faithless.

'I'll go tomorrow,' he said. 'The early ferry. I'll take her home where she will be remembered.'

'Take her home and grieve, my dear,' said Helen. 'Then return when you're ready. You're a child of the islands. After winter the herbs bloom on the bare rocks. Like these people, your heart has the warmth of rosemary and thyme.'

Dimitri stubbed out his cigarette with unnecessary force, '*Oti nanai*,' he said. 'Whatever. You're nothing but a romantic, Helen, like her.'

'Ah,' said Helen, 'what does she say about *nothing but . . .?*'

Rufus yawned with a little whine and stretched out on the warm stone floor. Faintly the chimes of the island Tannoy system floated across the harbour. *Ding Dong.* 'People are informed,' said the officious young woman who made these announcements, 'that there is to be a sale at the Home and Garden store at Little Bay on Saturday. The folk dancing will start after nine o'clock at the town square tonight. The monastery of St George in Parani has a name day next Wednesday. The last island bus will now run at ten o'clock in the evening and the Samagdios dog has gone missing again. Will anyone seeing this dog please ring the Samagdios house. This dog is the brown one with three legs and does not go far from the village.' *Bing Bong.*

Dimitri caught Helen's eye, 'Oh shit,' he said, smiling. 'These islands.'

The Harmony of the Stars

...τα ώτα μου ακούουν μελωδίας,
...εκ του χορού των άστρων μουσικήν.

. . . my ears hear music . . .
melody from the harmony of the stars.
By the Open Window C. P. Cavafy

They had come every June and constructed the island, as couples do, with their favourite beaches, bars and restaurants. Over the years they made friends with others who visited annually. The Greeks were extras in this regular romantic comedy, busy in kitchens and boats, amusing and irritating them, the material for stories which they told when they were home.

When he left her they had been married thirty-three years. She was sixty. It was March and the next holiday was booked. In grief, shock, rage and terror, she emailed and spoke with the closest holiday friends.

'Why don't you just come?' they said. 'We'll be there.'

So she went, finding out how much she had relied on him to check in and lift luggage and get tea at the airport and manage the overhead lockers. She was exhausted when she arrived, not simply by the journey, but also by the effort of smiling at the driver who met her and the nice English girl who managed the bookings and the plump cleaning lady who gave her the keys, who all said how sorry they were and held her hand or patted her shoulder. She was used to the fact that everybody seemed to know everything on the island.

'Are you settled in?' Jenny had texted. 'We'll be at the *Pomegranate* after nine.'

It was her least favourite bar, three small rooms and a courtyard, almost exclusively English in clientele, filled with cigarette smoke, loud bragging men and the screaming laughter of women. There would be more sympathy. She decided to have a very stiff whisky at the bar near her house.

At eight she sat down at a table and contemplated the elaborate pharmacy sign next door which flashed twinkled and whirled in an endless display of coloured patterns and endorsements of various products, like a miniature Piccadilly. After five unattended minutes during which, again, she understood how alone she was, Petro came out and she smiled as he shook her hand and said he was sorry. She ordered a large whisky and a small bottle of water, no ice. He brought a very generous triple.

'Difficult for you, I think,' he said, as he put it down. 'First night?'

'First night, yes,' she said.

She went to the *Pomegranate* feeling ridiculously wobbly and had to focus carefully on the steps and uneven cobbles. Jenny and her husband were not there but, unfortunately, Charles was. Charles grabbed her and hugged her in a prickly embrace and ordered her some wine without asking and regaled her with a marathon monologue about the disintegration of his marriage. Jenny did not appear and, finally, in desperation she pretended that she was meeting someone at a restaurant and made her way, smilingly, out of the bar.

Abruptly desolation enveloped her. There was nothing to console her. The warmth of the evening air, the bright harbour lights, the sociable noise of the tavernas, the dark, glinting sea, all the sights and sounds which they had revelled in and enjoyed seemed simply to emphasise her alien abandoned state.

'I'll go home,' she thought. 'Tomorrow.'

She could tell that sleep would not be a match for the darkness in her mind so she determined to drink herself as close to sleep as she could, at the bar near the house. As soon as she sat down, Petro brought her an even larger whisky without being asked, for which she was surprised but quite glad because she did not trust herself to speak. There was a screaming howl hurting her throat.

It was quiet at the bar and she had drunk almost all the whisky when she realised that he was standing by her table, 'May I sit?' he asked.

She indicated Yes.

'Quiet now,' he said and when she looked up she saw that there was no-one at the other tables.

'Sorry,' she said. 'I'll go.'

'No,' he said. 'I get you another?'

The gnawing pain of her loneliness was dragging at her stomach and she was sure she needed at least one more hefty shot to anaesthetise it for the night, 'Can I take it to the house?' she managed to say. She and her husband, No, ex-husband, had often done this before.

'Of course,' he said. 'I will walk with you.'

The howl was still wanting to burst out of her mouth, so she did not attempt anything more than a smile.

Solemnly they walked down the small paved street, he carrying another large whisky and she making every effort to walk straight and not lean against a wall and slide down into oblivion. She knew there was a small flight of steps to negotiate and began to summon all her concentration. At the bottom of the steps she took a large breath. He put the glass down, 'OK,' he said, 'you hold onto me.' He took her hand and made her hold his arm. They managed three steps in this way and the remainder with his arm around her waist. At the top he sat her on a wall and went back for the glass. Her door was a few steps away. 'You have your key?' he asked. Mutely she gave him her handbag and he found it.

He opened the door and lifted her over the steps into the sitting room where she made her way to the sofa with the aid of various pieces of furniture. He put the glass and her handbag carefully onto a low table.

'You sleep, now,' he said. '*Kali nikta*,' then he vanished, but, as she discovered in the morning, only after taking off her sandals, which were neatly placed beneath the table, and covering her with her bathrobe, which she had left in the downstairs shower.

On her second day, she dosed herself up with paracetamol, vomited twice and showered three times, before she set off for the agency to book herself out and arrange a flight home. Passing the table where Petro sat, he stood up and indicated a chair with such a kind and graceful gesture that she sat down. Silently he brought her orange juice. At another table were Lauren and Heather, a gay couple whom she knew by sight. They called her over and invited her to eat with them that night.

In the next two weeks she discovered that her couple friends were no longer friends. Meetings were vaguely planned but never materialised. If she met them on a beach, they often seemed about to get the early boat. If she asked where they might be dining, they were unsure. She had heard from widowed and divorced friends that they were dropped like plague victims by their married friends, but the cruelty had seemed unbelievable, until she experienced it herself.

Charles popped up everywhere and she resorted to scanning every venue for his battered panama in order to avoid him.

Through Lauren and Heather she made deeper acquaintance with other gay couples, who did not see her as a threat. She discovered a different island in which she was vulnerable, afraid of hurt and appreciative of the small considerations of others. If she went to the bar alone, Petro appeared at her table instantly, smiling, however busy he was.

On her last night she had a nightcap with her new friends. They were all a little drunk.

'This woman,' said Lauren to the crowded bar, patting her arm, 'this woman will have a new man next year. Who's for a wager? Isn't she lovely, Petro?'

He was flying about with trays and drinks, but he paused for a second, 'Of course,' he said. 'But good man, not like first bastard. Yes?'

She started to giggle and then to laugh and then she got hiccups. They took her to her door, kissed and hugged her and left her trying to drink a glass of water backwards.

It was a bad year. For three months he said there was no problem, she could keep the house. Then it was very expensive for him living in London and the house must be sold. This meant losing the paddock and the horses. Livery charges were out of the question. The pony was in his thirties and the gelding was twenty-five with ligament problems. Neither were worth anything to anyone other than her, for whom they were almost as precious as her children.

Her part-time job in the village shop paid her what it had cost to have her hair and nails done each month. Other than that, the necessity of producing a dinner party at a few hours' notice and keeping the house at five star hotel standard, for the business contacts, had been enough to keep her occupied after the children left.

The children rang from Japan and America, angry, bewildered and pompous with advice. A mutual friend informed her that her husband, No, ex-husband, had been seen with a blonde. Almost immediately he rang to say that he could offer her a settlement which she should accept, or the whole lot would go on lawyers.

On Christmas Day she sat at the bottom of the stairs in her pyjamas, with the pages of figures and requirements in her hand. She had stood out for the paddock, but the house was sold. She was waiting to exchange on a flat over the Co-op on a main road which hurtled out of the suburbs accompanied by drab houses, petrol stations, kebab takeaways, warehouse outlets and gas reservoirs.

Heather and Lauren emailed regularly and it was their faithful concern which persuaded her to go out in June. The children, of course, issued peremptory and almost angry invitations, but she needed a familiar place. The agency had a small bedsit with a balcony and a view, not far from the house they had always taken.

On her first night at Petro's bar, she stopped him before he bounded off to get whisky, saying she would have wine.

'How are you?' he asked.

'Alive,' she said. 'Just.' Charles's panama appeared, wavering round a corner. 'Oh God.'

'Come. Come,' said Petro urgently, beckoning her to follow him into the small room which housed the loos. 'You go,' he said, pushing her toward the ladies, where she hid for such a long time that she wondered if he had forgotten about her, but finally he knocked on the door, 'He is looking for you,' he said laughing. 'I tell him you have gone to Little Bay. He has to have a beer but he drinks it quickly because he must catch the bus to go there. I think first night, you don't want Charles.'

'First night or any night,' she said, giggling.

'You have a new man?' he asked.

She looked at him in complete astonishment, 'Of course not,' she said.

'Lauren said you would have a man this year,' he said.

'It was a joke,' she said.

Lauren and Heather arrived soon after and they went to Stavros's restaurant for courgette fritters and beef with metaxa.

Her budget was small, but it was possible to live very cheaply and her friends treated her generously. Her one indulgence on this island of luxurious beauty, was a whisky each night to take to her little bedsit, where she sat on the balcony, drinking in the malt and the view.

On her last night, 'This is for you from me,' he said, giving her the glass.

'I never thanked you,' she said, 'for looking after me when I got so drunk that night last year.'

'It is an English game, to get drunk,' he said smiling.

'I don't play any games,' she said.

'No, you are good woman,' he said.

She stared at him, puzzled because he looked incongruously serious, 'Well, *yeia mas*,' she said. Raising her glass she walked away.

That year the gelding had needed disastrously expensive treatment, but luckily the village shop had decided to branch out into coffee and cakes, giving her more work.

There had been embarrassed visits from the children who tutted and frowned at her tiny flat and burst out with indignant accounts of their father, telling her things which she knew already but preferred not to dwell upon.

The first night at the bar Petro brought her wine and asked to sit with her.

'Do you have a man now?' he asked.

She was not as astonished this time, 'No,' she said, 'in England, at my age, there is no possibility of a man.'

'This is very strange,' he said. 'You don't want?'

'I don't even think about it,' she said. 'I've got my horses, that's enough to think about.'

'Horses?' he said, clearly amazed. 'You go with horses?'

She laughed so hard that the wine spilled out of her glass and down her front, 'No. No,' she spluttered, 'I mean I keep them. In a field. They are my friends.'

He laughed, 'OK,' he said. 'I am glad because I am big, but not as big as a horse.'

She had no idea what she could say to this, so they sat for while in friendly silence until more customers arrived.

Her last night was unusually boisterous with folk-dancing in the town square ending with everyone joining in. She was standing with Grant and Jim, jigging about at the sight of the dancing circles.

'Hi Pete,' she heard Jim say, 'you abandoned the bar?'

'I come for one dance,' Petro said, holding out his hand to her. 'They can wait.'

He led her to a small space and, raising his arms, he danced a few serious steps in the decorous circling way in which the men dance for the women. Grant and Jim whooped and laughed. She was entranced and embarrassed and glad when he took her in his arms and swayed her around like the other couples. He felt warm and sturdy, like her old pony.

'Thank you,' he said in a solemn whisper, when the music stopped. 'I glove you.'

'What?' she asked leaning closer, her astonished brain racing through bewildered semantic links.

'I glove you,' he repeated, in a tone of voice which made it impossible for her not to understand.

Then he was gone.

Jim and Grant laughed and hugged her, 'Wow,' said Jim, 'when you dance like that over here, you have to get married.'

She shrugged off the warmth, laughing, 'Oh come on,' she said. 'He's at least fifteen years younger than me.'

Grant shook his head, 'Nope,' he said. 'Last birthday, sixty-five. Sevasti made him a cake. Mediterranean diet, you see. Can't whack it. Widowed. Lives with Mum. He's a nice guy. He'd do you good.'

'Stop it,' said Jim. 'She looks as if she's going to faint.'

That year she lost the pony. She found him dead in his stable one soft November morning and sat with his cold hard body, stroking his black mane, saying his name without tears because it was a good way for him to go and he had been loved for so long. Knowing the gelding would be bereft without his companion, she asked around and found a girl with a cob mare and no money, who gladly came and offered to share the work in exchange for the stable.

The cakes and coffee business was quite a success with the young mums and a number of people who arrived with laptops and phones, apparently needing somewhere to work. She began to make snacks for lunch and enjoyed listening to their concepts and projects and self-motivational processes.

Both of the children announced pregnancies. She was summoned to be a suitable chorus of approval and delight, when the grandchildren were born, thankfully well and bonny. The man who used to be her husband also announced a pregnancy, but she tried to put that out of her mind.

The first night on the island, she debated whether she should go to the bar at all and decided against it. She had battled to make some sense of Petro's declaration, but he remained a mystery of supposition and suspicion. She made arrangements to meet Lauren and Heather at the new oyster bar.

At midnight she was sitting on her small balcony, when there was a quiet indecipherable noise and everything went simultaneously dark and light. She stood up in surprise unable to understand what had changed. Her room was dark although the light had been on. A power cut. Even the street lights up the hill had gone. There were nothing but ghostly images of the painted houses and the independent lights of the yachts in the harbour and yet light was streaming around her from a moon which looked so large and luminous that it might have been a balloon floating yards above her head. Beyond the moon, the sky was covered with a host of stars, an arching cascade of glittering diamonds. The beauty flooded her body. She had never seen a night sky unadulterated by ambient light.

Someone was knocking and she went to the door.

'Are you OK, my sweet woman?' he asked.

'This is so beautiful,' she said, stepping out into the cobbled lane, reaching out her hands to the sky.

'I make it more beautiful,' he said. 'Give me this night of stars.'

So, there was no last night.

They had to separate for several months while she went to England to make arrangements. The girl with the cob mare was trustworthy and devoted so she left her gelding with tears and promises that there would be detailed reports on his health and necessary treatments.

The children exchanged disgusted emails about the irresponsibility of the old, blaming the swinging sixties for the shocking lack of decorum which both their parents had finally exhibited.

The dismal flat seemed to have escalated absurdly in value. The money bought a house on the island, near to his mother, where they grew roses and jasmine. Her cakes became a feature at the bar.

Lauren and Heather and Jim and Grant came to the wedding, along with so many Greek relatives that she gave up trying to remember their names, but it did not matter. Everyone was laughing and singing and hugging and dancing and the stars were shining in his eyes.

Afterwords

καί κάποτ' αίθερια εφηβική μορφή,
αόριστη μέ διάβα γρήγορο,
επάνω από τούς λόφους σου περνά.

and, sometimes, the chimera of a youth,
misty, moving fast,
glides over your hills.
Ionian Song C. P. Cavafy

'Did you know *all* of them?' asked my young friend incredulously, as we drank metaxa in *T'Asteio*, on our way home from a meal with the women whom I have called Angela and Helen. He had spent the day on St Nick's beach reading the stories, which was his penance for six days gratis on my living room couch. He writes serious stuff and, like all the young who think too much, suffers considerable melancholy from time to time.

'Hardly,' I said, laughing at him. 'When did we last go to Angelo's restaurant where the ex-President of the USA pops in and the house wine is *Crystal*? And no, I don't think I ever said one word to Gloria Porter, except perhaps Excuse me, when she may have been flat out on the lavatory floor at the fishermen's. But I know Sevasti quite well now. I'm very fond of Sevasti. And Irini. And Mrs Samagdios who knows everything, believe me! They're hardworking women that lot. I admire them. I met Elli through Irini. She was teaching embroidery in the Women's Group. I went one summer.'

He shook his head, 'Ah, that poor woman whose husband was screwing everyone?'

'I don't think she feels particularly worried about that. He isn't nasty. You should see him with the grandchildren. Anyway she didn't talk to me about him. I heard a bit of it from one of the English girls.'

'So many people unhappy, betrayed, abandoned, neglected, ignored. What a picture of inhumanity.'

'You're a romantic, beloved child. You love a victim. We get what we ask for.'

'But no-one talks about being a murderer. How did you find out about that?'

'Well just one of those really weird things. I knew Sylvia before Angela did. She told me that story, after a bit of a girls' night out and a lot of wine. The awful Lady Parthi came to me straight from Sylvia, who has a great way with words, as you'd expect. Anyway you must have met the Lady Parthis of this world. Most of us have.'

'I'm Bulgarian, we do not have such creatures in our particular menagerie.'

'Are you sure? No iron ladies? No monstrous women? No unreconstructed Stalinistas?'

'And the poor man whose wife is refusing to have sex with him for years and she goes out all the time and he has to break into his own house. She makes him so ill he has a heart attack!'

I slapped the table in irritation, 'Stanislas. The man was a fool. He deserved all he got and anyway he got whatsername . . . Celia . . . in the end, so all's well that ends well. You be careful. Megan is around here somewhere. She might take a fancy to you. Celia was the one who took the video of Ari. I've still got it on my phone.'

'But . . . ' he shuddered, pondering the awful depths of Megan and Clive's marriage, '. . . the poor man had been married for years! And these wives who leave their husbands to die! I see it is very dangerous to marry an Englishwoman.'

'It is very dangerous to marry anyone.'

'The Reg story I understand,' he went on confidently. 'It is well known in your boarding schools that the little boys are sodomised and then they grow up to love each other better than their wives, who have to pretend to be boys and so on.'

'You're rather out of date,' I said. 'The sodomising is much more likely to go on in the care homes nowadays. And the hospitals and the foster homes and the prisons for young offenders. All those places where we make sure of the next generation of sociopaths to keep the social workers busy. Dickens must be spinning in his grave. He was the master of the sadistic world of Care and the Looked-After. Has anything changed?'

'Have a drink and get off your rocking horse,' he said.

'Hobby horse,' I corrected.

'Anyone would think,' he resumed, 'that there are no happy marriages.'

'No. No. Jane and Tim were a very happy couple. And look at the wedded bliss of Petro and Diana. All those cakes. He's getting seriously fat. And I think Elli's happy with Angelo and he with her, and Michali with Maria, although he can be rather bad tempered. It was a shame about Reg's sister. I did know her quite well. She told me all about it on email, after she went to Brazil.'

'And so . . .' he said leaning back and waving his hand at the crowded buzzing tables in the noisy warmth of the evening, 'you are telling me that this is what everyone is doing here?'

'Are you getting your hopes up, beautiful child? A population of three thousand and three or four times as many tourists each year? What should we say? Six thousand women? Plenty of scope, I agree, but look at them. Not adventurers on the whole. Who is, when you get to fifty and thoughts turn to pensions and varicose veins? There's a lot of photography and water colouring and walking around in huge boots and bird watching, which is relatively safe although someone always breaks an ankle or an arm. Not terribly exciting to write about, though. To quote Angelo, you have to be lovely *and* crazy to paddle any deeper in this pond and most of us are too old to be either.'

'Or stupid,' he said. 'Like the woman in the shop. Please don't tell me that dreadful old man is anywhere near us. How could you have heard about that?'

'Come, come, he's a dear twinkly old thing. I'm very fond of him. She married again. Poor Tim died of pneumonia, "the old peoples' friend". . . No, she didn't marry Mr Tavrakis, you idiot. Someone from another island in UK, where her son lives. She told me all about Mr Tavrakis when I went up to stay with her. I think it's a charming story.'

'God,' he said. 'Will I ever understand the English and their love of the grotesque.'

'When in Rome, dear, or rather, when in Greece . . .'

'Let's have another,' he said hastily, 'I really don't want to think about that shop.'

I looked at my watch, 'I would,' I said, 'but it is getting perilously close to the time when Charles comes for his night cap and I don't think . . .'

We drank up and paid Silenus, who was transfixed by the basketball on Sky and ignoring his customers. From his chair he waved out a hand for his money.

'Why do you call him Silenus?' Stani asked as we walked past the takeaway. 'It isn't his name. His name is . . .'

'I know his name,' I said. 'There's something of the night, don't you think? Do you know I have never heard anything about him? Of course, it takes me years to learn things which they've all known about for ever. But that guy . . . nothing. But there is something. Look how he moves. Sometimes he's come up to the table so quietly that I've nearly jumped out of my skin. Still his wife is beautiful and he dandles the grandchildren just like Angelo. But I can't help feeling there's a story there. He's got a lovely smile, when he bothers to use it.'

As we laboured up the steps to the temple ruins, beneath which my house hides behind the bougainvillea, Stani said, 'And the child. Where did that story come from?'

'I've known her a long time,' I panted.

'She's only ten or something.'

'Is she?'

A tall man came toward us, tripping nimbly down the dark steps, muttering a cursory 'Evening' as he passed.

'Horrible Hal,' I explained. 'On his way home from further liver damage with Tom, who really dislikes him but can't find a way of avoiding him. I've sat beside those two for hours at Petro's bar, doing my crossword. Really, you know,' I said, taking his arm, 'I just listen. I sit and listen and watch. The stories come floating along.'

'I suppose I'll find myself in a story one day?' he asked.

'Everyone I love ends up in a story,' I said, 'along with some people I hate. It's what they call processing. Some people dream, some people write.'

'I can't think how you find the energy,' he said. 'I would just sit and stare. It's such a beautiful place.' He stopped and threw his arms above his head as if to gather the benign magic of the night.

We trudged on up the narrow steps between the warm stone walls of the houses, with the moon ahead of us above the bulk of the sheltering mountain ridge which was outlined in the faintest white glow from the remains of the sunset far away across the sea.

Occasionally, when I have had one too many of Silenus's generous metaxas, I have seen Hermes leaping along that ridge flashing his gold heels. Or perhaps it is just one of the mad American joggers in expensive Nikes. I choose to believe it is Hermes.